A NEW GOLD DREAM

E.C. GIBSON

For my sons, Benjamin, Jacob and Isaac

1

HIS FIRST THOUGHT WAS A fragment. A fragment of a dream. In a medicated brain fog, he was aware of faint light waves forming a lit, barred window. It loomed in the vague space of a darkened cell. Then he was in blackness again. Time passed, had been moving along. Much time. His beard was thick, and he knew he shaved.

The issue was, well, there were many issues, but the big question was that he did not know who he was. A large part of who he was felt missing—gone. Was he dead? If so, that would explain a lot. A ghost of a memory formed. It vanished.

Also, he kept falling asleep; that was another big problem. He needed to do something about that.

Either I am going out of my mind, or I am already there, was his first coherent thought.

⟡

So, am I dead?

A half-familiar female voice whispered in his mind, *when you wake up, you will find me. Who is she?* It made his head hurt. He passed out again.

His next coherent thought after another long sleep convinced him that he was not dead.

If you do not know if you are dead, he reasoned, *you are alive, and ergo, you cannot be dead. Right?*

Besides, unless the afterlife was a sterile medlab cell with a barred window and a medical robot in attendance, this was not it. If this was hell, he was disappointed in all the hype. The thought of spending eternity locked in an infirmary was hellish indeed.

There is a large part of my mind missing, and I need to find it. I need to make sense of what has happened. A name, "Britt," floated out of his memory, and he thought, *I killed him. I killed Britt. But why did I kill him? And who the hell was Britt?*

For the first time, he laughed at his confused state of mind. *If I saw this in a holomovie, I would be amused.*

He feigned sleep to observe this new reality. Feeling trapped and threatened, he wondered why he felt that way. There was a rage inside him, below the surface. Where was that coming from?

After a long time, a person in white clothing came in to do a procedure of some kind on him. He released his suppressed rage and realized that he knew some essential martial arts. In an instant, he neutralized the young man and exchanged clothing, places, and identities with him. He also knew how to reset a med robot and fry its motherboard.

Am I a robotics engineer? No, that is not it.

His unlikely name, according to his stolen passport, was Serono Moussa—address Zone 10 Calle 15, in Klystron City. He looked nothing like Sereno's holopicture. Sereno was clean-shaven and much lighter-skinned, but it would have to do for now. "Call me Moussa," he whispered to himself.

Klystron City did ring a bell. *K-City—fleshpots, dope dealers, murders.* He knew he had once lived here. Struggling to pull a recollection from his blighted memory had produced a headache. It was worsening.

Moussa's passcard unlocked the door.

In the hallway, the hospital was silent. Even the med-bots were sleeping.

He made his way into a corridor. In the hushed hallways, he realized it was nighttime. He made it to an elevator and down to the lobby, where he walked away like he worked there. Right by the security officers and out the front doors.

Sereno's pockets had yielded various denominations of Klystron zetzals, a colorful—but filthy—currency. He hailed a robocab and asked the interface to take him to Zone 10 Calle 15.

After fumbling with the stolen cards, he was able to enter the building and Sereno's modest apartment. He left most of the money he had taken on the countertop by the kitchen sink.

Sorry about all that, Moussa.

In the bathroom, he got a chance to look at his face in the mirror. He was about thirty-five years old, give or take. Longish brown hair covered a high forehead. Dark circles around bloodshot green eyes triggered a memory.

Blunt force trauma? Recent? Might explain the partial amnesia. He was about two meters tall and weighed approximately one hundred kilos on Moussa's bathroom scale. Somehow, he knew he was underweight by about ten kilos. A vague idea of who he was crawled around in the back of his brain, but he couldn't get a fix on it. Trying to focus on the faded memory made his head hurt more.

He also had jagged sutures running from his right eye to his jaw. A group of pox-like scars formed small red and purplish craters above his stomach. He felt puffy incisions in the back of his neck and lower back. He touched them and felt the soreness. In his memory, he saw explosions, smoke, and fires flash in the darkness.

Okay, so someone shot me, he thought. Why did they do that? Am I a bad guy? I don't think so, but I'm biased. Someone shot me. What the hell?

Other than that, he was lean and muscular. He could sense that, until recently, he had been in much better shape. Before the shooting. Before the surgeries.

The sutures and staples were itching and starting to come apart. He figured if he took a shower, they would wash away. As he showered, he reviewed the slim available evidence. There was a strong possibility that he was, in fact, a criminal. This thought did not disturb him as much as the constant headache did. No armed guards outside his hospital room could only mean he was neither a dangerous nor a very significant criminal.

Damn it, he thought, I should have stopped and seen if my name was on the med scan wall outside the room. I am not hitting on all cylin-

ders—*or on any cylinders. What was your first clue? Oh, you mean the not-knowing-your-name problem.*

He stared at the new jagged scar and pressed the area around the wound. It was tender but not too painful. When did it all happen? Days? Weeks? *How long ago*, he wondered as he shaved the stubble. *If I don't try thinking too hard about it, it will come back to me, I hope.* He dressed in clothes from Sereno's closet. The pants were too short, and the shirt was too tight. It was time to get going and get reacquainted with K City. He went into the kitchenette, instinctively looking for a weapon.

In a drawer inside a liquor cabinet, he found a set of brass knuckles.

Moussa, you dog, these are illegal. Antiques but still capable. If I lived in this town, I wouldn't leave my crib unless I was strapped. Tough town, K City. He slipped the knucks on. *Perfect fit. Nice weight.* He removed them and slipped them into his coat pocket.

His further search of the apartment only yielded a choice of a dull steak knife or sharp scissors. He tucked the scissors in his hip pocket and left.

2

I GUESS I WILL HAVE PEOPLE call me Moussa until I remember my real name, he mused. Sereno was a bit unwieldy. This part of town was unfamiliar. He decided to walk until he recognized something. He felt like his memory could reveal his past life if he put himself in motion.

Do I need to find the right triggers?

He considered the issues confronting him and understood he was intelligent and well-educated. It was a comforting realization.

An immediate sense of self-awareness stirred inside him. He hoped it meant that his memory would soon return. It felt like he had currents of buried thoughts moving around in his mind, making his brain hurt. He needed to sit down somewhere and try not to think so hard. His head felt like his brains might melt right out of his ears. His thoughts fell apart and flew away like leaves in the wind.

The neighborhood deteriorated one block away from the medlab. A half-dozen police bots patrolled the block of dismal flats. Ragged people foraged in the trash. Some had to fight dogs for slimy scraps. Next, he walked by a chaotic shantytown of disposable containers and rickety shacks illuminated by the glowing campfires of desperately poor people.

Descending a hill of broken pavement and enveloped now in a low damp blanket of fog, he was alert to any sound. Tall buildings loomed behind him. Corporate towers disappeared in the gloom.

In the slum block ahead, on a corner, he saw that a small bar was open. *Bolas de Mono* appeared in bright neon-green foggy letters. He knew that the Spanish words meant 'monkey balls,' and thus, he realized he was bilingual.

"Curiouser and curiouser," he said as he thought, *Isn't that a line from something?*

He could almost see the passage from a book, a children's book cover in his distant memory. He was distracted by these thoughts as he made his way to one of the many available bar stools. He counted six other men and two women at the bar.

I know something about staying alert in unfamiliar places. He waited for memory to announce itself, but it broke apart before he could retrieve it.

An ancient digital clock on the wall announced the time as 2:05 a.m. if it was accurate. He ordered a cold beer and tried to summon the memory that had dissipated.

A woman intruded in his space before he could pursue the memory any further. A young woman in a turquoise pinafore, black micro skirt, and fishnet stockings sat down next to him. *Nice body. She's a working girl taking care of her assets,* he thought as he smiled at her.

"So, you looking for a party?" she asked in accented street patois.

"No, thanks, I just want to have a beer," he said.

"Two girls, you want?"

He smiled at the visual image despite himself and shook his head. He realized prostitutes had approached him before, more than a couple of times.

Am I a criminal? He considered it. A tattooed young man who looked like a criminal got up from his stool and left the bar.

The kid did not even look old enough to drink, but he remembered that there wasn't much of an age limit in K City, on anything.

The young working girl was not quite ready to give it up yet. "Drogas?" she asked.

Aware of a constant headache and pains flaring up in different parts of his body, he considered the question before replying.

I will need some painkillers, and I will need them real soon, like right now.

"What sort of painkillers do you have?" he whispered.

She gave him a fleeting smile before responding. "Vicocet, ultras, mitsyn…you want?"

"I want…I could use some vicocet," he said.

Damn, he thought, this girl is a walking dispensary.

"We never get highborn accents down here in the backfill. You must be lost. Watch your ass, fool," she whispered.

Highborn accent…I speak like I'm from the upper classes…so not a criminal…maybe a well-off criminal boss? Well, I would like to think so.

She smiled again as she held out her purse low under the bar and fished around inside of it. He saw that the bartender had walked to the other end of the bar, and this made him cautious.

Careful, he thought, there may be something else going on that you do not see. This could be a setup, and you could have blundered right into it.

She continued digging around in her purse and then smiled. She presented a small black plastic canister to him, and he opened it. Inside were more than 500 tabs of vicocet. He recognized the DC brand embossed on each one that meant the highest possible quality. *Ah, Dyeus Corp, famously known for The Pure.* He realized he had taken them before. Another memory of a large tent in a faraway desert welled up for a brief flash and was gone.

That desert war…where did that happen? I got hurt out there somewhere.

He had no idea of what the currency was worth that he had taken from Moussa. A feeling of danger was close, yet there was no time to find the source. Best to conclude his business. He opened the wallet and showed her the money. "How much for all?" he asked.

She paused and narrowed her puffy pale eyes, as if to say, 'Are you for real?' She snatched an unknown amount of cash from his wallet and tucked it away in her purse. She nodded at him, stood up, and left the bar. His clip was empty now.

I got ripped off, he thought. Oh, well, it wasn't mine anyway.

He pushed the vicocet into his left front pocket and considered the situation.

Act like you don't know what's going on he mused, *and that's easy, because you don't.*

He picked up his beer mug and scanned his environs while he sipped it.

Better take the vicocet now and see if they work, he thought, *before this pain becomes unbearable.*

During his drug deal, the bar had emptied. Just he and the bartender, and two passed-out patrons, remained. The bartender looked at him. Through half-closed eyes, he gestured at his glass. "Vodka shots. Keep 'em coming." The bartender did as he was told.

He drank himself into a mild vodka and vicocet-induced stupor. It was pleasant, like seeing old friends again.

My old buddies, Mr. Vodka and Miss Vicocet.

The antique digital clock now read 4:41.

He was alert, and the pain had melted away.

Damned good vicocet. I lost track of more than two hours somehow. Pretty pure vico. God knows I love the stuff. If whatever it is is coming, it won't come in here. They will hit me when I leave the bar. Might as well make them wait a little longer, he thought. *I'm ready now. I should feel nervous or scared, but I'm not, why is that?*

He had another shot. *Curiouser and curiouser.*

3

A FTER THREE MORE SHOTS, AND about a half-hour later, he got up from the bar and headed for the men's room. There was an open storage space to his right, and he ducked into it. Waiting in the gloom, he slipped on the brass knuckles. After a few minutes, he was comfortable that no one had seen him, and his eyes had adjusted to the darkness. Behind a stack of crates and beer kegs, he saw the outlines of a large, heavy steel door and made his way over to it.

It is extraordinary. Like I am following training or behavioral pro-gramming, but what kind and by whom?

He could hear nothing outside. He unlocked the deadbolts and cracked open the door to get some fresh air and see what was out there.

Not fresh air. It was a narrow gravel alleyway. It reeked of decaying garbage, rotting fish, and other unsavory odors. Feeling the vicocet and vodka kick in a bit more now, he was euphoric and quite relaxed. The alley was empty, aside from a half dozen feral dogs and a few wasted people pawing through the garbage piles.

Well, the bad guys went home, he thought. *Will I go left, or right? Since I'm lost, it doesn't make much difference.*

He chose left and picked his way through the debris, avoiding the crater-like puddles. He gave a wide berth to the dogs protecting their garbage from the shambling, battered people.

The sky was showing the first gray slivers of dawn over the city's shadowy skyscrapers. He neared the end of the alley. From each corner of the adjoining street, figures emerged. The one closest to him had a deep chest cough and a desperate look.

In reaction, he reached back and palmed the scissors in his right hand. He glanced around, looking for other potential weapons or escape routes. There wasn't anything available.

The man on the right had a small Gauss pistol, a little burner. Despite the danger, he calmly thought that a .25 could be survivable, depending on the range and the skill of the shooter. The other fellow held a nasty looking little needler with about a 20-cm vibroblade. He recognized the coughing guy as the teenager he had seen leave the bar.

"I cover him, and you take the money. If he tries anything, cut his throat. We have done this a hundred times," said pistol guy.

"He doesn't look drunk to me," said the teenager.

"Make it quick," the gun bearer said.

"Now, wait a minute, boys. You don't want any part of me, and I don't want any trouble. This is a mistake." *They must be desperate to do this,* he thought. *I don't want to hurt them.*

"Shut up. No one cares. Not unemployed clone soldiers. We hate you. Hate your existence." Mr. Gauss pointed the gun up.

Unemployed clones? This will end badly.

"Last chance. None of us want to do this. Besides, I don't have any money anyway."

"Throw your wallet over," pistol guy said.

He tossed it to the teenager with his left hand. Unfortunately, he could sense no fear from either of them. He held his hands straight out, palms down, scissors hidden. He would not raise his hands any higher, or they would see the scissors.

The teenager cursed, tossed it to the pistol guy, and said, "Empty."

"Check his pockets then."

Bastards, I fucking won't let you have my drugs. He tensed his muscles.

The teenager came in close, almost close enough, but then he coughed and said, "Something is wrong here."

"Listen to what I said. You don't want any part of me. Look for someone easier," he whispered.

"What? Just search his pockets. I have him covered," pistol guy said.

"No, wait a minute. He's not scared like the other ones."

"He's drunk."

"I don't think he is."

"I'll slag him where he stands then. Move out of my way."

The kid was close enough now and reaching toward him. He plunged the scissors into the kid's shoulder and took the needler from him as he spun the teenager around. Now he had the kid's body as a shield from the Gauss pistol.

"Walk away. Leave me alone, and I will release him." The kid was bleeding from his shoulder, but he had avoided hitting any major arteries.

I know something about anatomy, too, he thought.

The gunman stared at him and narrowed his eyes. "Who are you? Why are you smiling? Who are you with?"

"So many questions for so few brains." He started walking forward as he spoke, pushing the kid in front of him. Keeping the kid's arms pinned with the needler in his back. The scissors wobbled around in the kid's shoulder with every step. The kid was tough; he had to admit. The kid did not say a word.

A dog screwed it all up. If it had not been for the dog, things might have gone another way.

The dog growled from shadows to his left and shot toward the gunman, barking at all three of them. The dog spooked the gunman so much that he shot the kid, who flinched and went limp in his hands as he started to fall over. Two more shots went off, and all the dogs in the alley started barking and snarling. The shots were loud in the narrow, confined space.

More shots missed. Pushing the kid's body aside, he dove for the shadows, crawling low on all fours behind an overflowing dumpster.

The man with the Gauss gun regained some of his composure. He was now approaching with the pistol out in front of him.

He felt a fist-sized cobblestone underneath his shoe and pried it out of the ground. Crouching low on the balls of his feet, he waited for the moment.

The throw was near perfect, and it hit the clone with great force right above the bridge of his nose. Staggered by the blow, the gunman fired into the dumpster.

He stood up, moved in close, and fractured the gunman's jaw with the brass knuckles.

Well, that was awful. I need a moment to regain my composure.

He watched as the raggedy people emerged from shadows and began stripping his victims of their boots, clothes, and anything else of value.

The pistol guy was unconscious. Not dead. An intricate tattoo—a geometric pattern—extended from below his ear down his neck and inside his shirt. It looked like a compass made of spears.

That tattoo's critical — what does it mean? It's a brand. Dammit… It's like someone has been in my head, shredding my memories.

4

FEELING THE DRUGS BUZZ UP another notch, he was floating as he dropped down from street level into the free travel tunnel and boarded a tram. Unsteadily. He felt like he was on a boat for a second.

The system map confused him. He was the only person in his car. The vehicle came to a sudden halt, the lights went out, and the emergency strobe lamp came on.

Alarmed, he saw uniformed corporate cops board the car at both ends. The clear leader said, "Key Largo. For your safety, put down your weapons and stand up slowly."

Disoriented and confused, he did neither.

Key Largo. That's my name!

He was looking for a way out when a luminous interface appeared in front of him. He saw a woman he recognized floating in a paused holocall. It was Minerva Klyne, his one-time boss at Grand Design Corporation. Memories of her were squirming around in his mind, about to erupt.

Impassive, she looked at him, frowning, before speaking.

"Commander Largo. Behave yourself. Do not try to harm the only people in the galaxy who are interested in your welfare." She smiled. "We come in peace."

Instinctively, he turned to flee, but the cops encircled him and shot him with a neural net. The lights dimmed and went out.

He awoke in the back of an ambulance. While he was out, somehow, a dress uniform had replaced Moussa's clothes. An elegant gold-and-black corporate outfit. He was reassured to find the vial of vicocet still in his pocket. Whatever was in the IV was making him feel exhilarated. Shreds and patches of his memory started to emerge.

The side door opened on an expansive plaza of ornate fountains, exotic landscaping, statues. Surrounded by magnificent glass and steel skyscrapers, Lago recognized it. Grand Design corporate headquarters, a gleaming ziggurat of offices and luxury apartments for officer-level employees, loomed above him in the morning light.

His experienced eye noticed the GDC insignia, a stylized Komodo dragon. It was on patrolling gunships, parked APCs, and the flagpole that dominated the plaza.

I had an apartment and an office here at one time. They've hardened the security features since then.

Armed guards motioned for him to get out.

His attendants helped him up.

"Commander Largo. You will go with me to the CEO's office."

The guard pointed a PSG, a particle shotgun, at him. Largo recognized it as one of the most lethal weapons in the corporate portfolio. A PSG could erase whatever part of your body it hit. Also called a rail gun, it stimulated a troubling memory that stirred in the recesses of his mind before fading out.

"Looks that way. I won't be any trouble at all. But could you point that thing somewhere else?" Largo asked.

"Negative."

No words were spoken again until they were in the GDC lobby. Largo looked at the lavish post-neo-classic furnishings. The high arched windows trimmed in gold leaf were spectacular.

"Get in." The guard pointed at an ornate elevator door.

"Sure. I have been here before, you know," Largo said.

"How nice for you."

The express elevator took them to the thirty-third floor in seconds. The spacious and lavish lobby was empty. A 3-D floor-to-ceiling wall display showed all the major stock indices and news. After a few minutes, a burly guard led Largo in to see Minerva Klyne, CEO of Grand Design Corporation. She was finishing off a holocall as they entered.

"This whole deal is…suboptimal. Fix it now. Last chance before I withdraw him from service," Minerva said.

She turned and nodded at Largo; her face was an unreadable mask. Her voice was emotionless.

"Commander Largo. So here you are at last. What were you doing running around in the slums, partying in the backfill, consorting with criminals, whores, and droogies? Do you even know who you are? Did you know you have an opulent apartment here provided by the corporation? You didn't need to go into the slums last night."

"I am a bit vague on all that, ma'am. Suffering from a kind of amnesia." Largo shrugged. "But my head is starting to clear some. Maybe."

She did not tell him to sit down in either of the plush chairs, so he remained standing.

"Commander Largo, you are the product of Grand Design's best institutions. Although you started life as a ward of the corporation at the age of three, you soon demonstrated acute and relentless competitiveness. Rose to the top of your classes early on. Your parents died in a notorious attack in Graile City, the capital of the Nasheed. Do you have any memories of them? Or your home planet? Graile?"

Largo shrugged. "No." *Yet that is not true. I do remember a blinding white light and a building in flames.*

"Do you remember the mid-level exec who sponsored and mentored you?" Minerva asked.

He smiled and nodded. "You did, ma'am." Memories were returning now. It was gratifying.

"Well done. Let me see if I can help you a bit. Commander, you attended Deoule Castle, our best graduate school. Highest marks in our geology program, a PhD in two years! Followed by another PhD in theoretical xenoarchaeology—also in two years. Rather esoteric pursuits for the times?"

Largo nodded. "It is familiar, now that I hear you say it."

"You crammed a lot in during your four-year allotment. Next, you had a corporate combat staff position with me, do you remember that? Largo, you advanced through the ranks rapidly. Familiar with martial arts and all weapons classes. Fast-tracked (by me) into the CEO training program at Lausanne Business School. Top marks in business ethics, making you eligible for my internship. Pretty good program at Lausanne. I know. I went there a few years ahead of you." She smiled for the first time. It was a beautiful smile—the kind that could make you want to sign on the dotted line. "You understood back then that corporations were only as good as their people. You understood my view of our corporate mission. So much promise, Key!"

She walked over to the floor-to-ceiling glass wall and considered the hazy skyline of K City. Largo recalled that the windows were blast proof, fireproof, and impervious to all known weaponry.

Minerva continued. She knew his background by heart; it made him edgy that she knew more about him than he did himself.

"Corporate espionage school, where the comments in your file say you do not ask stupid questions. You do not make excuses. Also, you lean toward loosely interpreting corporate policies? Well, at least that is the Key Largo I knew…"

She sighed. "So then…so then" (she tapped the window) "you transferred to corp battalion security staff. The proxy war against the Port Amphora terrorist cells broke out. And that is where you were when the wheels came off. Correct?"

"Proxy war?" Largo was confused for a moment.

"Yes. That little war on Port Amphora was the last gasp of yet another nefarious nation-state system. As is standard, we sponsored all sides." Minerva shrugged. "We tested out weapon prototypes. I made considerable money. Tried to bring the enlightenment of the Grand Design corporate way to prosperity to their blighted souls. I tried, and I failed."

"It's all lost in a dope haze, ma'am. I remember that much." *I could use some more of that pure stuff,* Largo thought. *I could duck into the men's room and take a couple, maybe.*

"Right. You are one of the millions who struggle with synth-opioids. Also, highest-grade vicocet. The Pure, you dope fiends called it. It was legal, cheap, and plentiful in PA. Ninety percent of our people there were on it at one time or another."

She paused and considered her coffee cup.

"After your incident, to protect our investment, my investment, I had you placed in an induced coma and rehabbed for a bit. Commander, the corporation has held high hopes for you for some time now. I still do—but you refuse to conform to our expectations. You came out of rehab and went right back on The Pure last night. Why?"

Largo shrugged, saying, "I hurt, and it felt good?"

Minerva scowled at him.

He shivered. *God, she can be terrifying.*

"Incident, ma'am?" Largo asked.

I have no idea what she's talking about.

"I'm coming to that. Sit tight, Commander." She walked over to her desk and picked up the needler Largo had taken off the kid in the alley. Minerva turned it on and manipulated it like a baton in her left hand. She casually put on a skilled and comfortable display of how to use it. "Nasty little needle. In your hands or mine—quite lethal. One of Grand Design's most profitable innovations. 'Like holding the power of lightning in your hand.' Remember that ad copy?"

Largo stared at her, unsure of what to say.

"No? No recollection? Nothing? Ah, well, but I digress.

"So, we tried behavioral mod biochips on you. A standard practice, that failed. Acute physiological modification surgery—also a disappointment. A few other odds and ends. Finally, we tried combining it all with multistage surgical hypno-therapies. You seemed to begin a sort of slow recovery about two days ago. Well, at least you did until you had that rather violent episode coming out of your coma in the med lab last night."

"I am angry, ma'am. I don't know why I am. Maybe I can control it—" Largo struggled to sound convincing. He knew now he was in a battle for the highest of stakes—his life.

"Commander. I wonder if you can still command. Say, a geo-investigation project on an unexplored world? Are you fit enough?"

He looked hard at her. Difficult as it was, he met her fierce blue-eyed stare.

"Pardon me?"

She is talking about a mission. I may yet get out of here alive.

"Pardon? Well, that is what this is all about. Whether I should pardon you for all your past sins. Are you worth extending one last chance for atonement?"

He decided it would be best to remain silent. Half-formed thoughts and memories ricocheted around in his brain. The desert tent again.

"Commander Largo, can you still run a complex off-world operation? Yes or no?"

He thought that a mission might be the thing he needed to sort himself out. "I don't exactly know. I could be, ma'am. Do I know the planet?"

But what if it is a suicide mission? It doesn't matter if it's a chance to survive.

"No, a planet discovered quite recently. Classified."

"I assume it is remote?"

"Very. Way out past the frontier rim. Deep in wild space—a prospecting mission far beyond Raba. Dangerous, of course. An all-volunteer crew of many of our top specialists has signed on. Like you, none of them have any family attachments. All anyone knows is that it is to be a 'top-secret voyage of discovery.' This job needs finesse. Yet it could also call for blunt force should the need arise. You must be able to conduct irregular operations independent of close supervision."

"I could be your man," Largo said.

Intriguing, a chance to make some serious cash?

"Maybe you are, Commander. Tell me about your last post with Tailored Access Ops." Minerva folded her arms.

Largo paused before responding. It was long enough to make Minerva arch an eyebrow in his direction.

The explosion. The mission in the desert. I remember now.

"Ma'am. It's classified. Is it not? My time with TAO?"

"Yes, I know. I am the one who classified it." Her impatience was palpable. "Tell me what you can recall, please."

"It is all jumbled up in my mind."

She poured coffee for both of them. "That is likely a result of all the trauma and surgeries you have endured over the past few weeks. Here." She handed him his coffee. "Take your time. What comes to mind?" She whispered. It was almost disarming.

"I am supposed to say, first of all, I was never on Port Amphora, and no such operation ever occurred or existed?" Largo asked.

Minerva smiled and nodded. "Well done. Your training and conditioning remain intact, it would appear. Now tell me what happened. That is an order, Commander. Now, you may sit."

The chair seemed to embrace him as he sat down. He gulped his coffee before continuing.

Delicious.

"Well, we went to PA, Port Amphora. A standard security detail," he said.

Minerva did not sit down.

"Right. Who briefed you before you left?" She looked at him.

He tried to recall. Nothing came to him.

"It is uh, not uh."

"I did. Right here in this room." Minerva frowned.

Largo shook his head. "That sounds right, but I don't remember it."

Minerva nodded. "Okay. What do you remember?"

"My team was there to protect one of our SVPs, Kayle Korban. She negotiated the acquisition of a casino conglomerate, Clockwork Enterprises."

Kayle, he thought. A deep sorrow welled up inside him.

"Good. Yes, your memory is coming back. But Kayle failed in her negotiations. She was our lead negotiator, groomed to join the senior staff, as you were. So, what happened?" Minerva asked.

"Kayle was in front of me, a flashnet grenade exploded, and almost at the same moment, a siren went off." A memory surge hit him so hard it was painful. "And then…" He felt the pain wash all over him again.

"Continue."

"Debris rained down. Smoke. The place was burning. She was gone. Vanished. Blood began to fill my eyes." Largo winced at the memory.

"Kidnapped. Allegedly. The terrorists demanded an obscene amount of gold bullion for Kayle's return. You suffered severe head wounds, which is why you have an impaired memory," Minerva said.

"What?"

"Some of your memories from the incident may be quite painful to recall. But your body armor kept you intact for the most part," she said.

She poured more coffee. "Although wounded, you still functioned. Like the warrior you were always meant to be." Minerva's voice trailed off, and she looked out the window.

Were those tears she brushed away? Impossible.

"I killed a team member. I killed Britt." He saw the pallid face of Britt, the terror in his eyes as he cut the man's throat.

"The traitor. Yes. He was in on it. Britt Carr compromised your team; he set off the flashnet—you saw it. You killed him. I am glad. You saved me the trouble of doing it. But there's something more. Tell me about Kayle," she said.

Largo felt his heart pounding in his ears.

Kayle. Why?

"She is the only woman I ever…" he whispered.

"Please," Minerva interrupted, waving her hand. "Loved? More like lust? Either way, you violated one of the most basic of all the unwritten rules." Minerva frowned.

Largo did not respond. He felt the desolation all over again.

"Never get your honey–" Minerva began.

Largo completed it, "Where you get your money."

"You knew that one, Commander. I taught it to you. A suboptimal choice on your part. One that almost killed you, and one that did significant damage to your reputation. Worst of all, you were becoming attached. Most of your colleagues now consider you disgraced and no longer a member of the 'club.' But that may help with our mission cover. You are an afterthought now among polite corporate society, and if you go missing, it won't be noticed. Your colleagues think I terminated you. Most employees would have been. But I made an exception for you. I hate to give up on investments."

Largo nodded. There was nothing to say. He looked at Minerva, studied her red-and-gold hooded robe. Formidable. She appraised him. The coiffed blonde hair, her blue eyes, perfect bone structure. An impassive expression. Considering whether he should live.

"I loved Kayle in my way," Largo said.

Minerva shook her head. Largo noticed she still held his needler.

"You may not be ready for this." Minerva shrugged.

"The mission? Yes. I have a few doubts." He reached for more coffee.

"I have more than a few doubts, but I'm not talking about the mission. You need to know some of the things we learned about Kayle."

Largo braced himself.

"Had you been honest with yourself, you could have avoided the whole mess. You would have realized that there were many parties left in that party girl. You chose to ignore all the red flags. You escorted her around to some of the best nightclubs and casinos in the galaxy. Gambling, dancing, drugs—you two were the worst things that could have ever happened to each other. You sure had a good time while it lasted.

"Unknown to me, and the board, Kayle loved to take high risks. If we had known, we would never have sent her to PA with you. Too many temptations to which she succumbed all too easily. Somehow HR missed all that in her psych scans. The people who were responsible for that oversight are now unemployed."

Meaning they are as good as dead, Largo thought. *If you're not a corporate citizen, you lose your income, housing, and security. Your only options for survival are either crime or poverty. I do remember that much.*

Largo was afraid he knew the answer to his next question. "So, did we pay up?"

"No, Commander, we did not. The ransom demand was absurd. We discharged Kayle and extracted your mangled team from PA. Wrote the whole thing off as a loss."

"Is she dead, then?"

"Her bio-chip stopped transmitting within an hour. So, she could well be. It would be best if she were. We do not have a body. But, from a corporate perspective, Kayle Korban is off the payroll."

⋯◈⋯

Largo had to step out while Minerva took a classified holocall. He struggled to understand what he had heard. *I know her story is missing something crucial…if I could only remember what she is leaving out.*

While he had a chance, he swallowed two vicocets dry.

Within minutes he was escorted back in. Now Minerva had an armed guard in each corner. Also, a thin graying man in the black-and-red uniform of a senior corporate officer now sat next to Largo's chair. The atmosphere had changed. Tension hung in the air.

"Commander Largo, this is my chief of staff, Lath V. Yeoh."

"Honored to meet you, commander." Lath nodded.

They shook hands.

Minerva cleared her throat.

"So, Commander, I have to decide on whether you are salvageable." She said, pausing to sip her coffee, "I am going to test you—see how much more of this you can take."

The gold bracelet on her left forearm started to twist and turn on her wrist. Its emerald insets glistened as it emitted a low hum. Strips of green lightning coursed around her arm.

An interface portal was coming alive. Largo had never been this close to a gateway in operation before. It was one of the newest technologies.

As recently as within the last year or two. These things came out of nowhere.

Minerva whispered, "Let's replay the betrayal of Kayle Korban." She said this as she twisted her bracelet.

A rectangular space opened in the air between them. In a 3-D display, Largo, his crew, and Kayle walked across a casino ballroom. Britt dropped the flashnet, and shrapnel went off as smoke filled the room. His team hit the deck.

Largo staggered and fell. But he was the first one up. His needler glowed in his hand as he grabbed Britt by the neck and cut his throat. Five of his men were thrashing on the floor. Jaylen "Rent" Renteria, his second in command, was up on one knee, trying to wipe the blood out of his eye sockets. His eyes were bloody holes in his face.

Kayle was not there.

"W-What?" Largo stammered.

"Indeed. What," Minerva hissed.

"How?"

"Take us back. Replay. Slower this time."

The replay started over in slow motion. Now Largo saw the moment it had happened.

As the flashnet exploded, a gateway opened immediately in front of Kayle. A gloved hand extended, and Kayle took it and stepped through the portal. The portal vaporized behind her. It happened almost instantly. Hard to see in the roiling smoke.

"She was in on it," Largo said. He felt dizzy. Nauseated.

"She was. So, four of our best men are dead as a result. You and Rent are lucky to be alive."

Largo shook his head and rubbed his eyes.

I am getting another crushing headache. I do not feel lucky, Minerva.

"Calm down, Commander. Take some deep breaths if you like," Minerva said.

"I have questions, ma'am."

"Good. I expected you would. Your immediate reaction?" she asked.

"First, how is Rent?"

"He lost both eyes. He returned to duty a few days ago. He has synthetics now. His vision is being calibrated."

Largo nodded before observing, "I had no idea the gateways, those portals—could be so quick, so instantaneous. Few in existence as far as I know."

"They are called portals, and pulse gateways, among other terms. Compelling devices. There are nine in existence, to be exact. They are priceless, of course."

"And aren't they only held by the nine CEOs of the corporate council?"

"Unless something has gone very wrong, only the Council of the Nine have ever had access." She nodded.

"Kayle was working for the competition. So it had to be one of the nine that she was working for." Largo saw no other conclusion. Sadness consumed him.

I must have been in love with her, or this would not hurt so much.

"Yes. They compromised Kayle at the highest executive level. It cost us billions in unrealized revenue once the merger unwound. And, of course, Dyeus Corp swooped in and managed to grab Clockwork Enterprises away from us." She paused. "Then there's the human cost." She gestured at Largo. "And our stock price still has not recovered from it. A major soup sandwich all the way around."

"So, one of your colleagues…?" Largo raised the question.

"One of my most brilliant colleagues. This was a coup par excellence. Despite everything, I admire the sheer audacity of it. The artistry. I have stepped up my game as a result." Minerva stood and walked back over to the large window arch. It was getting dark outside.

"So that narrows it down to the shortest of lists. It has to be either Vanya Rusk of Globex or Ross Lasker, CEO of Dyeus Corp," Largo said.

Minerva nodded. "Commander, you passed my test. My money, of course, is on Lasker. As CEO of the last privately held company, he has no board, no shareholders to appease. I envy him that autonomy." She turned to address her head of security. "Any questions for the commander, Yeoh?" she asked, changing the subject.

Yeoh paused and cleared his throat before responding. "An observation, Minerva?"

"Go on."

"I fail to see how you can trust this man to lead an operation that is this critical. It is so sensitive that even your chief of staff does not know the planet's name or location. I don't even know the exact nature of the mission."

"Classified. A voyage of discovery." Minerva continued to look off in the distance. "Don't let it hurt your feelings, Lath."

"Well, I assume it is dangerous and high risk?" Lath asked.

Minerva nodded. "Less than a 10 percent chance of success. Only volunteers admitted to the team. Still, high risk equals high reward."

"Perhaps you consider him expendable and thus worth the risk." Lath paused and looked over at Largo. "No offense, commander."

Largo shrugged. "None taken."

Lath continued, "Now, I recognize that you and the commander go back years. And that he was one of your most promising protégés. Yet, his obvious character flaws and drug addictions are problematic. His abject failure on PA renders him unqualified, suboptimal."

Minerva nodded. "I see. Anything else, Yeoh?"

"I hope he is not your only hope for this mission. Please tell me you have a backup plan in the likely event that he fails," Lath added.

"Hey, Yeoh?" Largo said.

"Commander?"

"Go fuck yourself." Largo grinned. "No offense."

"Why, you insubordinate…"

"Are you finished, boys?" Minerva cut them both off.

Yeoh bowed before continuing.

That's a bit much, Yeoh, you brownnosing fuck.

"As your chief of staff and head of security, I must warn you. Once our board gets wind of this, your credibility, your brand, our corporate brand. As strong as it is—it could all be in jeopardy." Lath shrugged.

Minerva turned away from the window and glared at Yeoh.

A death stare, Largo thought. *Get ready for the chop, mate.*

"You want to do this now? Fine. Help me understand why the board should ever know, please? I have complete autonomy here. I can keep this under wraps. Right now, the only people who know Largo is being considered to be commander of this op are all in this room—five people at this moment. Also, to be clear, you know very little. Almost nothing."

"Well, of course, but—" Lath paled.

Serene. Emotionless. Minerva walked over to the guard closest to her and again, turned her back on Yeoh.

"Lath, your comm implant has generated a half-dozen encoded message bursts this morning. Help me understand why you are sending secret messages? Messages so encrypted that corporate security can't crack them. You might also explain who is getting these messages?" Her unblinking blue-steel eyes stared through Yeoh.

Yeoh grasped his left bracer.

What is Yeoh up to? Largo mused. *Damn. Wish I was strapped.*

He saw the now-familiar traces of a portal assembling in the space next to Yeoh. A faint yellow light throbbed as the interface began to hiss and float in the gap between them. The air sizzled.

"Seize him," Minerva ordered.

Largo bent low to tackle Yeoh. He felt a plasma beam electrify the air above his head as a guard missed Yeoh.

Minerva did not miss. Her narrowed eyes like ice, she hit Yeoh through his knee with the guard's PSG.

Yeoh screamed as the beam connected.

His lower leg vaporized into a red mist.

A gloved hand extended from the portal toward Yeoh.

Largo reached to stop Yeoh but halted when he saw who was attached to the glove.

Kayle Korban, still very much alive.

They both froze for a split second and locked eyes. Kayle looked bereft to Largo. Yeoh grabbed her hand, and the interface sealed behind his bloody stump.

<hr>

"Kayle grabbed him. If I hadn't seen it, I would not have believed it." Largo shook his head.

"Believe it, Commander." Minerva sighed, "I guess I need a new chief of staff. Many turnovers in that position of late. I will tap my new head of security, Jordi Donner."

Minerva took a deep breath. "Yeoh's performance was—suboptimal." She handed her rail gun back to the guard. "All Yeoh ever wanted was…everything."

"He's going to want a new leg," Largo said. A large pool of smoking blood, bits of bone, and cooked tissue marked Yeoh's former location. The smell of scorched meat hung in the office.

"The number of medlabs capable of handling that kind of work is quite limited. I will put those labs under surveillance. Too bad, I pulled my shot. I was aiming a little higher and to the left. But Yeoh squirmed out of here quicker than I anticipated. That portal seems lightning fast compared to mine." Minerva frowned.

"Could someone change it?" Largo asked.

"It is an extremely complex and somewhat fragile device. It could only have been someone the inventor trained," Minerva mused, rubbing her graceful jaw. "Someone yet unidentified. One would need, at the very least, a skilled microengineer and a surgeon to pull it off."

"And the inventor is?"

"Missing. Missing since early last year. A mysterious man who disappeared in the outer reaches of explored space. He was testing an advanced disruptor drive and vanished. Presumed dead."

"His name?" Largo asked.

"The mysterious Mesh Trouter. The design genius. You may or may not recall that he led the research team for Dominica Corp that came up with the first disruptor drive a few years back. And Dominica tightly controlled his access. So much so, that little is known about him to this day. But most people are unaware that he alone knew how to make the portals and integrate the bracelets. So, he alone knew how to hide from them."

5

ARGO'S NEW DREADNOUGHT, THE *CRIMSON Rhapsody*, orbited the deep blue planet of Raba. The aqua sphere was up at about eleven o'clock from the observation deck of the modified warship. Only a few small archipelagos near the center consisted of land. The rest was vast oceans and far-flung seas. In these remote scattered islands, the major corporations and vicious pirate clans competed. They pitted their fishing, mining, and combat fleets against each other. Often the competition was violent. Ships vanished. The wild frontier of Raba made it an excellent place to test out new weapon systems—far from prying eyes.

Raba was the final stop in quadrant four of the known galaxy, the last frontier planet. The map from here—unknown.

Somewhere out there is the planet Gereon, Largo thought. These past few weeks had been a blur. *Still so many holes in my memory, but I have had little time to dwell on it. Maybe that was Minerva's plan all along.*

The logistics crew assembled in the vast hangar deck before they boarded the shuttle to Raba. Largo said a few words before they departed.

"At some point, a courier will find me and hand-deliver the data cube for the next part of our mission. *Crimson Rhapsody* will remain in suborbital. We will be required to take on more cargo and crew members. Any comments or questions?"

Jaylen Rent asked, "May I make a trivial observation, Commander?"

"I would be disappointed if you did not, Mr. Rent."

"Ladies and gentlemen! This may be your only opportunity ever to eat the freshest seafood you can get anywhere. Make the most of it."

The crew nodded and laughed in assent as they boarded the shuttle.

Their shuttle came in low over GDCC outpost CS-315. It was about two dozen dusty, one-story, prefab domed buildings in a jungle forest clearing by the sea. The operations tower was three stories high and located next to the beach.

Eight heavily armed fishing trawlers and mining subs flanked the corporate pier. One was still unloading the morning's catch. In the marina next to the dock, luxury yachts, casino barges, and high-end floaters made up a colorful flotilla.

High-security armored combat bots patrolled the piers and beaches.

Four other shuttles and about a dozen luxury skimmers sat on the runway. Largo spotted two battle-scarred heavy bombers parked in a hangar nearby. Adjacent to it was a hardened bunker full of drones.

A smoldering volcano loomed in the haze on the horizon, dominating the jungle landscape.

The operations tower controller laconically directed Largo to land. "Wherever he could find an open space."

"This outpost does not seem too interested in following corporate protocols," Largo observed.

"I can see I'm going to like this place," Jaylen replied. "Did you see those Bugatti and Selwyn skimmers? These guys are raking it in out here."

"Higher risks, higher rewards," Largo acknowledged. "The bombers, drones, and missile pods strike a serious note, though."

He pointed to the open space at the end of the runway.

"Sit her down over there, Mr. Rent."

"Roger that."

They landed, gathered up their gear, and exited the shuttle.

The base commander was the same rank as Largo, so the protocol did not dictate a meeting with his landing party. Thus, Largo and Jaylen were a bit surprised when she pulled up alone on her vintage hoverbike. It was a white carbon-titanium alloy job with red trim, 'Emi' painted on the fuel tank in black script edged with gold. She removed her goggles, flipped her bright black hair back, and smiled.

"Commander Largo. I am Commander Emi Manaka." Her armored flight uniform was well-tailored and expensive looking.

"This is my XO and Chief Combat Engineer Jaylen Renteria," Largo said.

"Call me Rent." Jaylen smiled.

Largo and Jaylen bowed; Emi was impressive. "Commander Manaka, your name is familiar to me. Why is that?" Largo asked.

She smiled at him. "I am sure I don't know."

Jaylen interjected, "Are you the same Manaka who a couple of years back led the attack on the so-called pirates who tried to assassinate Minerva Klyne in K City? In broad daylight?"

She nodded. "I was involved in the fracas that ensued, yes. They were from Dyeus Corp…not pirates."

"I heard that," Jaylen said.

"We couldn't prove it, though."

Largo remembered it. "Right. Minerva's then head of security was poisoned or something, and you were the next one up. You stopped them in their tracks."

"I was part of a larger team. We were a cohesive unit. It was what we had trained for."

"I seem to recall it was a pretty big deal. You were promoted to commander very soon after it happened." Jaylen smiled.

"Nah, it was not all that much. It got me this anti-piracy post out here, though, which was an excellent outcome." She gestured toward the buildings and the harbor. "Would you like me to show you around the place?"

"Sure. But could you show me your hoverbike first? That is a classic BMW 300 GS, isn't it?" Largo asked.

"Wow, you know your bikes. It is an S model, though, not a GS. The differences are kind of subtle."

"I'm a fan. I have, uh, I had, a Ducati 800," Largo said.

Emi whistled. "Those are fine. What happened to it?"

Largo paused, unable to remember.

"It got shot up on Port Amphora," Jaylen added.

"I see," Emi said. "We heard about the casino abduction clear out here in the boondocks. Bad luck that. You know, I went to grad school with Kayle. I find it hard to believe that she was in on it. It is impossible."

"Largo does not talk about that incident, Emi. Later, if we have time, I'll tell you what happened. We all got shot up on PA. I got some new eyes out of it." As he shifted the color in his eyes to a bright purple, Jaylen grinned.

"Oh! I thought those might be the new synthetics." Emi squinted. "Any other tricks you can do?"

"Sorry, Commander. I cannot comment on that. My eyes are so sensitive and classified that they do not exist. Nor will they exist at any future time." Rent grinned.

Jaylen's charm offensive is in full force, Largo thought.

━━━◁◆▷━━━

Dinner was in the officers' mess of Manaka's flagship *Reverie Scout.* The buffet was a seafood extravaganza, stretching over three large tables.

Emi introduced her executive officer before they sat down at her table.

"Gentlemen, this is Claire Corsac, my XO." Emi gestured at a tanned, lithe, and reserved woman next to her. A deep scar ran from the corner of her mouth to where her long brown hair covered it up. "She makes everything run around here. She is also one of the most gifted combat medics in the entire corporation."

They all shook hands.

Claire could have that scar removed, but it does give her a unique lethal look. Wonder how she got it?

Claire bowed and said, "Gentlemen, it is a pleasure to meet you."

The dining hall had gold flourishes, an azure ceiling, and polished mahogany panels. Oil paintings in an antique style decorated the walls.

He asked, "Emi, what is this style? What is it called?"

"Baroque. Derived from the earth, mid-1600s France." She shrugged. "It is a bit much, isn't it?"

"It is, uh, different. Looks posh, I will say that. It reminds me of Minerva's office suite. So, it's from roughly six centuries and sixty light-years from here?"

Emi smiled. "Roughly, yes. But I didn't do the design. It's from one of my predecessors. Commander Povich. Now deceased."

Largo arched an eyebrow. "What happened to him?"

"Killed in a mining accident. The seafloor caved in under her tunneler." A steward offered wine to Claire and Largo.

"So, it was a gold mining project?" Largo asked.

"Is there anything else on this planet worth the risk or the expense?" Emi frowned.

Largo paused before responding. "I guess not."

Emi continued. "Yes, I am afraid that gold, always in limited supply on Raba, is about gone at this point. So, it was a rather meaningless, irrelevant death for all concerned." She reached for her wine goblet. "The fish and shellfish resources, though, are still almost untapped, as you can see from today's buffet."

Everyone paused to look at Claire's holobracer as it illuminated red and began pulsing. She pulled up an emergency holocall full of static. Someone was jamming the signal.

"…alert…incoming attack. Incoming. I repeat we have incoming ma…" A massive burst of static interrupted again. "Three squadrons… bombers and fighters in—unknown departure point."

Emi stood up and spoke into her bracer, "Scramble all interceptors and bombers. Order the fleet out to sea. Activate all digies."

"Digies?" asked Rent.

"Digital camo," Largo said. "You know, cloakers."

Claire continued with her holocall, "Get all bang-bangs to battle stations. Ready the burn bags."

Largo asked Claire, "How can I help?"

"Fly an interceptor?" She was now pushing away from the table and unstrapping her Gauss pistol.

"Been a while, but yes—I can also run guns and countermeasures."

"Right then. Six in the aft section. I'll take you with me. Let's go," Claire said.

Over his shoulder, Largo gave orders to Rent. "Jaylen, get our team back to the shuttle and get Rhapsody into suborbital. Stay concealed and on standby out there in case we need you."

"Roger that." Jaylen pushed away from the table and joined the air-crews running to the exits.

Largo put on his armored flight suit and climbed into the ATF Dragon Interceptor.

Based on the old needle/delta-wing designs that Largo had trained on, the dragon was a fleet standard. The new technology was several upgrades since he had last flown. The flight suit doubled as a survival suit and integrated with the ship's AI. This was his first experience with the next-gen AIs. He approached his task with trepidation.

Three crew members operated the dragon. A pilot, a copilot, and a countermeasures operator/gunner. Largo sat behind Claire and her copilot, a Lieutenant Commander Viggo.

Largo spoke to Claire to get an update.

"Any instructions before takeoff?"

"Have you oriented the AI to your voice?" Claire asked.

"No."

"Press the VA button and talk to our ship. Once the AI is engaged, tell her to assume a wing-point position for our formation," Claire said.

"Copy."

Largo pushed the VA button. The AI voice responded immediately.

"Speak, unidentified crew member. What is your name?"

"Largo."

"My name is Bette…assimilating…ready for orders."

Largo responded, "Lift off and take the lead position."

"Acknowledged."

The squadron took off from the aft hold and climbed to 3,000 meters above sea level.

Largo did not see any bogies yet on his focal array screens, so he took a moment to run a quick tutorial to get up to speed. He noticed that the shoulder pads on his flight suit held a Gauss pistol on one side and a needler on the other.

If it comes to that…things will be grim, he thought.

"Dragon Leader to all dragons. Turn on shield generators. It's going to get kinetic up here. Activate target discrimination overlays. Activate Twidget bots for possible equipment repairs," Claire ordered.

"Did you get all that, Bette?" Largo asked.

"I did, and we are good to go, sir. GTG."

He saw a curved red line appear at the top of his screen. It soon expanded to a sizeable 3-D dome-shaped formation. Fighters were on the curved edges, and about ten bombers were on the bottom line. Around fifty ships in total.

They will swamp us. This was a bad idea, Largo thought. *Who are these guys?*

"This is Dragon Leader. Be advised that we cannot identify the bandit formation. Their tactics look disciplined, military, but their identifiers show no corporate affiliation whatsoever. Consider them hostiles, possibly pirates," Claire said, then paused before continuing, "headed for our base. Move to attack formations now."

Their ship slammed into high-velocity intercept mode. A bomber appeared in the focal aperture. Largo stitched it with the dragon's big twin kinetic rail guns and watched it break apart on screen. An escape pod ejected out of the cloud of debris as they flew on.

It was getting dark over the archipelago as they climbed up to 5,000 meters. A writhing mass of fighters, drones, and bombers punctuated by explosions whirled below. The missile pods and subs engaged. Drones and missiles filled the air in the bogie formation. It looked like they had destroyed half of the force, but four bombers were still coming for their base.

"Largo, we have company," Claire said.

Largo saw the fighter rising to meet them and hit a button.

"Countermeasures deployed."

"Taking her down on the deck." Claire took the interceptor in a steep dive toward the runway. He felt the temporary loss of gravity as he floated in his harness.

Claire knows her ship, he thought, as he fired the tail rail gun at their pursuer.

Largo shot a piece off the wing of the bandit.

"Reaching untenable vector. Leveling out," Bette alerted. "Target has intersected our course and is…"

The explosion in the copilot's space was deafening, with a blinding white light. A pile of cooked meat, bones, and tissue filled Viggo's chair as blood splattered throughout the cabin. Stunned, Largo struggled to wipe the bloody mess from his visor.

"Recommend eject," Bette said. "Do you acknowledge, captain?"

Claire was unresponsive.

"Captain's vital signs unsustainable. Commander Largo?"

Releasing his harness, crawling into the bloody mess of the copilot's section, he could see that Claire was wounded and out cold. He scooped her out of her chair and held her tight.

"Bette, activate survival module," he said as the wings peeled off and the module deployed—dropping them like a rock.

The module engines pulsed and fired as Bette slowed their descent. Largo could see that the battle was all but over. GDC drones were mopping up. A shot-up bomber limped away from the action with no interceptors in pursuit.

He tried to raise Manaka's holochannel.

"Emi. Are you there? We will need med support when we crash land in about three minutes."

He checked Claire's vital signs. Her blood pressure was dropping, her pulse weakening.

"Captain Corsac's condition is life-threatening," he added.

The module drifted away toward the jungle's smoking volcano. No responses yet on the holochannel. Largo saw wrecks flattened against the volcano's slope. A demolished scorpion personnel carrier, an escape pod, and a bomber burned.

"Bette, adjust course. Bring us down at the base," Largo said.

"Nav system functions at 26 percent. Working on it, commander."

After a minute, the holochannel responded. Largo heard Manaka's tired voice. They had lost visuals.

"Commander Largo, we are tracking you and have someone en route to assist. Claire's condition now?" Emi asked.

"Internal bleeding. Blood pressure falling." He checked the volcano looming in his window. "We are having nav problems but will be down in less than a minute. Probably on the volcano slopes—south-facing side."

A cloud of frantic nocturnal winged bird-lizards, beaks full of saw teeth, flew out of their way.

Hope we don't feed the birds tonight, Largo thought as he checked Claire one more time.

The ground was coming at him fast as he braced himself.

"Impact—thirty seconds," Bette said as the crash cocoon deployed.

Largo pushed up on the gull-wing canopy and climbed out on the ground. Claire was safer in her survival suit enclosed in the crash cocoon than if he tried to move her.

He saw two tall, armed men approaching. They were not in GDC uniforms, so he unbuckled his Gauss pistol and opened fire on the closest one. They hit the ground in defensive positions and returned fire. Largo was already moving down the slope. He tried to lure them away from Claire and the crashed interceptor.

Shots filled the air above, and Largo could see guns flashing no more than fifty meters away. Explosions pounded the ground all around him, and he stayed low. He rolled over on his back in time to see a fighter flying back around to attack him again.

"Oh, man. We've got problems now," he said, rolling back toward the crashed interceptor. Blood seeped into his boot.

I guess the shrapnel nicked me.

He heard thrusters kick in above him and saw a GDC interceptor dive in and attack the fighter, rail guns tattooing its dorsal side.

Must be the one Emi sent over, he thought.

He saw that one of his attackers was no longer firing. He returned to the interceptor, realizing that he had lost track of the other fellow. Largo resisted a strong urge to sink into the earth under the interceptor and hide. Instead, he crawled toward Claire's side of the cockpit and kneeled beside her.

"How is she, Bette?" He was afraid to hear the answer.

"Claire Corsac is dying, sir."

"Can I do anything?" Largo asked.

"Defend us."

Shots ripped the wind around him. He picked up Claire's rail rifle from the restraint holster strapped to the interior door.

Someone was shooting at him, and he pumped the rail gun in their direction.

The rifle jammed, so Largo got his needler out and waited.

It was quiet enough that he heard steps running behind the interceptor. Now he could see the big fellow looming in the darkness, coming in low and fast. Largo's needler stabbed at him and missed, but his assailant hit the wreckage at full speed and went down.

Largo was on him in an instant and jammed the needler right through his head. The man gasped, convulsed, and gurgled, as a smoking hole emerged in the center of his forehead. "You were good, man," Largo whispered, "I was half a second quicker."

In the distance, Largo could hear a ship landing in the jungle.

Friend or foe? He wondered.

Claire lay in a med sphere, a complete healing system integrated with sensory foam wrapped to accommodate any patient. Her vital signs had stabilized, and she slept. She was out of immediate danger.

Largo and Emi sat on a couch nearby, catching their breath.

"Damn. Dinner was only four hours ago," Largo observed. "We didn't get to have dessert."

"Been a bit hectic," Emi agreed. "We suffered heavy losses. Lost your entire squadron. Plus two bombers, about thirty KIA, a sub, half of the airstrip knocked out—this thing was well-organized." She sighed, before adding, "We pretty much wiped them out. And they did the same to us."

"Thought I was going to lose Claire there for a while. Bette is the best AI I have ever seen. Wouldn't have been possible to save Claire otherwise."

Emi nodded. "And now Bette has integrated with and cloned herself into your flight suit. So, you get to keep her if you want."

"Oh, yeah. That's an affirmative, commander." Largo stood up and stretched. "Lucky that shrapnel only nicked my leg." He considered the bloody tear in his flight suit at mid-calf.

"We were all lucky compared to the bad guys." Emi stood up too.

"Take any of them alive?" Largo asked.

"Negative. We did recover two bodies near your crash site." She whistled. "Damn, Largo. You are an artist with that needler."

"Thing about a needle is, if you have to resort to using one, it means things have gone to hell." Largo shook his head.

Emi laughed. "So true. Want to go down to the morgue and inspect your handiwork?"

"Might as well. See what we can learn about the opposition."

The body of Largo's first victim had been incinerated from the knees up by his Gauss gun, so it was stored in a morgue capsule. Largo's needle victim, aside from a massive head wound, was intact and lay under a half-sheet on a table. Three forensic specialists were going over the corpse with every instrument available. One of them detached himself from the group when Largo and Emi walked into the morgue.

He removed his mask and bowed to Emi. "Commander Manaka. I have been expecting you."

"Captain Meadows." Emi returned the bow, introduced Largo, and asked, "What have we got so far?"

"First of all, this big guy is a clone. Metabolic and chemical trace elements say that he was bio-engineered in K City. A high-dollar corporate job. Costly unit. It looks like he led a well-bred life. He was privileged even. Lots of superior nutrients, exercise, musculature sculpting. Plus the usual tactical enhancements. He was close to twenty-one years old. I'm sure he attended the best combat schools. He was a significant investment to whoever sent him here—designed for heavy combat. A ranger. Or a commando.

"You see, they have done extensive work to conceal his origin. For example, the corporate brand? Gone. It is mandated and required of all clones. Been removed from his left pectoral muscle and his neck." He pointed to a long narrow skin patch burned where the brand had once been.

Largo immediately remembered the guy in the alley in K City.

Right. That's what that was—a corporate brand. So, he was a combat clone too at one time in his life.

"His bio-chip data? Lab sourcing? Signatures?" Emi asked.

Meadows pointed to a severe black and purple laceration behind the clone's ear. "See that? Self-destruct functions. One of the newer models. Pretty much obliterated all bio-chips and data trace the second he died."

"Dammit," Emi whispered.

"Indeed." Meadows nodded.

"Any other identifying marks?" Emi asked.

"We are still looking for those—several recent combat scars on the chest and abdomen. This guy has seen quite a lot of recent heavy action for one so young. Look at those enhanced biceps. Like the majority of combat units, not programmed ever to surrender, but this guy could crush you if he wanted to."

"That's what he had in mind. Damn near killed me," Largo said and then asked, "Can I look at his feet?"

"May I ask why?" Meadows answered.

"Want to check something. Something I almost remember." A submerged memory was rising in Largo's mind as he lifted the sheet.

He found nothing on the left foot. But on the inside of the big toe on the right foot was a small red tattoo. It looked like a compass perforated with eight radial spears. "Look at what we have here."

"Dyeus icon," Emi whispered.

"Yep. The Dyeus Corporation's logo," Largo observed. "It is hard to obliterate all traces of identification on fearless clones bred for combat. This guy was proud of his corp. The high-line units are known for their hubris. Not nice people. Yet, they aren't supposed to be." Largo laughed. "I've seen this before—back when I was in TAO."

"The audacity of that bastard." Emi was livid. "Ross Lasker orders a brazen attack like this with his troops disguised as pirates! Hasn't changed his playbook much." She looked closer at the tattoo. "Still, this will help our forensic techs. Good catch, Largo."

"Well, while I agree Lasker may be behind this attack, we cannot rule out pirates either. One tattoo on a dead clone is not enough evidence to conclude it was Lasker," Largo said.

"I guess not, but I suspect we'll find a similar tat on his mostly-incinerated colleague," Emi said.

"Now we know the best practices for screening the bio-debris. We are recovering stuff from the wrecks all over the island. Soon, we will have a clearer idea," Meadows observed.

"Do you think we should alert the CEO, Largo?" Emi asked.

"Immediately. Minerva will want to know what we could be up against," Largo said.

"In that case, I need to brief you up in my office first. Can you come with me please?" Emi started toward the door.

6

E MI'S OFFICE HAD A SWEEPING view of the volcano out a north-facing window. Largo noticed the comms detectors as they walked in.

"I see the usual security screens. Should I shut down Bette? Are we concerned about remote comm sensors?" Largo asked.

"I think we are good, Key. There must be a reason Minerva selected this site for your briefing. It is about as far out in the boonies as you can get." Emi gestured at the small conference table. "Pull up a chair?"

"So, you are my contact here? Ah, it makes sense." He sat down and removed his gloves.

"This is pretty much our first chance to meet in private. Events took over," she said as she set up a holocube. "I got this by courier the day before yesterday. Instructions were to activate it in your presence. No one else but you and me are to look at it." She pressed a side panel and initiated the transmission.

Minerva Klyne addressed them from her office. "Largo, Manaka, if things have gone as we intended, you are viewing this together on Raba, and no one else is present. Largo, when the message is over, please integrate the attached Gereon files, such as they are, into your ship's computer. Then proceed with Claire Corsac to the planet Gereon. Manaka, you will remain on Raba to provide long-range logistical support."

Emi sighed at the mention of her XO. "Well, there's the first spanner in the old disruptor drive."

Largo nodded.

"I will get straight to the point. We have every reason to expect that Gereon has massive gold deposits. Possibly more extensive than anywhere in the known galaxy. As your files will show, the gold is expected to be shallow. From a geological perspective, it's recent and quite pure. Easy to extract." She smiled into the camera and paused. "I bet I have your full attention. Are you riveted to your seats?"

Despite the setting, Largo and Emi both nodded as if Minerva were present in the room with them.

"What I would give to see your faces right now." She chuckled. "And what I would give to go on this mission with you. But, alas, such adventures are no longer accessible to me."

Minerva leaned in for a close-up.

"So, I know I need to address the next obvious question about payouts. Are the common prospector shares and percentages in effect for a corporate gold strike of this potential size? It is the first question I would ask. After all, wealth is the whole point of all this, is it not?"

Largo noticed they both were leaning closer to the cube.

"The reward structure is generous and simple. You will agree." Minerva paused again for effect.

"Just effing tell us, Minerva," Emi whispered through gritted teeth.

Largo laughed. *This is getting good. Got to love Minerva...*

"Logistics support will be worth 1 percent of net revenue for two entire years after operations begin. Field directors Key and Claire will get 5 percent and 3 percent. All gold processed in line with our project plan. Each of you will get an additional bonus of one billion credits and guaranteed seats on the board of directors. If anyone dies in the execution of the ops plan, their share goes to their estate per usual arrangements. If we pull this off, we will all be legendary. I do not need to tell you this— but I will anyway. As you might expect, once you are on the board, your stock options will be—how to put it? Well, they will be substantial.

"As you know, large amounts of gold are needed to manufacture the sophisticated circuitry in our next-gen disruptor drives. Other classified components also need it. The corporation has no greater priority than the successful completion of your mission. Good luck to you both. I am all in with you two. End of message."

Largo and Emi stared at each other, at a loss for words. It was sinking in that Minerva had changed their lives forever.

Emi spoke first after regaining a bit of her composure. "Did you have any idea?"

Largo shook his head, "All I knew was it was to be a frontier mission requiring a geological background. She had considered me for it for a while, and of course, I knew that it was a high-risk venture." He was still trying to process it.

"She holds you in great regard, and she trusts you completely, it would seem." Emi stood and looked out the window.

"I don't deserve it. I was Minerva's protégé until Port Amphora, and then, well, let's say I'm surprised she still trusts me at all…after what I have put her through. I'm sure the board is not happy with me. She is stretching her neck way out." He felt like changing the subject. "So, did we get any extra information with the delivery of this cube?"

"Yes. We are close to the far limits of the effective range for Minerva's portal. I am now supposed to contact her live by holocall, and we are to maintain mission integrity. No mention of Gereon unless Minerva brings it up." Emi paused. "What is it? You look worried."

"It's nothing," Largo said.

"Or not?"

"From the moment Minerva told me she wanted me for this mission, I have had this feeling." Largo struggled for words. "Like, why me? Also, why have I had so many memories taken from me? There is something wrong in my mind, something missing…ah…forget it."

"No. Let's not forget it. Let's have some med scans run as soon as possible," Emi said. "I need to be sure all is well with my partner in this high-risk venture." She smiled.

"How good is your medical staff?" Largo asked.

"Pretty good. The doctors handle everything from birth control to autopsies."

Largo felt in limbo again. "No, I will pass on the scans for now. I don't know what is going on in my head, but I do know it scares me, this mission."

Emi stood and said, "Well, hell, it is scary, Largo. Look, we had better call in. There is a lot to brief Minerva on. She is expecting to hear from us."

Emi pressed her bracer, and Minerva responded immediately in a holocall. "Briefing completed?"

They both nodded.

"Okay. I hate risking my portal here. I'm not sure if it will work out there on Raba, and using it might alert people I do not want to be alerted. But there have been some serious challenges for our company in the last twenty-four hours. Hold on a second. I'm coming through." The air crackled and growled as her portal opened. Largo held out his hand. Minerva took it and stepped into the room.

"That thing is amazing," Emi observed. "Never seen one in operation before."

Minerva wore her skin-hugging black armor and helmet with blue-and-gold accents. She removed her helmet and placed it on the desk.

"How soon can Key and Claire leave?" Minerva was all business.

Emi cleared her throat. "There is a problem, ma'am. Claire is currently recuperating from some pretty severe wounds."

"What happened?" Minerva asked.

"About eight hours ago, we fought off a significant attack by a force that wanted us to think they were pirates," Emi began. "Yet their tactics did not resemble those of bandits. They came in close to sunset. Never seen an assault like this before, never been a direct massed attack on our base."

"And what were they then if not pirates?" Minerva interjected.

"Ma'am, it likely was a sneak attack by DC, Dyeus Corp. We took heavy casualties. Claire was one of them."

Minerva grimaced. "Ross Lasker. Does he know that we know it was his outfit?" Largo could see Minerva calculating her next move as she rubbed her chin.

"No, ma'am. We discovered this about an hour ago," Emi said.

"What a strange happenstance that the attack coincided with Largo's crew arriving on Raba. Almost like they knew where you are and when you'd be here." Minerva paused before continuing. "I still have DC penetration in my corporate staff. This was no coincidence. There's a reason why I am dressed in armor. We have had many attacks on our assets since yesterday. One of our competitors is probing for weaknesses. Probably

Lasker. I want you two to sit down and tell me everything you know for certain and then tell me what your speculations are."

After they'd finished, Minerva started asking questions. "Emi, who is your number three? Your GCO?"

"Emil Demos, ma'am. Out of company security." Emi replied.

"Excellent. Would you say Demos is qualified to fill in for Claire until she's fit?" Minerva's eyes narrowed as she examined Emi.

"No doubt, ma'am."

"Good, that's done." Minerva was distracted by something.

Perplexed, Emi asked, "Pardon me, ma'am, what is done?"

"You will replace Claire. I don't like having a commander reporting to a commander. That can be awkward. But you two will make it work, I am sure. Largo will have operational command of the mission, and you will run comms, weps, and logistics for him. as Claire would have done if not for this unfortunate misstep by the soon-to-be-dead Ross Lasker."

"Yes, ma'am." Emi was doing her best to keep up.

"Largo?" Minerva asked.

"Yes."

"Rent will command *Crimson Rhapsody* after you shuttle to the surface of Gereon with your advance party. You can brief the crew about the mission, their project shares, and the like after you get underway. Speaking of that, I need you two to leave Raba inside of three days, please. DC may have got wind of what we are doing. Step up your security ops. I will remain here to hurry things along. I will also bring in heavy reinforcements while I plan our counterattack."

"Will do." Emi nodded.

"Emi, take any officer or personnel you need for comms, weps, and logistics support from your garrison. We will be beefing up and hardening the base here in any event. The war has started. Lasker doesn't know what we know—this thing is on."

7

Largo and Emi surveyed *Crimson Rhapsody*'s vast cargo hold. The last of the lozenge-shaped containers was loaded into the munitions bay. A well-known warship of Grand Design's merchant fleet, modifications in K City had given her troopship functionality.

"Largo, are we expecting a war on Gereon?" Emi asked. "That is an awful lot of heavy ordinance."

He shrugged. "I don't know what to expect, but it is what the corporate brain trust back in KC drew up. To the letter."

"I realize that, but we are leaving Raba almost stripped. Vulnerable."

"Minerva's call." Largo shrugged again. "You studied the Gereon file?"

"Of course."

"Then you know that the three probes we sent out there have returned almost no data about the planet. We lost contact with all of them shortly after they entered the Gereon atmosphere. The atmosphere may be the problem, for all we know. Part of it is volcanic. It also has plenty of oxygen, water, and could be rich in minerals—especially gold. At least that's what we know from three probes." Largo looked over the manifest "So, we understand nothing about Gereon."

Emi added, "Other than we will need to conduct much geoengineering."

"Right. So, since we're headed to an unknown planet, for an indeterminate time, I'm glad we're armed to the teeth. If we hit a major gold strike, word will get around," Largo said.

"And that will attract attention. I get it," Emi conceded.

"I'm more interested in all the stuff we loaded in the hold in KC. Everything from world-building equipment to clone embryos. We could last generations out there."

"Minerva's plan?" Emi mused.

<hr>

The amphitheater was standing room only as Largo prepared to address the crew. The floor-to-ceiling wall screen was blank for the moment. Soon it would fill up with images and footage of everything related to their mission.

Everything I'm allowed to say. And none of my doubts, Largo thought as he surveyed the audience.

Emi and Claire, seated in front of him, looked elegant in their red-and-black formal uniforms. Claire's left arm was in a brace. Still, she was recovering, despite her terrible wounds: a welcome addition to the senior leadership group. The Raba medical team had cleared her for the mission.

Still, we haven't told Minerva we've brought Claire along, but she did say bring any personnel from Raba. Like we sometimes say—better to ask for forgiveness than permission.

Everyone wore dress uniforms. The large cadre of engineers were in brown-and-green uniforms, med staff in pale blue. Even the clone battalions were dressed in their silver-and-gray formal armor.

I hope three combat battalions are enough, he thought, before beginning his speech. *Minerva has indoctrinated us to treat the clones like we would treat humans, but this trip, I don't know.*

"Welcome. We have finally reached our full complement of crew, and our ship is full to the gunwales with cargo. I don't think we could cram as much as another cryo grenade into the ordinance hold. Or another gun into a wale."

This met with polite laughter.

"I will make this brief. I find that speeches best be quick and informative. The questions afterward are much more enlightening.

"Disruptor drives. When Mesh Trouter developed the first viable means of long-distance space travel, it opened up the universe. Without question, the most significant invention ever. Even though it still takes months to get anywhere in this galaxy."

Most of the audience was nodding. Everyone was attentive.

"But most of us do not know much about the principles of disruptor drives. How does one work? Well, it constricts space at the front of our ship as it unwraps it behind us while we move through space-time. Thus, we travel vast expanses with massive speed, rendering the theory of relativity moot."

He heard a few groans from the theoretical physicists in the room.

"Okay, physicists. I know I'm oversimplifying it. Criminally. Physics, contracting space-time, or stretching it faster than light. These are not today's topics. I invite any of you experts to schedule a colloquium on this subject for any interested parties." Largo paused and looked around the room before continuing.

"I want to talk about the long pole in the tent. When it comes to building disruptor drives, it's their gold circuitry. Gold. You need massive amounts of pure gold.

"Most of the known gold we have is gone—consumed. There has not been enough gold to build one new disruptor drive in the last two years. Not by any of the nine corporations. All we do is recycle and upgrade preexisting drives at this point. Our refitted ship, *Crimson Rhapsody*, has a recycled drive running it, of course.

"The planet Gereon, our destination, possibly holds enough gold for us to corner the market on building disruptor drives."

Silence. He thought a dramatic pause was appropriate to let that point sink in.

"Also of significance is a high oxygen content and the presence of water on Gereon. Commander Manaka will address that aspect of the planetary environment. Commander?" Largo stepped away from the podium.

Emi addressed the crowd. "Water occurs throughout the cosmos. But liquid water present in an atmosphere is unusual. Water suspended in the air can regulate temperatures. It can create weather systems capable of rain and storms. The surface of Gereon appears to be diverse and complex. But it is volcanically and tectonically active. These conditions have obscured the planet's surface and made it hard for us to study it."

"Water combines with enzymes to make organisms. Because amino acids are present, we can expect life forms. These can range from simple unicellular entities up to apex predators. The planet is three billion years old. Much life can happen in that interval—abundant dividing and multiplying. Be on guard, stick to your security protocols, and assume anything is possible out there. You can expect occasional earthquakes and high winds at times. Sometimes sandy, ashy conditions. So use your optional oxygen tanks as the situation mandates. But generally, with an oxygen content of 26 percent and abundant water, Gereon is quite hospitable. Oxygen tanks and masks will be optional.

"In a few hours, after our advance party deploys, we will begin to answer many of our questions about Gereon. Thank you for your time and attention. Commander Largo?"

Largo said, "Please hold your questions until the presentation has concluded. Roll it, Jaylen."

The lights dimmed. The 3D wall presented a satellite probe heading toward Gereon, an immense grayish-brown sphere with streaks of blue and green. The white dwarf sun Acanthus loomed in the distance.

<hr>

Largo began the q-and-a phase immediately after the presentation ended. Emi, Claire, and Jaylen joined him on the podium.

"Identify yourself before asking your questions. That way, the 700 people here can start to get to know each other," Largo said.

Warm laughter ensued. The room felt a bit upbeat now.

One of my more inspired speeches? Hell, gold always inspires people. Has forever.

Largo pointed to a blonde woman from engineering in the second row, a junior officer. "Yes. You there in the second row."

"Hi. I am Michelle Curvois, and my questions are for you, sir. I understand, Commander, that your background is in our security and counter espionage divisions?"

"Yes, and before that Corporate Combat Operations," Largo said.

"A follow-up, if I may?"

"Michelle." Largo nodded.

"Commander Manaka has much planetary field ops experience. Why isn't Manaka our director?"

I would have to call on her first, Largo thought, turning to ask Emi, "Commander Manaka, do you want to field this one?"

"Sure, Commander. So, Michelle, any of the four of us up here can lead this mission. We are going to face hostile conditions. The leadership team could take casualties." She paused before continuing. "Commander Largo was selected by our corporate board as the commanding officer. Hell, I wasn't even intended to be here. I was supposed to stay on Raba. Claire was meant to be second in command, followed by Jaylen as commander of this ship. After Claire was wounded, Minerva Klyne herself slotted me into the second chair. We have altered our roles, but Minerva's chain of command is intact."

"So, what are your expectations of this mission, ma'am?" Michelle asked.

"We could all get quite rich or quite dead, who knows?" Manaka shrugged her shoulders.

Looking skeptical, Michelle took her seat.

Largo pointed to a man in a bio-med uniform in the middle of the crowd. "You there with the beard."

"Hello. I am Dr. Postrenal. My question is also for you, sir."

I'm a doctor too, but I never self-identify using my title, that is a bit annoying. Some guys never get over it, I guess. Largo smiled.

"Go for it," Largo said.

Please do not bring up Port Amphora, he thought.

"Xenoarchaeology. You wrote an important thesis while attending our most elite university a few years ago," Postrenal observed.

Largo smiled. "Yes. Is there a question in there somewhere?"

Postrenal smiled as well. "I read your thesis. Brilliant. My question is implicit. Xenoarchaeology. Are we expecting something along those lines? On Gereon? Is it expected to be inhabited?"

Largo paused before responding.

That is a damned good question, been wondering about that one myself. "You mean specific indications of an intelligent unknown or alien life form, I take it?"

"That is what I mean." Postrenal pulled his beard.

"I know this much—that Minerva mentioned it during my interview. She asked me about my entire background. Consider that we are heading to a world we know nothing about. Perhaps she selected me because of the minute chance that an intelligent alien species could be there. A slim chance at best," Largo sipped water before continuing. "It is said that Enrico Fermi once did some quick calculations on a dinner napkin. He showed that the galaxy contains millions of planets like Earth. 'Where is everybody?' Fermi asked. Centuries later, humans are still alone in the universe. Always looking for the answer to that question."

"But still a possibility. As you said in your dissertation, one day, we will encounter an intelligent alien life form. It is inevitable." Postrenal would not let go of it.

Maybe I'm encountering one right now, Largo thought.

"Well, I was living the life of the mind back then, as one is inclined to do in grad school, when I wrote that. But this is real life. And real life is dangerous and brutal, as we all learned back in elementary school."

8

"Hang on! She's getting frisky. A bit of chop," Claire said through gritted teeth. The shuttle descended, bumping hard through murky volcanic clouds.

"There's a hole in the clouds on the port side," Largo pointed out.

"Trying for it. Damn. It's like wrestling an oak tree," Claire whispered.

The engines were deafening as Claire used the thrusters to keep control. A steady undertone of scree reverberated, hitting the ship's hull like bullets.

"This atmosphere isn't dense. It's damned near gravel," Largo said. "This is gonna be a rough landing." He looked for a reading on the screen, but couldn't see it through dense clouds of dust. "Claire, we have lost all comms with *Rhapsody*. Nothing. Zip."

"Could you grab the yoke, please? The computer can't close on the surface. Help me keep her flying," Claire said with accentuated calmness.

"Two thousand meters to surface. Right here is pretty much where all the probes lost contact," Largo noted. "Well, aside from that one geologic that lasted almost a full three minutes on the surface."

"The one that identified the gold profile. The one that has led us all here," Claire said as the ship made a nauseating, stomach-wrenching elevator drop.

"Kind of shows how desperate we are for gold, doesn't it?" Largo observed. "Uh, Claire, number two engine is failing."

The AI was a nanosecond behind Largo. "Number two engine will shut down in fifteen seconds. Impact with the surface in twenty-seven seconds," Bette reported.

"Setting her down now. Going to be bumpy," Claire said.

All Largo could see through the porthole were whirling clouds of gray-and-white sand. The shuttle slammed hard and rolled over and over, burrowing into the unseen surface of Gereon with a deafening crash.

Choking on clouds of grit and gases, he tried to unfasten his seat belt.

Can't see. With a headache straight out of hell, Largo tried to get up. *Are my eyes burned? What is this place? Who are these light creatures with their fingers in my brain?*

Kayle was looking down at him.

I knew she would come.

"Kayle" was all he could say.

"Not Kayle. Disappointed?"

"Not Kayle. Who?" Largo asked.

"Hey, it's me. It's Claire."

Claire's beautifully sad, scarred face came into focus. She whispered, "You're hurt, Key. Nasty head and neck wounds. You must lie still now, please?"

Bette said, "Hull breach. Mission and crew in peril. Sealing all remaining intact compartments and bulkheads."

"We crashed, Key. You've been out a few hours. Still bleeding. Bette and I have almost got you stabilized," Claire said.

"Commander Corsac?" Bette asked.

"Yes, Bette."

"Commander Largo has a strange, ruptured implant in his neck. It is a device I do not recognize, but it must come out immediately. It has moved close to his jugular. I repeat, the device must come out now."

"Thank you, Bette. I'm on it," Claire said.

"A cautionary observation. My scan shows Commander Largo has five other implants in his torso, also of unknown origin. They may comprise a sophisticated system. Possibly an endorphin injector connected by micro-bio-filaments. We risk a compromised systemic effect of all his implants if the one in his neck comes out. But it still must go. You need to anesthetize him partially. Too risky to put him under."

"Stop, Claire," Key whispered. "Report. What has happened? Casualties, damage?"

"Regrettably, we lost five security clones. Not sure how many wounded. Crashed and rolled into a box canyon. The shuttle is beyond salvage, but it will serve as temporary shelter while we regroup."

"Our supplies. Provisions?"

Claire paused and applied pressure to his wound before continuing, "We lost part of the armory. The atmosphere processors and botanicals are intact. Phase one of those just launched." She paused to put a scope on his neck. "Hey, look, we must take this thing out of your neck. Do you know why it's in there or what it is?"

"No idea. It could have happened during my coma…Claire…send a drone to *Rhapsody*. Apprise Jaylen of our situation. Make a statement to our surviving crew members here." Largo mumbled as the anesthetic numbed him from his maxilla to his scapula.

"Already done," Claire replied.

Strange to hear Bette and Claire talk about me and be unable to comment.

"I'll put you right, Commander." Claire spoke between gritted teeth. She placed the med-scan necklace around his neck and went to work. After a couple of minutes, she said to Bette, "Okay. I found another implant at the C1 spinal nerve. It looks quite old. Likely been there for many years, embedded in his bone tissue. It appears unconnected and unrelated to the group you detected."

"Commander Largo has more implants than most people," Bette observed. "I recommend we do not disturb the C1 implant. Remove only the dislodged implant in his neck tissue."

"Almost there, and…we've got it!" Claire said.

Largo felt a momentary flash of stabbing pain and passed out.

⎯⎯⎯◈⎯⎯⎯

After a nightmare featuring Kayle alone with him in a burning city, Largo woke up to a fogged mind.

"Ah, you have returned to us," Claire said. "How do you feel?"

"Like a monster needle went straight through my head." He struggled to get out of bed.

"Stay put, Commander. You are in recovery," Claire said.

"How long was I out?" he asked.

"Nineteen hours and twenty-six minutes total. When we removed the implant, you had a seizure and passed out. Before anything else happens, you must go through a thorough med scan." Claire was adamant.

"What has happened since the surgery? The drone went to *Rhapsody*, yes?"

"Yes. Nothing from Emi or Jaylen about that yet. Local network comms are back up. But the planet's atmosphere in this region is almost impenetrable for the moment. To clear that up, I have deployed sixteen atmospheric processors in a grid pattern around us. They appear to be having the intended cleansing effect. The base camp dome module is up, and we have all moved in from our wrecked shuttle. That is where we are now."

"Claire, you've done well. Thank you," Largo said.

Claire paused. "Um, I haven't done all that well. I sent out a recon squad. They are overdue to return."

"How overdue are they?"

"Almost three hours now. We had comms with them for thirty minutes and then nothing. They have a drone shadowing the convoy, but we have lost contact with it."

"Were they well-armed?"

"Two trams. Heavy ordinance. Should be able to handle anything," Claire said.

"Who is leading it?" he asked.

"LC Austen Nesh. Our most seasoned combat veteran."

"Good choice. I overlapped with Nesh in grad school. He's capable and clever. You've done what I would have done in your shoes," Largo said.

"So, what would you do now?" Claire asked.

"All we can do. We wait. But let's get my med scan over with so I can get back to work, shall we?"

—♦—

"Commander, your brain and nervous system have had major augmentations over the years. It started with a behavioral mod installed at the base of your neck when you were about three or four years old. Mods continued to be added over the years, with five more installed recently." Claire studied a tablet with Largo's results. "I have never heard of a behavioral mod implanted in someone as young as four. Usually happens to teenagers."

"I have no recollection of that ever happening," Largo said.

"Of course. Also, it is well-disguised. It is so embedded now, it has become part of your spinal structure," Claire said.

"Undetected for years. Who put it there? The recent ones must have been implanted while I was comatose. But what are these things doing to me?" he asked.

Claire pushed her hair back and tied it in a tight ponytail. She studied his face before asking him a question. "You were a ward of the company, correct?"

"Yes. I grew up in the system."

"Who was responsible for you?" Claire asked.

"Minerva Klyne."

"Wow. Pretty good mentor!"

"Well, she was not 'Minerva Klyne' in those days. She was one of many thousands of mid-level executives. She hadn't clawed her way to the top of the corporate food chain yet."

"And when did you and she connect?" she asked.

"I was around five years old, but I don't remember it at all. It's what I was told over the years. You hear something so many times as a child, it takes root in your mind. Memory is ephemeral."

Largo wondered, *Has my mind ever been my own?*

"And is it malleable?" Claire asked.

Largo shrugged. "Yeah."

"So, it may or may not have been Minerva who put that thing into your spine," Claire mused.

"I have no idea what happened when I was four. But Minerva had to have authorized the ones that were put in during my medical coma," he said.

"What are you going to do about them?" Claire asked.

"Have them removed at the first opportunity, including the oldest one. Also, confront Minerva if I ever see her again," he said.

"All of that could have dangerous consequences, especially the last part."

"My life has been a series of dangerous consequences."

"Can you tell me what you believe you remember about it?" Claire asked.

"Trying to be my analyst? All who tried have failed," Largo said.

"I love a good mystery." Claire smiled.

She's right. This could help, Largo thought. "Okay. Since I'm not going anywhere anytime soon, let's give it a try."

"Go as far back as you can recall."

"I remember the corporate grade school lessons from when I was six. Our motto was 'be more…'"

"—Than you seem.' It was everyone's motto," Claire added. "So, did you ever have questions?"

"Sorry. Still disoriented. Questions about?" he asked.

Claire paused. She touched his newest scar. "That was a close call, you know."

"Questions about what?" Largo repeated.

"Let's drop it. Maybe you don't have any questions. That would be amazing, but what do you remember about school? What was important?" she asked.

"The willingness to sacrifice oneself in an extreme situation, because the individual does not count, only the corporation."

"Pretty standard material. We all got that," Claire added. "Ever wonder about that stuff?"

"How so?"

"It has long been plain to me, to many of us, that our corporate educational system is built on coercion. It is programming, not educating, us. The purpose of the system is not stability, but compliance, even domination." Claire whispered, "We have no freedom as a result. We've never had any freedom. Freedom is an illusion."

"Why are you whispering?" Largo whispered too.

"We all know the penalties for disloyalty," she said.

"Disloyalty means contract termination, expulsion from the corporation. How is this conversation disloyal? We're just talking. Also, who could be listening to us out here at the edge of the galaxy?"

"Do you think that this corporate society of ours is the pinnacle of human evolution? That it's the best we can do?"

"You're still whispering, Claire."

"You knew Kayle, yes?"

Largo nodded, not wanting to say anything about all that PA stuff.

"She has long maintained that we must treat the clones better. They are more than slaves. You ever think about that?"

"Can't say that I have. But I do remember Kayle's feelings on the matter."

Claire shook her head and shivered a bit. "This kind of conversation falls way outside the lines of 'acceptable' moral corporate conduct." Claire paused. "You should know that."

"I do not," he said.

"What did they do to your brain?"

"I don't know, and I'm afraid to find out."

Claire's bracer activated with a holocall from Austen Nesh.

"Corsac. This planet is nothing like what I expected."

"Report, Nesh," Claire said.

"Get your combat medics ready. We have casualties," Nesh said.

"Numbers?" Claire asked.

"Many."

9

KAYLE KORBAN, FORMER SENIOR VICE president at GDC and current COO for Dyeus Corp, slept securely in her apartment. Suddenly, Minerva Klyne's face hovered over her bed. Floating. Grinning.

Am I still asleep? Dreaming? No. This is a nightmare. Why can I not wake up?

"Are you having trouble sleeping, dear? Does what you did to Key and the rest of us keep you up at night?" Minerva smiled, revealing her perfect white carnivorous teeth.

Kayle shook her head and said, "No. This is not happening. It is not happening. This is not real." She rubbed her eyes. Blinked hard. Minerva and her portal were still there. She was still floating next to her bed.

"Ah, I see I got your attention, Kayle," Minerva whispered, quite entertained. She could reach right through her portal and grab Kayle with ease if she wanted to. She caressed Kayle's hand to make her point.

"Ticklish?" Minerva laughed.

"Where? How? My bio-chip was—they removed my bio-chip." Kayle shuddered and swung her legs out of bed, looking for her sidearm.

"Did they? Are you sure?" Minerva's hands disappeared inside her flowing black robe.

"They took it out!" Kayle took a deep breath. "This scar on my neck." She felt for the small bump on her neck. It was still there.

So how is this happening? How did she track me?

"Are you sure? Have you checked everywhere? Made a thorough search, darling?" Minerva laughed and stepped through the portal.

Kayle leaped out of bed and ran to her kitchen. Her Gauss pistol was in a side drawer.

Minerva moved like a cat. Her rail gun was pointed at Kayle's head in seconds. "Hold it right there, dear. I don't trust desperate women in their kitchens. Do not move. Don't even breathe." She lowered her gun and laughed. "Okay. That was over the top. You can breathe."

Minerva glided over to the window and looked out at the beach and ocean below.

"Raba. Nice view." She nodded. "Good choice. I take it we are inside the famous pirate base. What? Do they hand out eye patches when you join?" Minerva laughed. "Rather luxurious for a pirate's apartment. I kind of like it here."

"Minerva. You have not killed me." Kayle braced herself.

"Not yet anyway." Minerva placed her gun on the bar and removed her helmet. "I miss you, darling. Miss your skin, so brown. Your enigmatic smiles."

"What do you want?" Kayle whispered.

Minerva pulled up a chair at the bar. "Kayle, I want to put you back on the payroll. Pour us a drink, will you?"

⋘━◆━⋙

It was early morning. Kayle stared at Minerva's violet lipstick-stained cocktail glass.

Yes. That was real last night. It happened.

"I am trapped," Kayle said to the empty kitchen, as she examined Minerva's lip prints on the glass. *Of course, she has perfect lips. Why am I not surprised? I wish I could talk to Key. Minerva seems a bit obsessed with him. That could be bad for your health.*

"If I do what she wants without getting killed, I could see him again someday. If Key lasts that long." She shrugged. "If any of us last that long."

A triple agent.

It seemed Minerva had figured that Kayle was more useful alive than dead. It unnerved her to know that Minerva could show up in her bed in the middle of the night.

Or anywhere else for that matter? There has to be a way to block a portal. Or, failing that, to go somewhere beyond its range.

I need to look into that in my copious spare time. Now I need to brief Lasker. If I don't tell him, I guess I've made my choice. Kayle realized she had no idea what she would do.

Dr. Ross Lasker, the wealthiest man in the galaxy, dressed almost like a monk. Simple clothes. No jewelry, kept his thinning hair cropped, and had a permanent beard shadow. It never seemed to grow. He was small-boned and wiry. Fat free. His concerns for personal security were obvious. Ten armed clone commandos in full armor ringed the room.

Does he even know what the word 'fun' means? Kayle thought. *All that cash and he pays no attention to it. Power, on the other hand...*

"I don't care what it takes to get our agent onboard that relief shuttle, Yeoh. Look. Don't bother me with the details. Just tell me when it's done! You will get him on that shuttle, or I will end your employment. Got that?" Lasker finished up the first conference staff call of the day. A crucial conference call with their embedded double agent on the *Crimson Rhapsody.*

Double agent, Kayle thought. Only a double? Try a triple, you slacking, unambitious sloth.

He pounded the table before he addressed Kayle. His bodyguards did not react to the histrionics.

"Ah, Korban. Sorry for the delay. Also, the theatrics. Yeoh is such an imbecile. He still fails to grasp what we are trying to do here." He sighed and smoothed his nonexistent hair. "I need you to immediately work up how and when we can form an off-world expedition to a recently discovered planet. Geo-engineering, gold mining, war force, the whole package. I'll be assigning my best man to assist you."

"Excuse me, but you did say gold mining?" Kayle asked.

Lasker almost smiled. The corners of his mouth twitched. It was the best he could do. "Yes. How about that? DMC, Dyeus Mining, might finally come out of mothballs. Most of that old equipment is stored here at Crema Bay, isn't it?" Lasker asked.

"Yes. Raba was our last major gold exploration project. Total bust. You fired all the senior managers and engineers involved." Kayle frowned and continued, "So am I to understand that GDC already has an operation with all the latest in exploration tech? And that they are actually there? At the site?"

"We don't know for sure, but we must assume so. If not now, GDC soon will be," Lasker said. "I must kill Minerva Klyne and take over all her assets. We must own GDC.

"Are you familiar with the dreadnought *Crimson Rhapsody*, Kayle?"

She nodded. "Yes. She's a powerful warship."

"She's recently been modified to take on a troopship and exploration functions. She left Raba two days ago. Fully loaded. An old friend of yours, Commander Largo, is in charge."

"Do we know where she is headed?" *Excellent assignment for Key,* she thought. *That explains why Minerva was so obsessed with him.*

"We need to get that, but so far, nothing on the destination." On his holo, Lasker said, "Peroni, get in here now."

Kayle got to the point, "So GDC has the jump on us, maybe an established base by now, all the best equipment. And all we have is…"

"Stop right there. The solution is simple," Julio Peroni interrupted as he walked into the room. "We bring overwhelming force. Take it all away from them."

"How many bodies are you thinking constitutes 'overwhelming' force?" Kayle asked.

"We draw down from all our subsidiaries, all bases, security forces, and vendors. Elite clone rangers, marines, only. About 2,000 bodies should more than cover it. Our intel says they have a little over 700 combat personnel on board that ship. Two thousand clones should be enough." Peroni shrugged before continuing, "Also, every ship and weps system that we may need, including prototypes."

"This could take a while to assemble. Also, as you probably know, Peroni, prototypes can blow up in combat situations," Kayle said. "And are we planning on using our clones in an expendable role again? Cannon fodder? Because that's a bad idea."

Peroni glared at her. "Look, Korban, this is my plan. I'm all in. If you have doubts, you can get out now."

Kayle stood and started toward Peroni, her hand instinctively drifting to her needle's hilt. "Ross, who is in charge here? Me or Peroni?"

"You are the first lead, and Julio is your XO. Kayle will lead the expedition to the planet as soon as we locate it. Peroni, you will stay on Raba in a support role."

Peroni scoffed and started to object, but Lasker cut him off.

"Peroni, you will accept this structure. Period. Your job now is to provide all necessary due diligence for inclusion or exclusion of weps and all logistics that Kayle needs to be successful. You have five days to plan."

Peroni stammered, "But Ross, I am her senior."

"Peroni, you will carry out her orders. Or how did you put it?" He snarled, "You can get out now. Now go make it happen. Immediately!"

⋘◆⋙

Kayle reclined on her balcony overlooking the beach. It was sunset, and Raba was putting on a spectacular show. Off to the south, thunderheads built up as lightning flashes strobed inside them and lit the clouds up like rainbow lanterns.

She heard the now-familiar crackling-in-the-air sound of Minerva's portal rasping and growling behind her. The two of them had come to an understanding. Kayle would spy for her, but there would be no further nocturnal intrusions. She felt Minerva's hand on her shoulder as the portal closed behind them.

Minerva struck an imperious pose, hands on hips, as she surveyed the view, the beach, the sunset, the patrolling gunships. Like she owned the place.

She breathed deeply of the ocean air and exhaled.

"I need a place like this, Kayle. I love the air here. Think I'm going to build one when I get a chance. When this is all over."

Kayle placed her drink on the table and stood very close to her. Minerva looked at Kayle, eyes alight with amusement.

"But it is never going to be all over, is it, Minerva?" Kayle whispered.

"No, not likely." Minerva shook her head, still smiling. It was not disarming.

"I have a question. You never bring a bodyguard with you. Don't you feel a little exposed out here? At an enemy base? All by yourself?" Kayle asked.

Minerva's eyes narrowed. She jumped up on the balcony railing. Lithe as a cat. Now she loomed over Kayle like a predator and spread out her long arms like wings.

"Want to have a go at me, darling?" The breeze floated her thick, blue-black hair in strands around her pallid face. Her thin muscular-enhancing meshed armor matched her hair. The ebony-and-gold needle in its sheath at her side was as beautiful as it was deadly. She pushed her hair back and held her hands out, balancing on the thin rail. "I have studied your background, Kayle. I know all about you. You would be a worthy adversary. Why not take a shot? I promise not to harm you." She grinned. "Well, maybe a bit, but not too much. Wouldn't want to harm a hair on that pretty head."

Kayle considered Minerva's laughing eyes.

The truth is I admire her. She is without question one of the most beautiful women in the cosmos. Quite possibly, one of the deadliest as well. But it's a lose-lose situation if I kill her. GDC assassins or an endless supply of bounty hunters will get to me if I kill her.

"We don't have a choice, do we, Minerva? We have to do this now. I cannot refuse your challenge. You know that don't you?"

Minerva grinned. "Like I said, I know all about you, Kayle. Your culture. Your background."

Kayle paused. "Ah, well, I don't have much of a shelf life anyway. Like anyone would care. I have betrayed almost everyone who ever relied on me." Kayle readied herself.

"Poor little Kayle. Feeling sorry for yourself?"

Kayle kicked out hard with her right foot and connected with Minerva's midsection. She grabbed for her needle but just missed it as Minerva went over the rail.

Minerva never stopped grinning. Her hands caught the rail at the last possible moment, and she backflipped behind Kayle. Before Kayle could react, Minerva's needle pulsed against her neck.

One second quicker, and I would have had her. Very close.

Numbed by Minerva's chokehold, Kayle could not move. The smell of her burning hair filled the balcony.

"Apologies for searing your beautiful hair, but that kick was not very sporting," Minerva whispered in her ear. "Now, Kayle, are we to behave ourselves? Or do you want to have another rumpus? I am fine either way." She released Kayle.

"I think that playtime is over for now," Kayle said. "We could give it another go when things settle a bit more?"

"Anytime," Minerva whispered. She sheathed her blade. "Are you ever going to offer me a drink? We have business to discuss. Make it a traveler. I want to take a walk on the beach with you. It is so lovely right now with that blue moon."

Kayle looked at Raba's only moon. "Azuri. It's all water, no land up there, Minerva. No gold."

"Let's get down to the beach, shall we?"

⸻◆⸻

Azuri glowed bright blue in the night sky as they walked along a narrow black sandy beach. Minerva had adjusted her armor to digital stealth mode. From a distance, it looked like Kayle walked by herself on the lonely shore.

Kayle summarized what she knew of Lasker's plans. Minerva was silent for a while as she considered all that Kayle had told her.

"It's cards on the table time." She pushed her hair back and stretched. "It's so relaxing here, it is making me sleepy." Minerva kneeled and splashed water on her face. "We need to assume that with his talented spies, Lasker will soon know Gereon's exact location. So, you better get on that mission and get off Raba before the week is out."

"I've already assigned myself to it." Kayle paused. "Wait. What's the hurry about getting off Raba?"

Minerva ignored her question. "And you need to be with the invasion crew. You need to land on Gereon in the first assault." Minerva was firm.

Kayle considered her options before responding. "I had not planned on that. I guess I can arrange it. Why, though?"

"Kayle, things will go so much better if you do not use that word with me." Minerva stared at her before continuing. "Finally dear, when it's all settled, you will get the same share of the proceeds as Largo. Five percent of everything."

"Generous. Thank you, Minerva."

I just might get rich. Now all I need to do is not get killed.

"There are a couple of stipulations, of course," Minerva added.

"There always are."

"You must sabotage Dyeus Corp at every opportunity, and you must not get caught. If you identify any overt threats to your safety, you will eliminate them immediately," she said.

Kayle hesitated to bring up her most pressing concern, but thought, *might as well clear the air now*. "What if that threat comes from someone on your leadership team?"

Minerva looked out at the ocean. "If it assures the success of the overall mission, you are authorized to terminate."

"Even if it's Largo?"

Minerva appraised Kayle with a fresh look. "Negative. If it is Largo, you will have to get clearance from me first."

"Fine. But you told me yourself that so far no comms from Gereon. Maybe the distance and dense atmosphere block everything, holos, your portal, even radio. So what if I cannot contact you, Minerva? What then?"

"Key will solve that atmospheric blockage problem. I guarantee it." Minerva grasped Kayle's forearm and looked in her eyes. "Let me make it crystal clear, Korban. Only I can authorize the termination of Key Largo's command."

10

"IT'S COMING UP ON THE screen now," Claire observed. "Notes for the logbook. Our first experiences on Gereon were a disastrous crash, with bloody combat immediately following."

Largo watched the drone cam footage. All he could see were APCs—two tram trackers moving through dust clouds on a featureless plain. The distant blurry white orb of Acanthus settled over the horizon. It provided scant illumination in the gritty twilight. Everything seemed normal. Uneventful.

Something twitched next to the lead vehicle.

"Hold up. What was that? Claire? Pause it, please."

A thick black claw attached to a long tentacle emerged from under the track. It grabbed the vehicle midway up its flank.

"That's some kind of large animal, Key," Claire whispered as she let the footage resume.

Claire gasped as four more massive tentacles gripped the vehicle. They jerked it underneath the planet's surface. An explosion of dust obscured the rest of the scene.

"Fast forward it," Largo said.

The dust cleared, and a cavern opened as the tracker and the tentacled beast disappeared. The drone hovered above the scene, capturing the action. Gun flashes and heavy ordinance explosions lit up the walls of the cavern. More troops deployed from the second tram and rappelled into the flashing firefight. More massive explosions concealed the fighting.

The firefight ended, and the recon force emerged. They ran flat out with their wounded and the corpses of two of the beasts in tow.

Nesh stayed behind and set charges. He sealed off the crater, burying the creatures under rubble.

The vehicles sped back to base camp and began unloading in real-time.

"Let's get down there, Claire," Largo said.

"Commander, you are still recuperating. I advise you not to…"

"Noted. Let's go."

⸻◆⸻

Nesh concluded his report to Key and Claire in the ops room.

"Confirmed. There are life forms and water present on Gereon. The tentacled grippers are quite hostile and thick-skinned. Like some amphibians, they have claws that emit toxins that are fatal to humans. Hemotoxins and neural toxins. We were lucky to escape without fatalities. Our medics…"

"Are the absolute best," Claire said.

Nesh nodded in agreement before continuing.

"They are. True. Takes a lot to bring those grips down, in any case. They tore that tram to pieces. All kinds of bacteria in that cavern too. No traces of gold in the sands, unfortunately."

"Well, it's early days." Key interjected.

"You did well, Nesh." Claire rubbed her jaw and considered what they had learned. "Any idea what the cavern dwellers eat? What else is down there?"

"The water samples may give us clues as soon as they are processed," Key said.

"We should have initial results within the hour," Nesh reported. "The beast autopsies will take a bit longer."

"So, the good news is the planet has an unknown source of subterranean water," Key said.

"And the bad news is that the water has nasty grippers in it. And I mean nasty." Nesh said.

Key nodded. "Did these grippers seem sentient in any way?"

"Grips seem to behave like ants or bees. Semi-coordinated. Hive intelligence."

"Common sentient intelligence," Key said.

"Common." Nesh concurred. "A lot more were coming down that tube, based on our thermal detectors. Dozens of them. That's when I hit them with the heavy weapons and made a tactical withdrawal. Then I dropped the roof and collapsed the cavern on them. It was too close Largo."

"Grippers are difficult to kill?" Claire followed up.

He nodded. "Skin is like plate armor. You can slice the tentacles with a needler when you're in close and then drop a sticky on their heads. That'll blow their shit up. But rail guns only seem to piss them off." Nesh laughed.

"Killing them at close range seems suboptimal," Claire deadpanned.

Nesh laughed. "Most definitely suboptimal Corsac. We need a better method for sure."

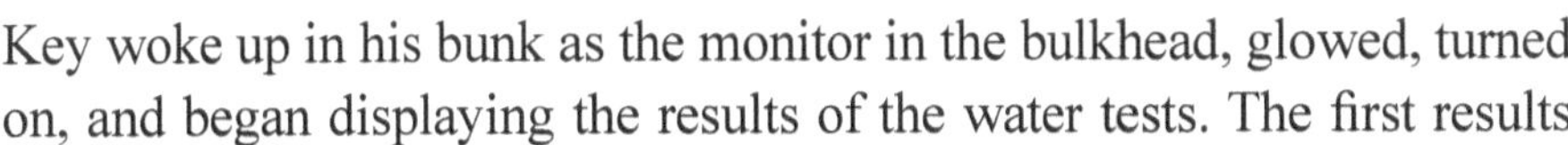

Key woke up in his bunk as the monitor in the bulkhead, glowed, turned on, and began displaying the results of the water tests. The first results were surprising.

Volcanic origin, many gold flakes.

DNA sample traces in the water were listed out next with adjacent phenotypical projections of what the life forms morphologically resembled. Some things looked like fish, eels, and tadpoles. The fish apex predator, a small piranha-like creature with turquoise scales, looked nasty. The amphibian's alpha predator appeared to be the creature everyone called a "gripper or grip." There were only four mammalian forms represented so far. A fanged tiger-like being, a massive quadrupedal herbivore, a canine/feline looking animal, and a furry, blurry, biped.

So, who are you? I wonder.

Key started a holocall.

Claire answered. "Hey. Looking at the results?"

"Curiouser and curiouser," Key mumbled.

"Sure, Alice," she said.

"What?" Key asked. "Alice?"

"Alice. *Alice in Wonderland*? Lewis Carroll?" She asked.

"That's it!"

Claire was perplexed. "Yes?"

"It's been a gap in my memory since I woke up in the medlab. I could only think of the words. I had no idea where they came from," Key said.

"Removing that one implant may have released more memories," Claire suggested. "And from watching your recent behavior. Well—"

"Well, what?"

"The implant removal also seems to have made you less compliant to GDC's commands. From what I have recently witnessed, in any case." She paused. "We may have started our way down the rabbit hole." Claire tied her hair back in a tight ponytail, while she spoke, "You know, I was five years old when I read *Alice in Wonderland*." She paused and checked her report. "Someone tampered with your childhood memories, Key."

"But who? And why would they?"

"Whoever did it they want you to forget what happened in those days." Claire mused.

"Well, it worked." Key rubbed his forehead. "But let's get back to the report. What is this furry looking biped on the screen, Claire?"

"It's a default image when the AI can't conclusively make an ID. It is a placeholder until we get a better sample. The one we have is degraded."

"All we know is that it walks upright?" Key asked.

"Pretty much."

⊰◆⊱

The next morning, the team meeting was standing room only. Key, Claire, Austen Nesh, Postrenal, and Michelle Curvois were sitting around a small conference table in the base camp surrounded by combat officers and staff.

Curvois had the floor.

"The gold grains recovered from the underground river are indicative of high-grade gold ore deposits. Regrettably, these grains also suggest that the major ore deposits that they eroded from are many kilometers away from here."

"How far? Estimated?" Nesh asked.

"Indeterminate? Unknown," Curvois said.

"Which one? Nesh nodded.

"Both." Curvois kept the floor. "We have taken a tiny slice of life here. It's a lot to process. However, I can tell you that the solid gold core these flecks and grains came from will likely be immense and probably originate in a volcanic mountain chain. It is as pure as can be, has a reddish-gold hue to it, and I mean, it is six nines fine 999.999 pure!"

No one said anything for a few seconds.

"Unheard of." Curvois added for effect.

"Which direction are these mountains?" Key asked.

"Who knows? Pick one."

No one spoke as they considered the implications of Michelle's comment.

"On another front. I have some news about our friends. I may have discovered some vulnerabilities in the *Testudo catafractata*." Postrenal interjected.

"Armored amphibian, roughly," Claire said.

"What?" Nesh asked.

"Latin for what we've been calling grips, grippers."

"I call them dead," Nesh said.

"I'm still calling them grips. It's easier." Claire smiled.

Key changed the subject. "We need to send out long-range drones to probe all directions for the mountain search. Austen, how many LRPs do we have operational? Including replacements?"

"About two dozen."

"Deploy all of them," Largo said.

"A bit risky, don't you think?" Nesh asked.

"Do it, Nesh."

———⬖⬗———

Postrenal finished fitting Largo with his very own vicocet graft pump. Worn as a narrow belt around his right calf, with intravenous implants, all he had to do to kill the pain from his numerous wounds and injuries was press the belt with his left shin. Immediately, a pure, peaceful wave of highly refined vicocet numbed his pain.

"I think I am in love, doc," Key said dreamily.

"I will be monitoring you for signs of drug abuse, Commander. If I see any, I am bound by corporate regs to cut you off." Postrenal tried to be stern.

Key's eyelids narrowed. His face relaxed. He appraised Postrenal. "Doc, if you do that…I will be obliged to…uh, terminate your position." He nodded. "Yep."

"Commander. You have already overmedicated, and you are high as a kite. This is a recipe for disaster. The Pure will ravage you. I have seen it too many times. If you abuse the pure, your body will demand larger doses."

"Which you will provide Doc. If not you, I can find someone who will," Key said dreamily.

11

KAYLE HAD PUSHED DYEUS CORP hard, round the clock, to get everyone armed, launched, and on time to take over Gereon. She had brought half the planned force, arguing that there was not enough time to get everyone else ready.

Now for the big finish, Kayle thought as she paced the DC dreadnought *Antares'* deck.

Burr Glass, the captain, called for battle stations.

Crimson Rhapsody was right where she was supposed to be. Twelve o'clock off the bridge of the *Antares.*

We have an exceptional double agent, Kayle thought. *Wonder who it is? Someone high up for sure.*

Kayle assumed Burr's counterpart and her former colleague, Jaylen Rent, was commanding his ship to respond.

He will dive for the surface and launch countermeasure. It's what I would do.

That was when Jaylen did something unexpected.

Burr cursed, "Bloody hell. He's come to a dead stop. Insane. Why?"

"Suicidal?" Kayle quipped. "But seriously, Jaylen, what in the actual fuck are you doing?"

"Attack. All fighters, all ordinance, everyone engage *Crimson Rhapsody,*" Burr snapped.

Kayle looked at the doomed ship hanging there in space.

All alone. Beautiful, lonely vessel. Such a shame. Ah, the reddish-gold body with crimson accents. Superb. So sad.

"Where did she go?" Kayle stared at only emptiness as the ship vanished before their eyes.

"Evasive action. Impact of incoming missiles in uh, eighteen seconds," the exec stated as if he were ordering lunch. "Countermeasures deployed."

Kayle was impressed by Tyr Roga, Burr's exec.

Just the kind of guy you want in that chair.

"There's that bitch," Roga whispered.

Rhapsody reappeared on their forward screens.

Oh, no. Jaylen is better than our guy. It might be time to head for the exits.

Perplexed, Burr said, "That is a hell of a digital camo they got. How did she get so much closer?"

Kayle offered an observation, "Burr, Jaylen Rent is likely two moves ahead of us, consider…"

"*Rhapsody* hit by three of our missiles," Roga said.

Kayle watched a fiery seam burst on the port side of the fast-approaching ship.

Both ships may never recover from this. Rhapsody is closing fast.

Burr whistled. "Four more strikes on her."

Roga interrupted with his report. "*Antares* has taken hits in our upper portside quarterdeck…uh, Skip, she's turning into our path."

Burr was stunned. Baffled. "What in the hell?"

Roga continued, "And, uh, a dogfight involving about 100 interceptors engaged right now. Swarming all around us. We have massive damage to the starboard data center." Roga took a sharp breath. "Skip, is he trying to ram us?"

Before Burr could answer, all the alarms on *Antares* went off at the same time. "Collision! Collision! Air-seal all compartments!"

Rhapsody was so close now that Kayle could see Jaylen Rent standing on the flying bridge.

Jaylen. There you are, smiling. All sardonic. It is a good look for you.

Kayle gave him a smile and a gentle wave. Jaylen grinned and casually saluted her, as the bow of the *Crimson Rhapsody* filled their screen.

The two ships collided, and chaos broke out in the skies over Gereon.

12

I N A DISTANT BURNING CITY, explosions, people burning, running on fire in the streets. Trapped. Lost. No one could help him. Key felt a gentle hand on his cheek and heard a voice far off in the distance.

"Hey, wake up. You're having a nightmare," Claire said. "A bad one."

She shook him awake. He came up flailing, but Claire hugged him. Hard. She was holding him steady. Key relaxed in her embrace.

"I've had it many times before," he whispered into her shoulder.

"Do you know where it comes from?" Claire asked.

"Tangled up in my earliest memory of Nasheed. But I'm not sure. In my dream, I'm abandoned, and buildings are blowing up, burning. Someone is carrying me, but it's not my mother. People are on fire in the streets."

"Is it your father?" Claire saw him hit the vicocet pump. Hard. "Key, do you need that thing more for physical or for psychological pain?"

"As the physical pain subsides, it's more of a way to take my mind away from things that still hurt," Key admitted.

"You know you will have to detox and withdraw, and that could be a problem out here at the edge of the cosmos," Claire said. She caressed his cheek and moved his hair out of his eyes.

Largo held her hand, whispering, "The desperate lover can hope no redress. Where beauty and rigor are both in excess."

"What's that from?" she asked.

"Don't know, bubbled up from somewhere deep inside my scrambled brain."

She said, "Is that what you think of me? Beauty and rigor in excess?" She laughed.

Key shrugged. "Yes. Rigor. Vigor. And all in excess."

"You're a poet too?" Claire asked.

"I have many talents," he said.

"Oh, yes. Yes, you do." Claire smiled, pushing her hair back. "But flirting is not one of them."

They burst out laughing.

Claire stretched. "I should get back to my quarters."

"Are you sure that's what you want to do?" he asked.

"No." Claire laughed. "But I'm going anyway."

◆

Key sipped his coffee and studied the data from the drone recon program. He decided it was best to abort the plan for now. After a week, they had lost half of their probes. Two promising mountain ranges in the distant northern and western sectors required follow-up. All the drones sent to the southeast had gone offline shortly after launch.

What the hell is going on in the southeast area? he wondered.

The atmos-processors around the base had cleared off a forty square-kilometer area. Some of the more active regional volcanoes were dormant. As a result, the base spaceport, now known as Camp Crimson, and as "Crim" colloquially, could be seen from space. On a clear day, it was possible to communicate by holo with *Crimson Rhapsody*. Key had tested the relay network a few times and was able to reach Minerva, who remained on Raba, via holocall.

Minerva still could not use her portal to reach Gereon. She accepted the limitations with a detached serenity. Her intel inside Dyeus had warned of an attack on Gereon in the next seventy-two hours. All forces were on high alert. Hair-trigger.

The general quarters alarm sounded throughout the base.

Claire called him on the holo. "General quarters! Key! We need you here in ops!"

Is that thunder in the distance?

"On my way," he said.

The thunder was louder and closer.

Those are explosions—heavy ordinance.

The staircase vibrated as he made his way to the ops deck. The floor-to-ceiling display showed a massive attack on *Crimson Rhapsody* in the sky above them, as an unidentified capital ship and different drones, fighters, and missiles swarmed. All kinds of mayhem were erupting above their base.

"Claire, can you holo Emi?" Largo asked.

"Signals are pretty much jammed. But she's coming up now," Claire answered.

Emi greeted Claire and said, "Make this quick. We're in trouble. Luckily…thanks to Minerva's warning, we were at alert status. They have brought many friends with them."

Key cut in, "Who are they?"

"The dreadnought *Antares*. Out of Dyeus Corp. She's got at least fifty interceptors engaged. Two squadrons just peeled off on their way to the surface. Brace yourselves. Manaka out."

Key looked over at Claire, sitting at the ops desk. "Claire. Are we suitably braced?"

Claire focused on the screen. "We are ready. This should be enlightening." Wrecks began to plummet from the skies. "Quite a show, Commander. We seem to have a slight advantage for now." Claire paused with a brief intake of breath. "What the hell is Rent doing?"

They all watched as *Crimson Rhapsody* rammed the *Antares* at flank speed. "Kamikaze. Not the recommended move at war college, Rent," Claire said. "I think he just blew himself up, and our only ship went with him. Commander?"

Stunned, all he could say was, "Fuck!" His first thought was a concern for Jaylen's safety. They were like brothers.

His second was *Jaylen, if you survive this, I will strangle you myself.*

Largo stared as white-hot explosions racked the ship's bows. Hundreds of escape pods ejected and rained down on Gereon. The fighters from both ships descended toward their base in a spread-out continuous dogfight.

"I guess Rent skipped class that week," Claire said as she deployed the force field over the base. "Battle stations, everyone! Fire at will."

13

KAYLE LEFT THE SMOKE OF *Antares'* burning deck and headed for the auxiliary bridge. She had to fight her way through a terrified crowd running in the other direction. Red-helmeted corporate clones–Elite Deck Guards—tried to impose order on the evacuation. She grabbed a PSG from the closest deck guard and fired a warning volley in the air.

"Stop, all of you! No need to panic. Remember your training. Guards, if anyone jeopardizes your ability to do your duty, deadly force is authorized."

Now the guards' efforts to control the mob met with some success.

A few heads have to roll, but soon the lines for the escape pods will be organized. The corporate slaves to the wages will fall in line. The clones, of course, will be the last ones off—after they try to save all our asses. Genetic programming. Got to love it.

"Deck guards, your escape pod is filling up. After your assigned evacuees leave, save yourselves!" Kayle ordered.

Kayle made it to the emergency yoke. She strained to pull it back, as she tried to slow the descent of the *Antares*, and stop it from rolling over.

Tyr Roga joined her and grabbed the yoke too. Together they lifted the nose a little. "She's gonna land rough, mam. All we can do is try to soften the blow," Roga said. "We only have three thrusters operational. Main engines are off-line. We are adrift, Commander."

Kayle kept fighting with the yoke. "Tyr, I must confess, I'm afraid of escape pods. There is no way I'm leaving a good ship for a large bathtub."

"And then there's the fact that you have no control over the pods. You have to trust the onboard AI. I, of course, have severe trust issues." Roga shook his head. "Look at that. She's almost level, and we have two kilometers to spare." He notified the crew, "All personnel, this is the exec, surface impact in, uh, eighty seconds."

Kayle checked the manifests. "You and me, Tyr, are all that's left on board of all our corporate citizens."

"How many clones left?"

"Full complement of Deck Guards." Kayle whistled. "Almost 100 battle-hardened clones. We have what we need to guard the ship, GDC could be here in a few minutes."

Roga ordered the guards, "All security personnel. Redeploy to ship bunkers. Expect company soon." Tyr paused and looked over at Kayle. "Wait. How far are we from the GDC base?"

Kayle looked at the HUD map and gasped, "Far. Also, drifting further. We are 540 kilometers south, southeast from their outpost."

"It may take them a while to get to us. What with all the various skirmishes still going on…" Roga observed.

Kayle pulled up the view screen of the surface below them. In the twilight of an orange sunset, it displayed a massive black lake surrounded by a barren volcanic rim. "Roga, that is a lake in a collapsed volcano. It should not be there. Our patchy intel included no mention of any such geomorphic features."

"Place is full of surprises. Can we make the other side of the rim, or are we gonna hit the lake?" Roga asked.

"Gonna be close," Kayle observed.

"And bumpy," Roga added. "All personnel–brace for impact."

Antares' dorsal fin caught the edge of the ancient palisade. She hung on the lip of the crater before turning hard to starboard and rolling over into the lake.

⟨◆⟩

Emergency stabilizing foam injected into the airtight compartments. It offered some flotation protection before *Antares* sank.

Kayle opened a hatch and pulled Tyr out.

Tyr stood and pointed at the dorsal surface of the ship. "Many of our clones are going to make it out. Disciplined and orderly. Look at that." A methodical platoon of guards made their way off the port side.

"We're going to need every single one of them." Kayle nodded. "The *Antares* is sinking fast, Tyr."

Roga nodded. "There's not going to be much left to salvage. I sure did love this ship. My first post as an exec, and now look at her."

"Want to swim for the shore now?" Kayle asked as she dove into the inky waters.

They swam together and reached dry land in minutes. They both lay on their backs on the black sand, gasping for breath. A rail gun fired off to their right, illuminating the aft section as it made its slow slide into the lake.

"What is that thing?" Kayle asked, pointing at a barely discernible tentacled blob. It grabbed two Deck Guards and took them underwater. The guards that had reached the beach immediately opened up with everything they had. A spotlight drone made the scene as bright as day. Hundreds of creatures were tearing *Antares* apart piece by piece. They grabbed a few of the remaining guards and took them underwater.

The Deck Guards' commander set up a defensive position on the beach, and the ensuing havoc was staggering. Smoking chunks of the creature's flesh and guts rained down on the beach.

Still more came streaming out of the black water.

"Kayle let's get over there. Add our firepower to the valiant effort of our guards," Tyr said.

Kayle shot into a squirming mass of dark creatures near the beach.

"Run. We're only pissing them off!" Tyr grabbed her hand, and together they sprinted to the defensive perimeter the guards were setting up.

"Sir. Mam. Glad to have you with us," Collum, the guards' commander, said between rail rifle shots.

"Collum, this formation looks a bit like a British hollow square," Kayle said as she shot into the mass of creatures trying to get traction on the beach.

"Yes, ma'am. It is a classic, but it works well with mobs. Chaos. That's what this is." He pulled out his needler as one beast got too close and incinerated its head. "Seems to be an endless supply of these buggers."

A muscular tentacle wrapped around Collum's ankle and pulled him toward the water's edge.

Kayle left the protection of the square—firing into the beast's head, ripping up creatures all around it. She lay flat on the sand and kept firing until a blazing white explosion behind her flattened everything on the beach.

She was stunned and disoriented. The grenade's concussion wore off a bit when she felt a burning pain in her calf and realized she was being pulled toward the water feet first. Another tentacle grabbed her hand, but Kayle was able to get to her needler and sliced the creature's entire limb off. Now her martial arts training and her will to survive kicked in as she leaped up and ripped into the beasts.

"*Fulcra cubo*. Korban. Nice," Collum said. His ankle was a bloody mess. He fired continuously at the attackers. When Kayle charged into the mass in front of them and wielded her needler with unerring accuracy, he paused to watch.

"*Fulcra cubo*. The Needle Dance of the Nasheed. Never seen it before." Roba whistled. "She's good. Hell. She's magnificent."

"It is a sight to behold," Collum concurred. They both watched Kayle carve the beasts to pieces. Her needler became a blue-white rapier flashing in the dark dealing death, lopping off tentacles. She whirled and pirouetted and killed.

Her glowing weapon lit her face with a grim beauty.

"Lookout, they've got behind us!" Collum alerted the guards. The black sand beach was awash in guts, blood, and ichor. It was difficult to stand without slipping.

Three of the beasts were on Collum. Two were on Roba.

Kayle fought her way to Roba and dispatched one of the creatures. Roba took care of the other one.

They freed Collum from a mass of entwined tentacles, but it was, it seemed, too late.

The beach was silent—no more beasts for the moment. Kayle and Roba gently turned Collum's body over.

His face was a bloody mess. Dead. His eyes closed…then they popped open.

Kayle gasped, not believing it. "Tyr, do we have a medic? Or even medical supplies?"

"I'll check. We've lost more than half of our guards on this bloody beach. He's pretty far gone, Kayle."

Roba went looking for a medic.

Collum whispered as Kayle put her ear against his lips.

"*Fulcra cubo.*" He coughed. "I've only seen the needle dance once before. You are *Nasheed Dominae*?"

Kayle nodded. "Yes. Save your strength," she whispered.

"I thought you were all wiped out years ago. The company sent me to Graile to do just that."

"Shh."

"It's funny. Ironic, you might say." He sighed.

"Shh, Collum. Rest."

"The Nasheed ethnocide. You survived it…to think I was supposed to be your protection. Like you needed it." He laughed. Coughed. A bloody froth formed around his lips.

He whispered, "Radix Lorca nil nostra."

His eyes rolled back. This time they didn't reopen.

"Radix Lorca nil nostra corso," Kayle whispered back in Nasheed. "I'm all that remains of a warrior's dream." She stood up and realized she had tears in her eyes. "Collum." She sighed. "Now, you know what's on the other side of the sky."

⬦

The guards pitched an emergency camp about 400 meters from the beach on a long gradual slope. Tyr prepared to lead a squad back aboard the *Antares* to see what they could salvage.

Kayle climbed out of the large hole they were digging. It would be a mass grave soon. The guards dug it in silence, intent on giving their colleagues a final resting place.

They have a secret brotherhood, rituals, and religious practices that only they can attend. Like we do on Graile. This is a good time for me to go do something else.

Tyr was sitting alone on a boulder, clipping cryo grenades to his vest as she approached. "Commander. How's the work going?"

"The grave is about finished. It was time for me to clear out," Kayle said.

Tyr nodded. "May I ask you a personal question?"

"Depends on how personal."

"Are you Nasheed? The stuff of legend. I mean, that planet, Graile, is the beginning and end of Fulcra Cubo, isn't it?" he asked.

"That's what I've always understood. But many myths about the Nasheed are out there, you know," Kayle said.

Tyr stood up and grabbed the rest of his kit. "Right. Right. You didn't answer my question, or did you?"

Kayle smiled.

"Aren't there still bounties on the heads of any Nasheed survivors?" he asked.

"I guess there would be if any such survivors existed." She laughed. Kayle decided to change the subject. "I should come with you."

"I would love to have you, but you know the command protocols," Tyr said.

"Yeah, but you and I are the only command protocols left alive out here. So, I'm coming with you." Kayle was firm.

"Okay, but if I get the COO of Dyeus killed, Ross Lasker will fire me." Tyr shook his head, grinning.

Kayle laughed and clipped two grenades to her belt.

"Lasker is the least of our problems."

14

THE FIRST BATTLE OF GEREON was over. GVC was the winner hands-down. Emi Manaka was on a holocall with Key and Claire. They made their way in an APC tracker toward where Emi had belly-landed *Crimson Rhapsody*. They had about seventy kilometers left to go.

"In summary, Jaylen is MIA with about sixty others; he may have made it out. I hope he did." Emi finished her report.

"The foredeck emergency module?" Key asked.

"It was seen ejecting below the bridge seconds after the collision. Jaylen may have had time to make it," Emi said.

"We haven't picked up his signal yet," Key said.

"We still might, and Jaylen may be trying to get to us since our ship is salvageable if we had parts."

"Which we don't," Key grunted.

"How did the base fare?" Manaka asked.

"It wasn't all that competitive," Largo said. "Minerva has a high-up source in Dyeus. She gave us almost three full days of advance warning. It was all the edge we needed."

"I am setting up a defensive perimeter. I will leave a skeleton crew to defend the ship. We can start ferrying the remaining provisions back to our base. I hope to get there soon without any further incidents." Emi sounded on edge. "And, of course, we will keep looking for Jaylen."

"Find him. Find him so I can promote him for destroying DC's ship. And then demote him for destroying ours," Key said.

Emi nodded, half-smiling.

"Any trace of the *Antares*? Any idea where she went down?" Key asked.

"No traces yet. Search parties are out looking, but so far, we have nothing," Emi replied.

"We will all have to check for survivors at the various pods and wrecks that litter the surface between us," Key said. "Not sure how long it's going to take."

"Be advised, strange animals are roaming around in the desert. Manaka out."

Key and Claire continued in the tracker, looking for survivors in the endless dunes.

Red sands for as far as the eye can see. Without water, no one's going to last long out here.

"How high up is Minerva's source, do you think?" Claire asked.

"Senior management. Senior staff. That intel was closely held. Six people in Lasker's entire company knew when that attack was coming," Key mused. Then it hit him.

No, it couldn't be. Kayle couldn't be our agent at Dyeus? Her and Minerva? A one in six chance. Let's face it. Everything's possible with those two.

"Where'd you go, Key? You were here a minute ago," Claire asked.

"What?" Key came out of his trance. "Uh, I was thinking about Minerva."

"And Kayle?"

Largo did not respond. He was lost in thought.

Dammit. Of course, it's Kayle. It's not unthinkable—this entire thing has Minerva's fingerprints all over it. Unbelievable. Except it isn't. She's manipulated me my whole life, but even for her, this is…

"Turns out ramming the *Antares* was Jaylen's stroke of brilliance," Claire observed with a faint smile.

Key looked over at her to see if she was joking. Her face revealed nothing.

"Or a stroke of absolute bona fide dumbass luck," Key said, looking through the drone's visor. "This looks like a dry salt lake, this lakebed. It's huge. The climate was once wet enough to sustain this giant lake.

So much to learn about this planet. And we haven't learned much of anything yet."

"Still, it's nice to get a chance to study Gereon's geomorphology," Claire said. "Okay. Time to stop. Everyone, let's walk from here, this pod ahead of us is one from *Antares*, Red 6."

The team deployed from the tracker. Everyone wore light desert armor. Most held rail rifles. Key knew every one of the clones was thinking about how there were no laws of salvage on Gereon. So, it was wide open finders' keepers for GVC. Lots of rewards were in the offing.

"On screen, I'm picking up two Dyeus personnel beacons rushing away from us to the north," Bette said. "They are moving erratically."

"Keep tracking them," Key said.

Claire sent two guards to investigate the pod. Everyone else covered them.

The pod's hatch was open. The guards looked inside and motioned everyone forward. Inside they found an interior drenched in blood. The pod's floor was covered in strange little armored rodent-like creatures.

"Scavengers. Look a little like big armadillos," Key said, and raised his pistol to shoot. Thinking better of it, he said to the clones, "Capture a couple for further study. What the hell?"

The scavengers squirmed out of the escape pod.

"Look at these stalks." Key pointed at the scavengers as they extended their eyeballs out on segmented stems and frantically looked about. Like insects. Their eyes wheeled about, and the animals made clicking sounds.

"That's an apt name for them," Claire said. "Stalkies."

Bette said, "Commander, we have an unidentified large group of fast-moving quadrupeds. Approximately one kilometer. The drone has them in focus. To our northeast."

Key looked at the display and saw a pack of more than twenty creatures moving through a field of boulders. It was hard to see them in the dust and the shadows. Several of them were carrying chunks of meat in their jaws. About one and a half meters tall on all fours, they looked deadly.

Felines? Canines? Some mixture of both?

"Bette, what is your best estimate of where they came from and where they are going?" Key asked.

"Not enough data sir." Bette replied. "They have headed toward that long escarpment ahead. Tracks, behavior, and animal morphology indicates they are large canids. Or something resembling wild dogs."

"Let's get in the tracker and follow them," Key said.

"Everyone back in the tracker," Claire ordered.

They fanned out and followed the bloody tracks up a boulder-strewn gulley. The shadows grew longer in the dim afternoon sunlight. Up ahead, dead trees arched over the narrow path. The crew dismounted.

"Trees!" Claire exclaimed. "We will be getting samples."

"Water was available up here not that long ago," Key said.

"Have determined that these canines are predators who travel in packs," Bette said. "Our drone indicates they are 400 meters ahead of us. The gulley widens out into a gorge up there. Many boulders and trees. Living trees."

Their clone detachment used the rocks as cover as they moved up the trail.

"Be advised they have detected our presence and are approaching. The drone is dropping canister bomblets on them." Showers of explosions echoed in the gorge up ahead.

A large canid appeared in front of Key, bloody jaws agape. Close enough to be dispatched with a needler. Another one was approaching Claire. She fired her pistol, and the creature's head vaporized in a pink mist.

"Another pack is coming from the gorge. I have determined that these canids do not fear us," Bette said, as another brute loomed in Key's pathway. Key's needle flashed through the toothy snout.

15

THEIR LAST REMAINING RECON DRONE hovered over a cave that Kayle and Tyr wanted to check out. It was inside a low, weathered volcanic butte. About three kilometers from the crash site, the butte held many caves and rock shelters. Their small convoy of five vehicles pulled up at the foot of a shallow talus slope in front of a long, flat volcanic outcrop.

A scorpion APC, the prize of the *Antares* salvage effort, led the way. Kayle and Tyr were in it with a six-person crew. It looked like its nickname, a segmented all-terrain tracked vehicle. Stored in the forward holds were twin pincers that could lift 20 metric tons apiece. A pulse cannon formed the tail section. The *Antares'* priceless disruptor drive was now secured in the cargo hold. Using the scorpion, they were able to fill up two massive cargo haulers. One of the flatbeds carried three rail cannons. They had enough ammunition and rations to fight a small proxy war.

"You know, Kayle, this rock formation could be an excellent temporary shelter. Covered, almost hidden, close to the water and whatever swims in that water," Tyr said. They watched the guards set up a temporary camp at the foot of the slope.

"Think those grippers are edible?" Kayle asked.

"One of the guards has already tested that hypothesis."

"Did he die?"

"Not yet," Tyr said, "he only tried it at breakfast…said it tasted like—"

"Chicken?" Kayle smiled.

Tyr laughed. "He said it was like eating licorice potatoes."

"We will have to get way low on rations before that's a possibility for me," Kayle said.

"I'm gonna eat the licotato tonight if that guy is still alive." Tyr shrugged. "Might have to stretch the rations, you never know."

"Licotato?" Kayle chuckled, "Right, but…" Kayle's bracer glowed a dark red. "Ugh. This holo has to be from Lasker."

"Yeah, but might as well get it over with," Tyr said.

Lasker glowered at them. "Why have you not contacted me, Korban?"

"I've been busy trying to survive, sir," she said.

"Mission status?" Lasker asked.

"Disastrous." *Actually, it's worse than that*, she thought.

"Tell me what happened," Lasker growled.

Kayle took a deep breath and gave him the condensed version.

⬥

When Kayle finished, Lasker was impassive and silent. He then addressed Tyr. "Anything to add, Roba?"

"Just a strong impression that GDC seemed ready for us. On alert. Waiting for us to show up. *Crimson Rhapsody* immediately went to digital camo and…"

"You sure about that?" Lasker interrupted.

"Not certain, but…"

"Well, I am certain. The details of this operation were known only to my direct reports and you and your captain. Any word from him?" Lasker asked.

"Burr Glass is MIA. Likely ejected from our ship with all the other corp citizens," Kayle answered.

"So, I have terminated the three people here on Raba who knew anything about our Gereon ops. Of course, my son Hugo is not a security risk. Neither is Peroni. So…"

Kayle nodded. *Think I know what comes next.*

"I need to seal this off now. It's an open wound. You two are liabilities, and at this moment, you are out. All official duties terminated. All rank stripped. Eligible for reemployment only after you are investigated and cleared of any wrongdoing. The only reason I have not ordered your termination is that you are there at the scene of combat. You risked your lives. So, it seems unlikely that either of you could be GDC's agent. Still, I can't be certain, and until I can be, you're done. On your own."

"What the hell?" Tyr asked.

"Yesterday morning, GDC flattened our Raba base. They destroyed everything here. But they missed the fleet inbound from K City. Their intel was pretty good. Not perfect, but not bad. Minerva has agents on my staff. Thus, I'm replacing all direct reports, and all their directs, two levels down. I'll let you know if you are eligible to be rehired."

Lasker ended the call.

"So, what do we tell the guards?" Tyr asked. "They will likely abandon us if they know we are no longer full-fledged corp citizens. We have no authority now."

"Nothing. We tell the guards nothing. We need to buy time," Kayle said.

"To do what? Lasker will already be organizing a new mission to come here," Roba asked.

"To clear our names and find the gold."

Roba nodded. "I guess you're right. Under the circumstances, what else can we do?"

"We must get reinstated, Tyr. We clear our names and ready ourselves for the next more massive Dyeus invasion," Kayle said.

"How long before that happens?" Roba asked.

"At least a month, but I'm guessing," Kayle said. "Maybe sooner. It could be expedited. I mean, it all depends on how much force Lasker wants to bring."

"We can hold out that long, I'm sure," Roba said.

"I'm not."

Roba laughed. "You do not know how lucky you are, Korban."

"Why?"

"I am the highest-rated survival trainer in the corp. We are going to be fine," Tyr said.

"Let's get to proving it, then."

16

EAD ANIMALS JAMMED THE NARROW pass. Fewer attacked as the fighting died down.

"We lost three clones so far, Key," Claire said. "These things dragged their bodies away. I will take some of the dead canid specimens back for analysis."

"A permanent source of water is 500 meters ahead. After that, this pass opens up into a narrow sheltered valley," Bette observed. "A herd of shaggy bovine-like creatures is running up the valley."

"We will hold here until the rangers bring up the hoverbikes," Key said. "Bette, show me an overview of the valley on screen."

"The two Dyeus personnel have not moved for twenty minutes. They are about thirty meters ahead," Bette replied.

Largo checked the screen. A small stream flowed in a secluded, sunken valley encircled by volcanic tuff for about ten kilometers. The tuff formed a ring of outcroppings around the drainage. Twenty kilometers away, the volcano that had ejected the tuff long ago made a perfect cone. Tall reedy trees with oval-shaped leaves grew on both sides of the stream.

Claire came over and looked at the screen with him. "Well, this is inviting and well-hidden. Good place for a base camp."

"So reading the geological signatures, it seems that this valley has been here a long time. Thousands if not hundreds of thousands of years," Key noted. "A recent eruption of ash covered it for a time and was then eroded and compressed. That's how you get the volcanic tuff ridges that almost conceal it. The water looks permanent and originates in an underground spring not far upstream."

"Ah. Here are the hoverbikes," Claire noted as the flat-bed tracker pulled up.

"Okay, let's you and me and four of the clones get over to that side," Key said.

They mounted up on the bikes and rode over the pile of dead canids.

"Unexpected low-level nonlethal radiation detected ahead in this valley," Bette reported.

"Source?" Claire asked.

"Unknown. I can determine that the exposure happened approximately 2,000 years ago," Bette said.

They stopped as they came to the top of the escarpment and into an open area. The view expanded several kilometers. The path swept down into a broad expanse two kilometers distant. It then continued on through a hilly, intermittently forested area.

Key looked back at the stack of dead canids. "There's more than a hundred of those things in that pile."

"In two instances now, we have encountered predators that attack in hordes until they die. What kind of selective evolutionary pressure can account for that kind of behavior?" Claire asked.

"One that is out of whack and runs contrary to established evolutionary theory," Key said. "Something to do with these unexpected radiation readings?" He put down a large specimen bag and spread it out on the ground, forming a rectangular pad. "Claire, Bette, help me do a quick field exam of one of these guys."

They selected an average-sized individual of approximately 1.5 meters in length and carried him over to the pad. Bette began a quick scan.

"The most notable feature is the large canines in this male specimen. Weight is approximately 100 kilos. The fur is gray to black, thick and wiry. Quite unexpected," Bette observed.

"What is?" Key asked.

"Underneath the fur are thick interlinked layers of osteoderms, interlocked bone armor-like scales. Three different forms of osteoderms cover the head, and they have a light-sensing pineal eye in the forehead area. This creature is arboreal, a tree-dweller, in essence. These are not canids. I am unsure of how we are to classify them. They are comfortable in diurnal or nocturnal settings. A pack of these trailing you at night would be…suboptimal," Bette said.

"If they are up in those trees down there, we will need infrared scans to spot them," Claire added.

"Okay. That's enough analysis for now." Key gestured at one of the clones and said, "Tag him and bag him. Let's move on, everyone."

"Before we go, Commander Largo, this specimen over here has a Dyeus homing beacon." Bette lit up a massive carcass with her laser pointer.

"Where?" Key asked.

"In his abdomen."

"Guess I'd better cut him open. Where do you recommend I make the incision?" Key asked.

"The osteoderm layer is thinnest below the sternum. Better use your needle for this," Bette recommended.

Key opened up the animal, and the contents of its stomach spilled out on the mat. The beacon was upside down, drenched in blood. Key flipped it over. It read 'Lath V. Yeoh, Commander, Dyeus Corporation.'

Key grunted. "Looking a little worse for wear there, Lath."

"You knew him?" Claire asked.

"Met him once. The previous chief of staff for Minerva Klyne. Traitor to Minerva as well," Key said. "Torn to pieces by the tree dogs."

"Is that what we are calling them, tree dogs?" Claire asked.

"For now, I guess."

"The other beacon is still moving about 500 meters further up the valley," Bette reported.

"Let's ride up there and check it out," Key said.

They mounted their hoverbikes and came to a small grotto off to the left.

"The beacon is in there," Bette said.

Crushed, bleached bone fragments and red leaves were strewn about the entrance. Inside they could hear a rustling sound and a low growl. Key advanced up the hill with his pistol in his right hand. He looked inside and holstered his gun as he chuckled.

"It's a tree dog puppy chewing on the bloody beacon." Key whispered to the pup in a soothing voice, "Let me see what you got there, fella." The animal growled but wagged his tail all the same, as he released the beacon. Key retrieved it and read the identifiers.

"This recently belonged to Commander Burr Glass, Pilot of the *Antares*, Dyeus Corporation." He scooped up the puppy, who did not resist.

"So Glass and Yeoh were in that pod. They left it, a suboptimal choice considering that the tree dogs ate them," Bette observed.

Claire laughed. "This 'suboptimal' stuff is a thing now? Right?"

Bette did not respond.

Key looked down the hill toward the flat plains and the stream bed. "Something about the stream looks odd to me…what do you think?"

"It does, but I can't figure out what it is," Claire said.

"It looks too straight to be natural," Key said. "Like a canal or something. Bette, send the drone over there and hit it with lidar and thermal imaging." Lidar was the pulsed light device that worked similar to a radar.

"Yes, Commander."

Key's and Claire's bracers started glowing. "Let's take it on mine," Key said as Minerva Klyne appeared in their holo. She was in dark robes on a balcony overlooking a deep blue sea. Pensive.

"Key, Claire, you're both looking well. Key, are you holding a puppy?" Minerva asked.

"Yes, ma'am. We found this guy. His older cousins have a nasty disposition." Key rubbed the puppy's belly. It made him go limp in Key's arms.

"So cute, I want one," Minerva said. "He looks well-fed."

"He recently dined on Dyeus Corp execs," Key said.

"Oh? Who? Anyone I would know?" Minerva grinned.

"Your former chief of staff, Lath V. Yeoh, and the captain of the *Antares*." Key showed her Lath's blood-streaked beacon.

"Delightful! Might give the poor thing indigestion, though." Minerva laughed. "Okay, you two, catch me up."

<hr>

When they had finished briefing Minerva, she was quiet for a time.

"So Jaylen is still missing, and the fate of the *Antares* is unknown?" she asked.

"Yes, ma'am. The ship's crash site has not been found," Claire said.

"It would be nice to get her disruptor drive," Minerva observed.

"We have scoured the planet's surface. Wreckage and pods are scattered over a vast area. We don't know how far the debris field extends," Key noted.

"There's someone else I want you to look for, Key. Kayle Korban is out there somewhere." Minerva folded her arms and narrowed her eyes.

Too stunned to reply, Key stared at Minerva.

Claire reacted first. "Kayle was on the *Antares*, ma'am?"

"Yes." Minerva nodded.

"She was your Dyeus source, wasn't she?" Key said.

Minerva nodded.

"Why was she on the *Antares*?" Key asked.

"To sabotage their mission in any way possible. Kayle was successful, as you know. Lasker still doesn't know. We need to keep this information between us."

"If any of our soldiers managed to find her, they would treat her as a hostile. As an enemy," Claire said.

"And for the sake of appearances to Dyeus, that is exactly how I want her to be treated." Minerva was firm.

"This is a dangerous game we are playing with her life, Minerva," Key said.

"Minerva shook her head. "Not really. The chances of anyone finding Kayle are slim. She is a competent and highly skilled agent. I can't connect to her via holocall. She's so much like her mother, it's amazing."

"You knew her mother?" Key asked.

"I will explain it all sometime when I see you, Key. Some things are best discussed face-to-face," Minerva said.

"So, Kayle is hiding from you?" Claire asked.

"Oh, she is hiding from us, but I suspect her biggest problem right now could be Lasker. He suspects something, given our recent attack on his Raba base. If I were her, I would do my best to lose myself in the vastness of Gereon for a time," Minerva said.

"We attacked Dyeus on Raba?" Claire asked.

Minerva nodded. "It was the least I could do, all things considered."

Largo was overwhelmed with emotion. Repressed memories of Kayle bubbled up from the darkness of his consciousness. Some lights were turning on.

"Why, Key, you look like somebody walked over your grave," Minerva said.

Largo did not reply for a few seconds. "How do you know Kayle's mother?" he asked.

"You want to do this now? I knew her, yes. She was a skilled Nasheed assassin. No one knows what happened to her after the troubles. Same coppery skin, same black luxurious hair. Her devious ways. Her high intelligence. Dangerous to herself and to others."

"Did you know my mother too?" he asked.

"Key, that long scar on your neck. What's that all about?" Minerva asked.

"An implant of some unknown function ruptured. It had to be removed. Of course, I was unaware that it had ever been installed. Were you aware of it, Minerva?" Key asked.

She paused before responding.

"Well. I see I have disturbed you enough for today. We will resume scheduled calls tomorrow at 1600 hours." The call ended. Minerva faded out.

"Hey, are you all right?" Claire asked.

"You know Minerva never tells the whole story."

"What do you mean?"

"Now that she has got what she needed from Kayle, Minerva considers her expendable," Key said.

"Commander Largo, here are the results of the scans you requested," Bette said.

On the tablet screen, faint lines diverted from the stream at intervals. They extended approximately 200 meters in each direction from the stream channel.

Largo was stunned. The ramifications of their discovery left him speechless.

Agriculture. Irrigation canals.

Claire looked at him as he pointed at the screen. She looked at it and let out a low whistle. "Someone's been here before us," she whispered. "An advanced society."

"Get Manaka on the holo. We are diverting the bulk of our explorations to this valley. Relocating the base camp…everything."

Claire contacted Emi while Key gave Bette new instructions. "Bette, I need a complete low-level geodesic study. I want every landform visible or buried in this valley. Anything that looks artificial needs lidar, geothermal, remote sensing, every geological method possible. When the rest of our field scientists get here, we will get started on the floral and faunal studies."

Claire got off the call with Emi and looked at Key, smiling.

He grinned back at her and asked, "What?"

"You are what. Look at you, Dr. Largo. You look euphoric, and this time you didn't need drugs to do it. I guess making the biggest scientific discovery of all time will do that to a fellow."

17

K AYLE AND TYR REASSEMBLED THE AI in the scorpion APC. Glitchy after being submerged in the lake, it had become unstable. So they had taken the AI apart and rebuilt it.

Parked on the shore next to the wreck of the *Antares*, they watched the guards' work gang continue to scour the ship for anything salvageable. They loaded recovered supplies and useful parts on to an awaiting flatbed.

"That should be about it," Tyr said after slotting the last socket back into the control panel.

"Reformat it now, right?" Kayle asked.

"Right. Strip it all the way down and then reinstall the OS."

"Okay. Here we go." They watched the monitor flicker, go through the prompts, reboot three times, stop, and do nothing.

Tyr laughed. "That's not what I had in mind. Got any ideas?"

"Since this scorpion is a prototype, it must have something new in its start-up protocols," Kayle said. "Wait, there's the cursor back up."

"What next?" he asked.

"Voice activation?" Kayle paused before continuing. "Scorpion?"

The AI responded, "Awaiting proper nomenclature protocol."

"I think step one is assigning the AI a name," Kayle said.

"Male or female or non-gender specific?" Tyr asked.

"You will be interfacing with it more than me, so you choose whatever you like," Kayle said.

"Okay, what do you think of Ambarella?"

"I'm fine with whatever, but that's a little long," Kayle said.

"How about Bella?" Tyr asked.

"Short and sweet, I like it."

"AI, you will be known as Bella," Tyr said.

"Acknowledged. Bella is reporting for duty. What is your name, please?"

"Tyr Roba."

"Kayle Korban."

"Who is primary?"

"Tyr is," Kayle said.

"He and I will need some time alone to get acquainted."

Kayle laughed. This was new, but she had to follow the protocols. "Okay. I will go out and survey the shore until you finish. She wants to be alone with you. Bye, Tyr. Watch yourself."

Kayle climbed down the side ladder of the scorpion and stretched. It was the most beautiful morning she had yet seen on Gereon.

As she walked along the shore with the warm sun on her face, she marveled at the strange flying creatures skimming the surface of the lake. About the size of her hand, they resembled flying lizards, except their wings were like those of hummingbirds. They glinted. Their aquamarine scales were iridescent in the morning sunlight. They dipped and dived at small beetle-like insects that skimmed on top of the surface. Up ahead, something glinted where the shoreline met the water—Kayle jogged over to where it was half-buried in the wet sand.

What is this?

She realized she was looking at an obsidian stone tool of some kind. Crescent-shaped with a tanged stem, it was a weapon.

But who made it? We didn't bring it on the Antares.

"Someone else has walked this beach before me." She was excited. She couldn't wait to tell Tyr.

"This opens us up to all kinds of possibilities," she whispered as she held the crescent up to the sunlight. It was translucent and streaked with blue and yellow bands. "So pretty. Whoever made you had to have been an artist."

She surveyed the shoreline, now alert to anything else that might be strange. Back from the beach on the first terrace above the lake, the soil looked different, not sand but a sandy loam. It had some fragile remnant grass tufts scattered in it.

So glad Key took me out to the archaeological sites on Port Amphora and taught me how to look at them, how to see them as an archaeologist sees them.

The soil was more substantial here, and grass had been growing there until recently. She found a partially buried bleached bone. It was a fragmented rib of a gripper, probably. Still, it had been exposed to the elements for a long time, pockmarked and bleached white, and eroded at either end.

This end is sharpened to a point! It's a spear.

She decided to walk up to the next lake terrace and look at the soil anomaly from a different angle. Reaching the summit, she heard something in the air, looked up, and saw an unfamiliar drone. Sleek and silent, it had to be a prototype.

Tyr and Bella working together. That drone's a good sign.

Down below, she heard the scorpion fire up and start moving on the shoreline as it turned toward her. She ran down the beach to stop Tyr from crunching the first nonhuman archaeological site ever found in the cosmos.

"Stop, Tyr!" she yelled as she ran out in front of the scorpion. Its tracks were chewing up the beach as it crawled toward her.

Thankfully he's stopping.

Tyr opened the hatch, climbed out, and jumped down on the sand. She stopped running and walked the rest of the way to the vehicle.

"What? Did you find anything? What's that in your hand?" Tyr asked.

She unclasped her fingers and showed him the crescent.

He whistled and said, "That's a beautiful piece. Handcrafted. But by whose hand?"

"That's the big question, isn't it?"

They both stood silent and looked out at the enormous lake stretching out beyond the horizon.

Finally, Tyr said, "Gereon is an enormous planet, and we know next to nothing about it."

"Except now we know some sentient creatures were here before us. We are not alone in the universe," Kayle whispered.

"You know what, Kayle, not even alone on this planet," Tyr observed. "I'm bringing the new drone that Bella told me about over here, and let's try a bit of geophysical remote sensing."

"You know who we need here? It's a shame he works for the competition. One of the best archaeologists ever produced by any of the nine corporations," she said.

"Who is that?" Tyr asked.

"Key Largo. He's on the planet somewhere. He would know the best way to proceed with this."

"Who says he's part of the competition? Our status with Dyeus is liminal at best pending Lasker's investigation," Tyr added.

"What are you suggesting?"

"I'm suggesting that if we can make contact with GDC personnel, we have some leverage to make a deal."

Kayle smiled. "I like the way you think, Tyr. Let's see what the drone is coming up with, shall we? Zoom out about 100 meters, please."

They watched as the drone displayed the area of ancient shoreline they were standing on from 100 meters above. An evident discoloration in the soil was apparent on the second terrace. It extended approximately half a kilometer on either side of them.

"Zoom out more and let us see where this discolored soil zone ends," Kayle said.

Now it was clear that the darker soil zone was localized to a narrow part of the lake terrace, except for a small strip that extended from the lake and went an indeterminate distance back to the escarpment.

"That looks like a path or road," Tyr said.

"This terrace might have once been an isolated hill overlooking the lake and connected to the escarpment by that road. Or it's a causeway?" Kayle suggested. "Hit this area with the hyperspectral imaging function."

"Aye aye, Skip," Tyr said.

Kayle laughed, saying, "I'm not your skipper. Remember, we are both without a portfolio now."

"Still, you are the senior officer out here, and that's how the guards see you as well," Tyr said.

Kayle grunted, not wanting to argue the point.

"Hyperspectral focus coming up now," Tyr said.

They both gasped. The image showed a series of buried circular structures covered the hillock.

"There is nothing random about these," Tyr said. "This is a pattern of some kind. Indicative of heavy usage."

"I think we better proceed carefully, but let's take a look under the sand and see what these things are," Kayle said.

"Shall we get help? Bring some guards over?"

"Not for the moment. Let's keep this to ourselves for now," Kayle said.

I think I know what these are. I wish we had not found them.

"Okay, I'm gonna overlay the whole area with the lidar and 3D reconstructive map functions, and play around with some rotations and views." The terrace came into sharp focus.

"They're domes," Kayle said.

Buried by ancient dunes, a few had collapsed, but most of the domes looked to be preserved and pristine. They had strange trapezoidal doors. Large, heavy stones sealed the vaults.

"We need to snake a camera into one of these things," Tyr said.

"I will get one from the scorpion as well as some other detection tools," Kayle said.

"Wait. I'll help…" Tyr said, but Kayle was already climbing into the scorpion. He shook his head and said, "Best stay out of the way when you're excited."

Tyr was still trying to enhance the images when Kayle returned with the tool locker.

She pointed to one of the collapsed domes nearby and said, "Let's try to get into that one. These other seals look tighter than a drum."

The camera system was in a long segmented cable and wrapped with microscopic rotors that caused very little disturbance. LED lights on the exoskin enabled boring into tight spaces and seeing where the camera was going.

Kayle and Tyr laid out the coil and fired up the rotors. Kayle used a joystick to navigate the camera into the sand. A tablet connected to the stick displayed what was in front of the camera. It tunneled so fast that the screen looked like a tiny sandstorm at first. Then it connected with a firm yellowish-brown surface. She followed an edge for a time.

"That's curious," Tyr noted. "What do you think it is?"

"It looks like hard adobe or some similar blended material to me," Kayle said.

"Can you break through it?" he asked.

"Not with this, but we could get out the microdrills. Wait. See that hollow space? Going to put it in there. Better turn on the lights," she said.

Something brilliant and shiny appeared. Kayle adjusted the camera filters. "Still too bright. I have to turn off some of the lights."

"Woah. That is bright," Tyr said.

"Something pale. That's a bleached white bone…a jaw," Kayle observed. "And whatever is gleaming is right below it."

Sand around the bone collapsed into an unseen cavity. Kayle was able to navigate the camera above the rounded jaw and around the high vaulted squarish skull. She looked down on a brilliant gold necklace blazing like a beacon in the ancient crypt. Strange symbols were engraved on its surface.

The silence was so deep they could hear the wind blowing and the waves lapping against the beach. They stood there on the ancient shore, trying to understand the enormity of what they had found.

Kayle kept staring at the necklace, filled with conflicting emotions. She realized that tears were streaming down her cheeks.

Tyr noticed. "Kayle, you're crying? What's wrong?"

She tried to hold it off, but her emotions washed over and overwhelmed her, and she shivered as she sobbed.

"I guess it's time I told you about my Nasheed people and how I came to be here, Tyr." She took a deep breath. "I am going to share with you something so sacred and secret that you must give me your word you will never tell anyone. Can I trust you?" Kayle asked.

"You can," Tyr vowed.

"On your life?"

Tyr paused. "Maybe you shouldn't tell me this. Why so solemn?" he asked.

"This is a serious business, Tyr. So I ask again. On your life?"

He shrugged and said, "On my life, then."

Kayle began her story, "There was a time when I lived on the peaceful planet of Graile at the other end of the galaxy. I was fifteen and living in the convent of Leivonne. My mother was a nun."

———◆———

Inside the scorpion, Kayle continued her story, while Tyr drove them down the lakeshore. They continued to search for more archaeological sites using the drone.

"In those days, the nine corporations had not yet formed the council. We were all about to begin the Great Unity War. As we all know, it was the last scramble for the outlier planets' limited resources, most notably gold. Our world was not famous for its wealth, but for its pristine beauty. We had mountains, vast glaciers, deep frothy rivers cutting through virgin forests. Graile was almost untouched.

"There never were substantial quantities of gold available on Graile. And what gold we had was made into art, jewelry, and religious artifacts. The religion and culture of the Nasheed were called *naelm*. This concept is where outsiders were often confused about Nasheed culture.

"We were exclusively matrilineal. For centuries Nasheed women lived in compounds in self-imposed exile from men. We would mate once and only once. Marriage was not part of the equation. If a man wanted to help with providing the resources for his progeny, that was welcome and encouraged. Once our men reached the age of majority, they were encouraged to leave Graile and seek their fortunes outside in the enormous galaxy. That is why so many of our men became pilots, gamblers, scholars, bounty hunters. They would return to Graile to perform reproductive duties and then return to other pursuits."

"So what about when they were young? What did the Nasheed do with their male children?" Tyr asked.

"Around the age of three, the mother, sometimes with the help of the father, sometimes not, would find a home for them. In the days before the Great Unity War, childless women of the corporations would adopt them; some would become wards of the corporations. It varied."

"Maybe some of my friends had this happen to them," Tyr mused.

"Yes. It is even likely. But if it were correctly done, only a very few people would ever know about it, would have access to that information. The Nasheed guard their lineage secrets well.

"Among the Nasheed women, there was an elite warrior class known as the Domina. We had a sacrosanct duty to protect our sacred queen. Domina females were raised in convents away from their mothers for secrecy and security. If someone knew who your daughter was, they could get to you. Domina mothers kept an eye on their daughters and contributed money and resources. The details of the matrilineage were classified by the convent's secret chambers and stored in their archives. Domina neophytes were identified by age three and placed in the sevens—the seven elite assassin schools. These schools were located in the high mountains in the north country. Way up in thick forests away from the prying eyes of the outside world. My education in the hidden arts began way up there many years ago."

"The stuff of legend. Are you Domina?" Tyr asked.

"I'm getting to that. A potential Domina was recognized early on in our childhood for specific skills. Agility, quickness, mental acuity, and physical strength. But most notably for a sense of spatial awareness that we called *serral*. Serral is hard to explain, but it's quickness and spatial awareness so keen that we can snatch a dragonfly from the air with ease. The foundation for serral is an acute awareness that things are not what they seem.

"I was among the last Nasheed women to be trained as Domina. Upon my graduation, I would meet my birth mother and be recognized in a week-long ritual known as the corsram.

"It did not go that way. Here is what happened…

"Graile City was the only port on Graile where trade with the outside world was permitted." Kayle paused and took a deep breath. "On the eve of the Great Unity War, all nine corporations had forced their way into having trade offices in Graile City. Triad, Dominica, Shanzu, Guatagua, Norvo, Snyder, Globex, GDC, and Dyeus. But only Dyeus and GDC dominated our local trade. Triad, the hired mercenary corporation, subbed out a lot of the dirty work for Dyeus. Even then, Dyeus verged on being an outlaw company."

"Triad has been doing that for generations. They're good at it. Had a few unfortunate run-ins with them," Tyr said.

"Tod Lasker, Ross Lasker's father, came to Graile to talk with Queen Danta. He wanted to expand trade and gain mineral rights to explore for gold," Kayle continued.

"For months, he tried to get a meeting with her. Although she was friendly and amiable and sent her ambassadors to meet with him, she kept him at bay."

"So, she generally grin-fucked him," Tyr said.

"Yes. That's a colorful but not inaccurate way to put it. In any event, she agreed to meet with him in Graile City to put an end to his pestering ways.

"He had been planning it for months when he kidnapped Danta and held her for ransom." Kayle's eyes flashed in anger.

"Now what I heard was…Danta ordered him to leave Graile and take all of the other corporations with him. Then she tried to arrest him, but there was a skirmish," Tyr said.

"None of that happened. Lasker held her for ransom, and the ransom to be paid was three warehouses full of gold. Absurd!" Kayle paused to collect herself.

"Well, we didn't have that much gold available anywhere. So Lasker altered his demands and said we must bring him all of our golden art-works. That included our sacred religious artifacts, jewelry, sculptures. We were to fill up only one warehouse at the Graile City Starport," she said, and sobbed.

"So we did that. We stripped our culture, our chapels, our convents, our museums, and we filled the warehouse.

"Then he cut Queen Danta's throat at the exchange ceremony. He threw her body off a balcony at the Dyeus trade building," Kayle whispered.

"Thus began our war against Dyeus," she said.

"So, that's not the way that history is taught at the academies," Tyr said.

"Of course, it isn't. But this is the truth. GDC tried to help us. Now, they didn't do this out of any sense of misplaced altruism. They did it because the Great Unity War had broken out, and GDC was aligned against Dyeus even back then.

"With Queen Danta dead, GDC had to contact each Nasheed community to build a coalition. This took too much time.

"Some of us were able to fight our way into the area around Dyeus Corp's building, and we retrieved our late queen's body. The royal cemetery was located outside of Graile City in a remote mountainous region. It is known as the Sepulchelles (named after the imperial tombs there).

"For generations, we buried the queens, princesses, and other female nobles, with some of their favorite things from their lives. These valuables were theirs to take with them on to the next life. Many of these artifacts were gold.

"You can guess what happened next.

"Lasker brought his military to the Sepulchelles and desecrated our tombs, looting everything that was not nailed down.

"So, in a period of a few weeks, he killed our queen and took away every single thing that was sacred to the Nasheed.

"We Nasheed believe that spilled blood demands vengeance.

"We retaliated by blowing up the Dyeus building with Tod Lasker in it. His oldest son Ross was in suborbital flight around Graile at the time. Ross proceeded to level Graile City. He also staged fake Nasheed, false flag attacks against the other corporate trade buildings. The short Graile Punitive War ensued. That is how the Nasheed diaspora happened, the total destruction of our culture. Survivors became refugees, and we were scattered to the four winds, hunted, persecuted with bounties on our heads. This last part sounds familiar, yes?"

"How could you ever work for Dyeus, Kayle?" Tyr whispered.

She stared at him in reply and watched the light come on in his eyes.

"Oh. I get it," he said.

"Right, the nine corporations are not the only forces who have assassins. The last of the Nasheed Dominae will wipe the Lasker bloodline out of existence. We have all taken blood oaths. It will happen."

"You tell me all this because..." Tyr was on guard.

"I should not have told you so much. I didn't mean to. All I can hope for is that you understand why I am opposed to disturbing these tombs on Gereon." Kayle sounded hopeful.

"I get it. But you have to realize, I mean, you know that's the whole reason we are all here, Kayle. It's all about the gold…" Tyr paused.

"If the guards find out about these burials, what will happen, Tyr? What do you think they will do?" she asked.

"Kayle, we came a long way for the gold. A lot of people died for us to get this far…on the possibility that we would find gold here." Tyr shook his head in disbelief. "You can't expect me to…" He reached for his collapsible shovel. "Look. Let me get this one necklace out before we make that decision."

"No. Not this gold, Tyr. It can't be this gold. We should concentrate on finding where the Gereon ancients mined for this gold. That's what we should be looking for. Let's leave this where we found it," Kayle insisted.

"I don' know if I can do that, Kayle. I don't see it the same way you …"

Her needle flashed through his head before he finished his thought.

"I will regret killing you for the rest of my life, Tyr," she whispered.

———◆———

Kayle drove the scorpion out to a sandbar on the lake and dropped Tyr's body into the black water. Shaken by what she had done, she tried to say some words to justify her actions but came up empty.

18

T HE EXPLORATION OF THE VALLEY continued unabated. Emi had joined up with her crew. Their forces were getting better organized now. As Key and Emi assembled a recon crew of seven, mounted on hoverbikes, he thought about all that had transpired in the last two days.

Key was concerned about how thin they were getting. A force of about 100 people was left at *Crimson Rhapsody*'s crash-landing site. Another 150 were at Camp Crim, the shuttle port. The remaining 300-plus were establishing a more permanent base camp in what had come to be called Green Valley or "GV" for short. It was unfortunate and risky to have the forces split into three different localities. Still, Key could think of no way to avoid it under the current circumstances. Remote sensing of the valley's archaeological resources revealed several buried circular structures. And several regularly spaced rectangular features that resembled walls. Fifty centimeters below the surface, a long causeway extended across the entire length of the valley.

They came to a shady grove of trees after about thirty minutes and decided to stop for a coffee break. Key sent the drone in a circling-defensive pattern above the crew.

"Whenever we have time, there will be a lot of archaeology to do," Key said to Emi.

"At what point do we stop looking for survivors from the battle, Commander?" Manaka asked.

"Let's give it a couple more days. We still have almost fifty of our people unaccounted for, plus who knows how many of the *Antares* crew? Assume they brought around 800 to meet us, and we have found, what, ten of them so far?"

"It's up to twelve now," Emi said.

"So, it's a big planet, and we need to search a little longer. I especially want to find Jaylen or his remains. He's the last friend I have left, believe it or not, so, yeah, it's personal." He mounted his hoverbike, and the rest of the crew followed suit. "And then there's the matter of Kayle Korban. Minerva put much emphasis on learning what happened to her," Key said.

"But that's not personal." Emi smiled and put her helmet on.

"Been talking to Claire?" Key asked.

"Well, she's about the only real friend I have left…on this planet, anyway," Emi said.

"Mount up and move out, folks," Key said.

⟨◇⟩

By midafternoon the causeway broadened out a bit as it followed a natural gorge off to the south. This area was less wooded and rockier. Large windswept boulders and rock formations changed the course of the road as the crew ascended the path up to an adjacent mesa.

They continued to move upward, turned a corner, and came into a high, immense rock overhang. The causeway ran underneath it.

They did not see the antler-men until they were in their midst.

The startled creatures were napping when Key's team came upon them. One of them shot at Key with a bow and arrow, and then it was chaos as the battle erupted into a close-quarters brawl.

Emi was knocked off her bike, and Key slung her up behind him. Another fellow aimed at Key, but a clone vaporized his head with a needler.

"Press on. Don't dismount. Let's get out of here and up on the mesa. Now!" Key ordered.

They stopped where the road met the mesa. Key checked the drone screen. The beast people were retreating down the trail in a disorderly horde. A jumble. They vanished into the deep woods.

Key motioned his team to stay mounted and form up in a semicircle. They waited, weapons ready.

Rail guns can do a lot of damage at close range, Key thought as he changed weapons.

In the woods, the beast people howled and screamed in fear and agony. They seemed to be closing in using the thick trees for cover.

"Were they wearing headdresses, or were those actual antlers in their heads?" Claire asked.

Key shrugged and got his needler out, and the rest of his team did the same. They waited, but nothing came out of the woods.

Key turned to Emi and asked, "Was it Boris that we lost back at the rock shelter?"

"Yes, it was Boris. Boris Beamon," Emi said.

Key pointed to the two nearest clones and said, "You two go back and retrieve his body and his bike."

"Yes, sir."

Bette interrupted his thoughts, saying, "Commander. We have an unidentified individual approaching from about 200 meters to the south. Here is a close-in view of him."

The screen showed a beat-up looking man in the grimy, shredded, and bloody uniform of a GDC lieutenant commander. He was wearing a bone mask fashioned from a pelvic ring of some kind. Scalps were attached to his belt.

Scalps? What the hell? He looks familiar. But is that—

He zoomed the camera in as the man waved up at the drone and removed his mask.

He was looking into the purple eyes of Jaylen Rent.

Key rode out to meet him on his hoverbike.

Jaylen smiled, held out his arms, and said, "So you finally got off your ass and looked for me, you lazy bastard."

Key laughed and said, "You owe me a new ship, buddy."

They embraced.

"Seriously, Key, those assholes almost had me a couple of times."

"What's with the bone mask and the scalps?" Key asked.

"Props. Intimidates the shit out of the stag heads. They fear me now. Want to debrief here or back at the base? Where the hell is the base, by the way?" Jaylen asked.

"We have a new base much closer now. About a ninety-minute ride from here," Key said.

"I wouldn't mind some real food for a change."

Emi arrived with the other bike in tow.

"Are you fit to ride, Jaylen?" Largo asked.

"Absolutely. But first, do you have your flask with you? A shot or two of whiskey would be wonderful."

19

JAYLEN TOLD HIS STORY TO the assembled officers at the OC. Minerva was present via holocall.

"The foredeck emergency hatch saved my ass. I dropped into the emergency module and fell out of the sky, trusting the AI to protect me. The collision destroyed most of the controls. I wore battle armor because of our alert status. So, I had integrated AI, full digital camo, needle, pistol, and three days of emergency rations on me. I would need all of it plus a little luck, as it turned out.

"My escape module drifted far to the west, and I lost sight of our ship and all the other escape craft. On the dorsal view screen, I saw a red circle surrounded by flickering orange flames looming below me. It was an active volcano. The module was going to land in it.

"I had enough time to grab an emergency jet pack and strap it on. Then I ejected and shot out of the forward hatch. I came out violently and almost passed out from the rapid descent. Somehow, during all this, my tracking beacon went dead, so I knew I was on my own way before I landed. I saw the volcano swallow the escape module and wished there had been more time to grab some extra rations.

"The AI slowed my jetpack, and I touched down about ten kilometers from the volcano. It was an area of jumbled up landforms. Windswept deserts interrupted by mountain ranges and deep river canyons. I had a strange feeling that I was being watched (which I knew was unlikely, but I felt it all the same). All I saw below me was a herd of shaggy bovines. They looked like buffalo but with longer hair."

"We haven't seen those yet," Key interjected.

"Big herds of them. Potentially, a great source of meat," Jaylen added. "So, I landed on top of a nearby mesa. I saw distant rock formations that looked like walls and towers. I figured they were windswept rock formations. So, I headed out that way, aware of the forty-eight-hour life span on the jetpack's batteries. Trying to keep down in the mountain shadows, I could not shake the feeling of eyes watching me. The hair on the back of my neck was straight up.

"So, imagine my surprise as I neared the rock formation and realized that it was not a rock formation at all. It was, in fact, a citadel with gleaming black walls hewn out of a granite mesa."

"Interesting," Largo said.

"That's it? It's interesting? I tell you I found a castle built by nonhuman intelligent life forms, and that's all you got?" Jaylen asked. "Damn. What a letdown!"

Largo laughed, "Well, we've found some remains as well. And then there are those strange antler guys who attacked us," Key said.

"Yep. I know those guys. I have their scalps." Rent paused and poured out a tumbler full of scotch and tossed it straight back, smacked his lips, and poured another one. "Damn good stuff, Key. Langlois whiskey?"

"Yep. Fifty years old." Key poured one for himself, Claire, Postrenal, and Emi. "Was the citadel occupied?"

"Not by anything alive. No."

—<♦>—

"After hitting crosswinds and violent updrafts, I landed on the highest parapet. I readied myself in case some defenders came rushing up the stairs to challenge me. But no one ever came. It was weird, quiet. The roof area is large enough to hold two of our dreadnoughts. Vast.

"I could hear the wind in the crosscurrents around the castle walls. Whistling through the shattered parapets, blowing sand and dust against my armor, it made an eerie howling sound. Strange acoustics in the tower. Like ghost voices were whirling and floating in the winds.

"My AI checked for life-forms. She detected none. But she did discover some dead forms in the turret below me. I saw an open doorway to some stairs, so I went down there to have a look. Four flights. The place has flights and flights of stairs." He took a more restrained sip of the scotch. No one else said anything.

"On the next door, I had to blast the lock to get in. After that, a lot of hard pushing and lifting to get to the next part. It was blocked by who knows how many centuries of sand and dust. Some of the sands had strange white streaks mixed in with the reddish and yellow hues. These streaks, it turned out, were pure calcium; I identified these as vaporized bone dust. There had once been a hell of a battle up there. Many life forms pulverized.

"The floor opened out into a sealed-up gun turret of some kind. Four massive cannons of unknown origin, design, or function, protecting each of the cardinal directions. They, too, were clogged with dust. The guns connected to a thick cable that ran down into the depths of the castle. No idea what those cables were all about, or where they went. Power, fuel, or ammo source. Here's the thing, though—a perceptible hum emitted from that cable. Electric machinery?"

"So, it's still connected to some power source?" Key asked.

"Apparently." Rent shrugged.

"Then we need to get up there and check that tower out," Key said.

"Did I mention that the guns were enormous, about nine meters high? There's a reason for that, I guess. Based on my measurements of the gunner's seats, the chaps who used them were around 2.0 to 2.5 meters tall." Rent paused and said, "Bette, on screen, next floor down, please show my study of the defenders of the Dead Castle."

"Château des soldats morts. Château Morte," Postrenal whispered.

<hr>

Rent's helmet cam footage displayed his next actions on the main screen.

The area, decorated and loaded with strange, unfamiliar objects, had a color palette consisting of amber, brown, gold, and yellow. Red dominated the halls and chambers. The old yellow curtains were drawn, concealing a view of the sea. On the left, in an antechamber, Rent looked in on the dead, large feet of three soldiers laid out in a row. Their dark leathery corpses stood out in stark contrast to the rest of the room.

Framed in the center were the remains of a luxurious and expansive palatial office. A messy writing desk was in the nearby background.

Arranged around the room were ammo boxes and the remains of two desiccated meals. The other cluttered objects were alien—strange and challenging to identify. In the immediate foreground lay a large suitcase filled with weapons. Abandoned. One dead defender sat in a command chair next to it. He was wearing a pastel orange uniform with red piping.

"Love that uniform," Minerva observed. "He must have been the head honcho. It seems to me that he was hiding from the world in this room. The situation reeks of desperation. It looks like he gave up. Any insignia or rank signifiers, Mr. Rent?"

"With all that dust on his uniform, he has about merged with the landscape of his office," Rent said. "On each epaulet, I could see what looked like the number eight on them. The top of the eight had a V-shaped hash mark. No idea of what any of that means."

"The dead soldiers' feet compared to his feet suggest a sense of loss, or of being lost, or both. Unlike them, he still has his boots on," Largo noted. "He sat down in that command chair and awaited the inevitable. Die with his boots on."

"It wasn't far away," Minerva mused. "Look at that. He has six fingers, as do the dead soldiers who have webbed feet. Remarkable. The squarish skull is very much like our own, except for the high cranial vault and the deep eye sockets. His skin is desiccated to the color of dried blood. I assume you took bio-samples, Rent?"

"Yes, ma'am. Results are in process. Not yet available," Rent said.

"So, how many unique sentient life-forms does that make?" Minerva asked.

"Two," Key said. "The primitive antler guys and these tall castle dwellers."

Rent said, "This place has many surprises."

"Who are the primitives?" Minerva asked.

"One will be coming up on the screen in a few minutes," Rent said.

Claire observed, "That suitcase is strange. It looks like an artifact of a bygone era, not his. Yet it lies at the center of this scene in his life. It is a weight that he carries. And he gave up on packing it. Why?"

"I think the room mirrors his mental state, confused, transitory," Key said. "It is as if he has been shot from the sky and crash-landed into this chair, awaiting rescue or death."

"Well, we know he wasn't rescued," Rent said.

"So, what happened next?" Minerva asked.

Rent continued, "The exit door looked like it was welded shut, seamless. There was no way for me to explore the castle any further. A crater in the roof and some fallen ceiling tiles suggested that a battle had penetrated at least this far into the citadel's interior. I got back up on the parapet where the heaviest fighting had apparently happened. As I put back on my jetpack, I saw something glinting in the bone dust against a wall. I dug it out and found an extraordinary thing. There was a shattered radius bone lying next to it. One of the guys who got vaporized must have been wearing it.

"Careful with this thing, it's got strange juju. I get a bad feeling from it," Rent said. He pulled a large solid gold bracelet out of his cargo pocket and handed it over to Key. "It doesn't like me. Won't let me wear it."

"You sound like you think it's alive," Claire said and laughed.

"Look, it acts like it's alive is all I know. It's a little tarnished, but who knows how long it lay exposed to the elements up there?" Rent said. "Hey, Key, don't."

Rent moved to restrain him, but Largo, against all his years of training, on impulse tried it on. It was a flexible gold band that contained dull blue jewels embedded in silvery rectangles. The bracelet moved, gave him a mild electric shock, and twisted on his wrist. It rotated 180 degrees and gently squeezed itself into his wrist—startling Key to his core. He felt two dart-like pains in his arm. He saw gold microfilaments embed under his skin as the bracelet began plugging into his body. The bracelet jewels had tiny gold lights blinking inside them.

This is like Minerva's, but how could it be? That one was invented by Mesh Trouter…

"I tried to stop you—" Rent said.

"What the hell? Did you all see that?" Largo asked.

Stunned silence.

Minerva asked, "What were you thinking? Dammit! Can you take it off, Key?"

He tried to untwist it and pull it off. It was too snug. "No, Minerva. Not without help," Key said. He held it up against his ear. "It's making a low static sound, almost like it is alive."

"I've seen something like it before. I see one every day. The first time I put it on—it acted a little bit like that. Regard my portal bracelet." Minerva held it closer for everyone on the holocall to see. They were similar in appearance, almost identical in structure.

"It looks enough like yours the same artisan could have made it," Largo said.

"And that artist was none other than Mesh Trouter. He made mine. I know that is certain." Minerva added,

"So, Trouter made it out to Gereon and dropped a bracelet here? "Rent asked. "Or made it to K City from Gereon?"

"Mesh is connected to the square heads somehow?" Key speculated.

"You know his skull was a little on the squarish side." Minerva mused, "But he had the right number of fingers, as far as I know. He often wore gloves, though."

"In the footage, I've seen of him, he looks about 6 feet and a half. "Rent said. "So, he would be tall enough. And no one knows what became of him or where he even came from?"

Minerva reached over to adjust her holochannel. "Dominica corp discovered him. Years ago. The consensus view is he was a prodigy, trained in one of their elite monasteries. They have always been hyper secretive about their activities, but especially so in all matters about Trouter. Rent, please continue your report to the others. I must step away for a moment and arrange immediate passage to Gereon."

"Wait, Minerva. We have some things–" Largo tried to stop her.

"Key, do not try to use that thing! An untrained hand on that bracelet can destroy himself. Claire, Postrenal, Meadows, I'm counting on you all to figure out a way to separate that bracelet away from Key. His survival may depend on it," Minerva said. "I will be in the fastest interceptor we have. Minerva out." Her holocall disconnected.

Postrenal said, "Commander, I need to examine your wrist. The bracelet...some alien microbes, possibly dangerous to your health may—"

Largo cut him off. "Later, Doc. We need to conclude this debrief. Dammit. I don't need Minerva coming here right now." Gritting his teeth, Largo said, "We have too much going on."

While Largo and Claire fidgeted with the bracelet, Rent continued his story.

"After I found that bangle, I got up off the wall and jetted high enough to get an overview of the facility. As you can see, it's not a castle, even though that's an easy way for me to refer to it. It is more of a colossal citadel fort built on top of a large rectangular ziggurat-shaped pyramid. Roughly, a 900-meters-long by 800-meters-wide walled structure. So, it must have had two layers of defenses. The construction material is massive red granitic obsidian blocks. The whole thing is cemented together with something like a hard yellow adobe material, but it's harder than steel. Harder and denser. I found the red obsidian to be unbreakable—the most substantial stone I have ever encountered.

"As you can see, the north side of the castle borders the desert dunes that give way to the ocean. It sits astride a deep spring that flows out of its depths and forms a river flowing toward the south. On either side of the stream are swamps and marshes with clumps of trees interspersed. They merge into some thick, dark forests on both sides. In the swamps, I saw the most bird-like creatures I've seen since we came to Gereon. They look almost identical to birds, except that they have iridescent scaly skin instead of feathers."

He showed a close-up of a green horned lizard-like bird with hummingbird wings. On-screen, they watched as Rent became distracted from the birds when he saw the tall grass move nearby. He caught sight of a tree dog then, a wildish juvenile that had jumped out of the woods. The dog sped away, disappearing back into the tall grass.

Descending to get a closer look, Rent saw a dark, vague shape.

"I could not identify it, so I closed in," Rent said. "At first, I only saw its humped back beyond the crest of a hill. But then I saw the rest of it, and I knew what the tree dog knew. It was a bipedal predator that was giving chase."

He froze the image. "Here is a good close-up look at one of our antlered primitives."

The creature looked up to where Rent hovered in his jetpack.

Everyone leaned in closer to the screen.

"He is not afraid of you, Rent. That's telling. Let's take a look at you, stranger," Largo said.

His limbs were in proportion and balanced. His sallow skin seemed to stretch across his sinewy, muscular skeleton. The humpback looked to be part of his muscle system. Skin so transparent, it was almost colorless. It showed the work of muscles and arteries underneath. Teeth shaped into pearly points; he had veiny, watery eyes. Large stag antlers grew out of his head.

The creature's eyes narrowed as he reached for an arrow, knocked it, and fired it at Rent.

"Accurate archer, this stag-guy. Athletic," Rent deadpanned. "He shot it like a missile."

"The arrow damaged my jetpack, so I decided to follow the streambed," he said. "I extended the pack's glider wings and looked for a safe place to land."

"As you can see, the stream starts straight, falling over those mossy logs. The solid land veers off to the right. To the left, there are scores of junked military vehicles. Later, I went out to examine them. A dense forest runs down a steep slope to a field of sandstone boulders. Farther up the trail, there's the first collapsed dome structure, then another, then a clump of five of them. And after that, more than I could count. The whole lot was encircled by more fragmented, rusted-out wrecks. A large battle happened here a long time ago."

"What are these domes?" Largo asked.

"They appear to be hardened bunkers and domiciles. The settlement pattern is scattered and exurban. I saw no signs of urban centers. It looks like it was once a landscape of agrarian villages."

"Pause the image there, Rent, and could we go back to the guy who knocked your jetpack out with an arrow?" Largo interrupted.

Rent paused it and rewound to the moment before the arrow shot.

"Reactions?" Largo asked.

"Their antlers and transparent skin are shockers," Claire said.

"Right. You can see the blood circulating," Largo said. "Weird kind of adaptation or mutation."

"I've been thinking about it," Rent said. "His skin is a bit transparent. So, is he an underground or under river dweller—for millennia?"

"Plausible." Largo nodded. "A beneficial or neutral mutation, in that setting."

"So, this stag-antler guy," Austen Nesh said, "has he any military kit besides bow and arrows?"

"Nothing that I saw. He seemed to have stone tools and weapons. This one had amazing strength, though," Jaylen said.

"What about that hump on his back?" Claire asked.

"It appears to be where some of his brain functions are located," Jaylen said. "He sneaked up on me later when I was studying the battle site, and I stunned him with a solid kick to the hump. Knocked him out for a few minutes. Long enough for me to escape, at least."

"Bette, give us a holographic, 360-degree look at this creature," Key said.

When the creature stood silhouetted against the forest background, Key said, "Freeze it right there please, Bette."

"Look at that," Claire said.

Barely discernible in the forest gloom, the creature's antlers merged with the tree branches. His transparent skin was almost invisible.

"There's your adaptive value of those features," Rent said.

"Right. He's got perfect camouflage for a forest environment," Largo observed. "Wonder how many of them are in the woods?"

"Quite a few. I picked up hundreds of heat signatures in there, and I'll tell you this too, I wouldn't go in that forest without an armored battalion and full air support," Jaylen said.

"Whenever we go, if we go, that's how we'll do it," Nesh said.

"Let's break for lunch," Key said. "Bette, get the galley to send us up whatever they have cooked for the rest of the crew. Jaylen, give your complete report to Bette immediately. I will edit it and disseminate it to the Senior Leadership Team as soon as you complete it."

Jaylen nodded.

Largo addressed the rest of the ops team. "Nesh, Claire, Emi. I need you to get with me in the lab. We are going to investigate the citadel as soon as possible."

20

Kayle approached their campsite, thinking about how she would explain Tyr's absence to the guards. Coming in at dusk, the long shadows of the escarpment offered concealment.

The drone's radar warning system picked up several large flying shapes emerging from the nearby rock shelters.

Before she could focus on them, an explosive burst of static blurred the screen just as she lost contact with her last drone. The screen was black.

"What the bloody hell—" Kayle muttered under her breath as she tried to reestablish contact.

Without warning, something struck the side of the scorpion hard and flipped it over on its back.

At the same moment, Kayle heard a message from the guards, "Be advised we are under attack."

Another deafening burst of static.

"Flying beasts breaching the perimeter. Many casualties. The situation is deadly. Korban. Do you read…" A thunderous burst of static erupted through the speakers. Silence.

Still stunned from the collision, Kayle activated the emergency defense response system (EDRS). A high-intensity electric arc of 50,000 volts emanated from the scorpion's armor. It blasted the unidentified life form clinging to it. A strong smell of ozone and burned meat filled the compartment.

An eerie scream pierced the twilight. Kayle, once more, tried to make contact.

"Calling the base. This is Korban. The scorpion has crashed, and I'm under attack," She attempted to unhook her harness, but this was made difficult by being suspended upside down. Another impact rolled the scorpion over a slope. She bounced hard inside the cockpit as loose objects ricocheted all around the cabin. Something hard struck Kayle's head and knocked her unconscious.

She heard a faraway voice say, "Where is your friend?" It woke her up. She thought someone was in the crashed APC with her.

I know that voice. Tyr? No, I killed Tyr.

Through a cracked windshield, Kayle could see the first streaks of pink light creeping across the morning sky. Sore and tired, she extricated herself from the debris and clutter at the bottom of the vehicle. The floor escape hatch was now overhead. Kayle was slow to climb out of it. Her right knee was throbbing from the collision.

A burned, dead bat-like creature was draped over the front end of the scorpion. It was smoking and reeking of rotten burned flesh. Kayle poked the corpse with her needler. Its body still smoldered from the bolt of lightning Kayle had shot into it the night before. Approximately eight meters in length with a wingspan of over seven meters, it was a behemoth. Thick-skinned, with bony membranous wings and a massive, fanged jaw, it was the stuff of nightmares: a giant, smoking, fanged bat.

"Dead, at least," Kayle said. "And as dead as I will be if I don't figure out a way to get the scorpion up and running." An idea of how to do this came to her. She remembered that the scorpion's claws were retracted and stored in the forward storage bins. They were situated against the ground now.

Each arm can lift 20 metric tons. Just have to do everything upside-down.

A half a kilometer from the base, she saw the smoke and smelled the stench. About two dozen of the bat corpses littered the cave entrance. Blasted and burned body parts were in grotesque piles.

The heaviest fighting was right here, Kayle thought. *Bits and pieces of clone bodies mixed with bloody bat parts. No survivors.*

We managed to get 100 elite combat clones killed out here. And for what?

Kayle extended the excavation claw and began to dig a mass grave. Although it was battered, damaged, and covered in dried blood, gristle, and guts, most of the scorpion's functions were still operational.

I am further away from completing my mission than I've ever been. Have I failed? Played a high stakes game and lost everything?

A holocall from Minerva interrupted her reverie. "There you are! I have been trying to reach you, Kayle. I have news."

Kayle surprised herself when she realized she was glad to see Minerva.

She managed a half-smile. "Hello, Minerva. It has been a bit hectic here. And chaotic. Much chaos since we last spoke."

Minerva waved her hand, saying, "Korban, you look like you were chopped up in a blender."

"That's an apt description," Kayle said.

"What are you doing?"

"Digging a mass grave for all of my clone commandos." Tears welled in her eyes.

"What happened?"

"Minerva, as far as I know, you are looking at the last surviving officer of the dreadnought *Antares*."

"I'm sorry, Kayle. I need to know how things stand between you and Lasker. Give me the main points, please."

<hr>

When Kayle had caught her up, Minerva said, "We can reasonably assume that you are almost back to the point where Lasker needs you again."

"How's that?"

"I will soon be landing on Gereon. In about seventy-two more hours, I'll be planet-side. I'm on a burner right now, and I am hopeful my portal will work when I get there. You and I could meet face-to-face," Minerva said.

"A one-way ticket?" Kayle asked.

"After a portal, it is the fastest transport possible, but a burner ship consumes its entire disruptor drive. Expensive as hell… Necessary given the current circumstances," Minerva said.

"Which are?" Kayle asked.

"Dire. Let me give you the short version. Dyeus and Grand Design now have the first declared trade war in half a century, and I am losing the war at this moment. Trillions in capital and millions of lives are at stake. To make a stand, and to strengthen our hand, I'm in the middle of consolidating a portion of our strategic resources on Raba and Gereon. Their remoteness may buy us some time. Over the next few months, we should be well-entrenched on both planets. I suspect Lasker is sending his second (and much larger) invasion force to Gereon even as we speak. He wants to deliver the death blow before we get established. At this point, Lasker is more committed to destroying us, destroying me, than he is to the gold."

"And you want me to contact Lasker and offer my services?" Kayle grimaced.

"Not yet. Let's hold off on making you look desperate for as long as possible," Minerva continued. "I have completed an exclusive deal with Aduvah Fattah, Triad's CEO, to tip the scales back a bit in our favor. She's been a friend since grad school."

"An exclusive? With Triad? Did you mortgage half the corporate assets to close that deal?" Kayle shook her head. "You've bet the farm on Gereon, haven't you?"

"I have done exactly that," Minerva said. "I have made a significant financial investment. The corp is all in on this one, and I have the board's support with me for now, at least. But it's getting a bit thin with them, I must admit. Still, Triad's hired guns should be enough to win the day."

It was the first time Kayle had ever seen Minerva worried.

21

N the lab, Largo and Postrenal looked over Rent's report. Arrayed on tables around them were some of the recovered artifacts from the citadel. The rest of the leadership team waited in the main ops building.

Postrenal cleared his throat. "The pathos of this fallen civilization combined with its sophisticated technology. It is a situation that demands that we come up with a unique name for such a magnificent culture."

"Do you have any suggestions?" Key asked.

"The *sacramentae*." Postrenal smiled. "I know you love Latin. And it is better than square heads."

"The mysteries. It's good. We'll use it for now unless one of us can come up with something better." Key nodded.

"First names usually stick in taxonomy, but this is a good one," Postrenal said.

"And what about the guys with the transparent skin and the antlers?" Key asked.

"I have not come up with one yet," Postrenal said.

"Of course, the troopers have started calling them stags, so that that name may stick," Largo said. "Is there anything else, Doc? We have a mission coming up. And I need to get my armor from my quarters."

Postrenal looked uncomfortable but didn't say anything.

Largo paused and asked, "Okay. What is it about? My vicocet pump?"

"Well, that's not what I want to discuss, but your vicocet abuse is something we need to talk about soon. Nonetheless, I have something more urgent on my mind…your new gold bracelet. It needs to be checked out, Commander."

"It's on my mind as well. And my wrist." Largo chuckled. "I can't take it off, can't move it at all, you know?"

"Would you mind if I scanned it?" Postrenal asked. "It would only take a few minutes." He opened his satchel and pulled out a medsleeve. "Look. Put your right forearm down here on the table and let me slide the sleeve over it. Won't take long at all."

Together they watched as the medsleeve did its work. At first, it displayed the bracelet as it appeared resting on Largo's wrist, a surface view.

"Commander, have you ever had one of these sleeves used on you?" Postrenal asked.

"No."

"This device takes thin cross-sections, magnetic resonance images of objects and structures in your body. It then turns those into 3D slices and reveals subsurface microstructures. These sections can be as thin as .05 millimeters." Postrenal paused before continuing, "Are you ready? This may give you an unpleasant shiver."

"Let's get on with it," Largo said.

The surface of the sleeve dissolved into a screen. It was immediately apparent that the bracelet had inserted microfilaments into Largo's subcutaneous deep tissue. These, in turn, had formed into a net-like structure that encircled the interior of his entire forearm.

Postrenal whistled. "The only way this is coming off is through intensive surgery. Or an amputation. Commander, I had no idea."

"Consider everything we learn classified, Doc."

Postrenal nodded.

The next cross-section revealed microfilaments entwined and connected with his nervous system. They had integrated via his radial, musculocutaneous nerve stem.

Postrenal shook his head. "It is almost like it's a living organism, see the dendritic treelike structure? They resemble organic crystals. Somehow it is plugging into your nervous system, and it has completely merged with you. It cannot be removed. I suspect it has reached your brain by this point!"

Neither of them spoke for a few seconds.

"Is it a threat? A parasite?" Largo asked.

"More research is needed, Commander. There are only nine of these bracelets in existence that we know of."

"Ten. Now."

"Ten. As far as I know, there are no published scientific studies on any of them. For all we know, this invasion of the host body is a standard operating procedure for portal bracelets. It is almost certainly affecting your nervous system. your higher-level cognitive functions." Postrenal shrugged. "As your doctor, I regard it a threat, until I know that it is not. Consider that it was worn by someone with anatomy quite different from ours. Alien."

"When Minerva gets here, she will allow you to take a look at hers. This one is different. I think. It seems heavier possibly more complex," Largo said.

"Examining Minerva's bracelet would be most helpful. Now, before we leave for the citadel, Commander, I must caution you on your vicocet intake; you must cut it back. Immediately."

Largo appraised Postrenal.

He is merely trying to be my physician.

"Maybe later, Doc. Right now, I'm a mass of aching muscles and screaming nerves. I even have an alien parasite embedded in my forearm. I need my vicocet pump more than ever. I need you to understand this too, and I need you to refill the pump. Now, before we leave."

Postrenal sighed, "Point taken. Still, we are only delaying the final reckoning, Commander. There will be a high price to pay soon."

"In more ways than one, Doc. In more ways than any of us know."

⊰⬦⊱

"Château mort," Postrenal had called it, and it seemed a fitting name as it loomed above them in twilight's early gloom. A company of clone marines accompanied Largo's archaeological crew on the recon trip out to the citadel. Two fire teams of four men, led by Austen Nesh, also deployed from their hoverbikes. They commenced setting up a camp and sorting out the provisions under Austen's direct supervision.

Claire, Postrenal, Michelle, and Meadows stood in the deep shadow cast by the citadel. They all looked up at the massive structure.

"Extraordinary," Meadows said. "Alien. I mean, it's incongruous. It shouldn't be here."

"And yet it is," Postrenal observed.

"There's enough light to put on our jetpacks and go to the parapet. Let's get up there," Largo said.

They retrieved their jetpacks from their provisions.

"I recommend rail guns for this venture," Rent said.

"Why? In your report, it was uninhabited, correct?" Michelle asked.

"That doesn't mean the stags haven't found a way into it in the interim," Rent replied. "Besides, I wasn't up here after dark."

"Break out the rail guns, folks," Largo ordered.

Armed and in their jetpacks, the archaeology crew landed on the parapets a few minutes later.

"There's the doorway," Rent said, and pointed to a squarish structure behind the walls. The door was open enough to squeeze through one at a time.

"Before we go into the citadel, I would like to do a study of this area. Let's set up our floodlights and look around up here," Largo said.

"You aren't concerned about attracting unwanted attention?" Michelle asked.

"Unwanted attention would also be part of our learning experience, wouldn't it, Michelle?" Claire grinned at her.

Michelle did not reply.

Largo gave Claire an appreciative smile.

"Let's spend about an hour up here getting oriented, and then we will head back to our camp," Largo said.

"Commander, I have found something over here," Postrenal reported. "Looks like some kind of weapon."

In the floodlight, Postrenal had uncovered a strange device. It consisted of crystal tubes and cables entwined around a barrel. The barrel was gun-metal black, and the crystals were a translucent blue.

"Leave everything in situ, for now," Largo said. "We need to try to get a sense about what happened up here before the structure was abandoned. In the morning, we will get the blowers up here and begin removing the metric tons of sand and dust."

"Did you see that?" Michelle asked.

"Alert! Large, winged creatures are deploying from a cave below us. Assume they are hostile," Bette said.

"We are inbound," Nesh reported in.

Michelle's wounded scream pierced the night.

A massive, black-fanged bat thing had her forearm in its talons, fangs gaping toward her head. It knocked over the nearest floodlight, plunging half the area into darkness.

Largo fired at it. Missed.

Michelle had her needler and was trying to fight back as a bloody foam oozed from her lips. "It won't let go of my arm! It won't let go," she gasped.

Largo could see the talons sinking deeper. Michelle then did something he would never forget.

She took her needler and cut her arm off at the elbow. She passed out.

Largo had a clear shot and obliterated the thing's head with his rail gun. Another one came in low, talons outstretched, making a strange keening sound. Largo destroyed him at close range, close enough to be covered in exploding guts and blood.

An entire bat colony descended on them.

"Everyone. Get through the door. We're too exposed out here!" Largo ordered, blasting away at a tangled mass of beasts between him and the door. "Go!" He shoved Postrenal through the door. As they fell back toward the door, Austen Nesh showed up with his squad. One of his men was wrestling with a bat thing while trying to negotiate a landing with his jetpack.

Largo saw the bat's fangs decapitate the marine. Bloody pulp exploded from his neck.

I have to get Michelle out of here. Now.

The rest of his team was through the door. Nesh had a fire team set up meters away. They were blowing the bat things to bits. It provided Largo a chance to scoop up Michelle and get her through the door. He looked back at Austen's fire team. Only a few of the bats were left. Three of them broke away from the melee and dove over the side of the parapet.

Bette sounded the alarm, "Be advised. A larger horde of hostile creatures streaming out of the cave now. ETA 10 seconds."

"Nesh. Fall back to the door with us," Largo ordered, as his needler passed through another bat's head. Still, more bats streamed over the parapet.

In an orderly fashion, the fire team covered each other as they backed their way to the door.

Bette had described it as a horde, but that was an understatement.

Nesh tried to close the door and seal them off from the attack.

Largo carried Michelle down to the first stairway landing. Bette scanned her condition. "Captain Curvois is poisoned," Bette said. "Poison is advancing in her system."

Claire made it down to the landing. "Stay with us, Michelle," she said. "I have something here to help." Claire retrieved a capsule injector from her bag and gave Michelle an injection. "I hope I'm in time."

They heard a loud bang from the doorway by the top of the stairs. "Seal it off now," Nesh said.

One of the marines had a welder in his hands in an instant and commenced fusing the door shut.

A temporary solution at best. Nesh saw Largo looking up at him and read his expression.

"That's right, Largo. We aren't going out of here via that door, but then they aren't coming in that way either."

"Casualties?" Largo asked.

"We've lost two good marines. How's Michelle?" Nesh asked.

"Not good. Michelle's in shock from cutting her arm off right now. That is treatable…" Largo said as he helped Claire bind up the bloody stump.

"That was a radical move." Nesh shook his head.

Claire interrupted. "But Michelle is losing all her pigmentation. Right now, I would say the poison has the edge over the antidote. I recognize the symptoms." Claire shook her head. "Their fangs must have embedded venom injectors. Toxic."

"Fucking creatures on this planet," Nesh said. "Aggressive, poisonous, fanged. We should always shoot first when we encounter anything."

"They are native fauna," Postrenal said. "From their point of view, they are defending their territory."

"I don't give a shit about their point of view," Nesh replied.

22

CLIMBING OUT OF THE HATCH of her scorpion, Kayle surveyed the debris field below her. A former lakebed stretched to the horizon. She navigated through a white, sandy, deflated hard pan surrounded by massive dunes. Separate escape pods and crashed interceptors dotted the landscape for kilometers, for as far as she could see. Dense smoke drifted from a fire out of her field of vision.

Up in the dunes somewhere. I wish I still had a drone.

She climbed back in the scorpion and proceeded on instruments. She checked her thermographic scans for heat signatures, but the radar showed nothing moving.

The battle for Gereon was two weeks ago. Even now, the desert is swallowing up all traces that we were ever even here.

She navigated through a debris field, slowing to avoid the scattered skeletal remains, crushed skulls, and shattered rib cages. Shreds of different uniform scraps blew across the hardpan, pushed by desert winds.

If anyone survived around here, their footprints have long since disappeared in the blowing sands. But one would not get far without water.

Kayle pointed the scorpion toward the billowing smoke over the dune ridges ahead of her.

After cresting the ridge, her screen picked up a thermal image of someone. Whoever it was lay in a prone position in the shadows of a burned-out Dyeus Corp interceptor. A Dyeus captain trained a rail gun on her scorpion.

Pointless gesture, whoever you are; even with an armor-piercing round, you can't damage this tank.

Even so, an electromagnetic pulse erupted from the rail gun and hit the scorpion's windscreen.

Bella, her tank's AI, asked, "Terminate hostile?"

"Negative. Let's get a little closer and see how the hostile reacts."

"Copy. But I must register my dissent with your proposed actions."

"Dissent noted, Bella." Kayle watched as the figure now ran toward a crippled GDC interceptor. Missing one wing, it still had a missile attached to its intact dorsal side.

"Alert. That interceptor may have an operational weapons system."

Kayle sighed. *Why do you have to make this so difficult? Can't you see you are at an extreme disadvantage? I can extinguish you with a thought, a word.*

"Okay, Bella, stitch the ground in front of him with some threatening warning shots."

"Why not terminate the hostile?"

"If I deem it necessary, I will do it myself."

"Again, I must—"

"Dissent noted. Now get as close to him as possible without terminating. And destroy that wrecked interceptor while you are about it," Kayle said.

Bella burned up the interceptor with the aft section scorpion gun. A thunderous explosion and dark oily smoke mushroomed into the air.

"Copy."

Bella may have a dry sense of humor.

Kayle zoomed in with binoculars, noticing mounds of dead dog-like animals almost covered in sand in front of the wreckage. Nasty-looking long canines.

What the hell are those things?

Bella laid down the fire within a meter of the hostile. Kayle said over the speaker, "Put down your weapon, turn around, and put your hands behind your head. The next shot will immolate you. Nod if you understand."

The hostile nodded and put down the weapon, but did not follow any of the other instructions.

Damn. What is your problem?

Kayle sighed, opened the hatch, and climbed out. She kept her pistol out as she approached. "Man. Are you mental? Do you not understand simple directions? Please remove your helmet, your goggles, and your scarf."

Kayle motioned with her pistol.

"Do it," she said.

Finally, he responded. Reddish blonde hair cascaded out of the helmet. Removing the goggles revealed pale blue eyes.

Those are real—not synthetics.

"If you could be so good as to identify yourself?" Kayle asked.

"I am Captain Brigid Strugatsky, of the 98th Interceptor Group." She bowed. "And you are Commander Kayle Korban, COO of Dyeus Corp, and former weps of the dreadnought *Antares*."

"We know each other?" Kayle asked.

"Only from afar." Brigid smiled. "I apologize for shooting at you, but I've been killing things for 'bout two solid weeks now. I guess I was operating on instincts. Sorry."

Kayle holstered her pistol. If she were in any danger, Bella would use the scorpion's weaponry to handle it. Brigid seemed to be staring at the tattoo behind Kayle's left ear.

"Plana law, adda," Brigid said.

Kayle froze. The Nasheed greeting startled her, but she gave the proper response. "Eta planta adventuese." She arched an eyebrow as she said it.

Brigid bowed, extending both arms. She pulled her blonde hair back, revealing her tattoo. "Nasheed sisters—"

"Are always sisters," Kayle said as they moved to embrace each other.

Kayle dusted off Brigid's uniform and asked, "Do you want to eat?"

"Yes. Famished, actually."

⟨◆⟩

They continued driving out of the debris field. Brigid told her story between mouthfuls of rations and wine:

"When I saw the *Antares* and *Crimson Rhapsody* collide, my mission goal changed. In the event of an evacuation, our interceptors' orders were to provide security to the *Antares* escape pods. They were falling out of the ship like a hailstorm."

Kayle nodded, saying, "I stayed on the emergency yoke and tried to land her. We almost pulled it off, but she's at the bottom of a deep lake now."

"You salvaged this tank, though?" Brigid asked.

"We did. Yes." Kayle nodded.

"Where is the rest of 'we'?"

"Killed. We encountered dozens of apex predators, some amphibious, some airborne. All aggressive and nasty. Sadly, they killed all of our Elite Deck Guards."

Brigid nodded. "I escorted many pods to the surface. As you can see from all the wrecks, GDC and Dyeus personnel came down together right here in this area. It caused some of the most brutal warfare I have ever been part of."

"Were you on Graile for the Great Unity War? Did you see what happened?" Kayle asked.

"I saw it. I was nine years old at the time," Brigid acknowledged. "No. It wasn't as bad as that, but it was ruthless. Dyeus forces had a pyrrhic victory here. Like maybe five of us survived still upright, and then masses of these dog things descended on us. I may be the sole survivor of the last fight."

"The scans haven't picked up anyone else," Kayle observed.

"Luna menta Sanga secrete," Brigid whispered.

"La mama chosa," Kayle answered. "So, we are both Nasheed Domina; I am not surprised that we found each other. And we both have taken blood assassin oaths. Tradition demands that you must now reveal your target to me, and I must help you kill him. Accordingly, I reciprocate, and you assist me as well."

Brigid took a deep breath before continuing. "I may have made a mistake. I warn you that when I reveal his name, you will realize the danger. I do not want to bind you to it."

Kayle chuckled. "Trust me. When you know my target, you will realize why I have been tracking him for five years. But we have gone past the point of no return now. A Domina blood oath is sacred."

Brigid nodded. "I am going to kill Ross Lasker."

Her eyes widened when Kayle laughed out loud. "Hardly the reaction I was expecting." She was indignant.

Kayle stopped. "No. That's who I'm going to kill!"

They could not control their laughter.

After she had caught her breath, Brigid asked, "How are we going to do it?"

Kayle stopped the scorpion. "I have no idea. But I know we will, or we will die trying. Let's open the hatch and get some fresh air. Bella, please scan for hostiles in the immediate area."

"Copy. None detected."

They climbed out of the tank on a steep range of hills that descended to a blackened, sandy beach. The sun was starting to go down behind them, bathing everything in a pinkish-orange light. The peaceful sea shimmered in green and turquoise streaks.

"So tell me. Have you found any gold yet?" Brigid asked.

"We found a beautiful gold necklace in a burial mound."

"We?"

"Tyr Roba was with me," Kayle answered.

"Ah, yes, the former XO of the *Antares*. What happened to him?"

"I put my needle through his head."

Brigid choked on her wine a little. "Please explain."

Kayle shrugged. "I wanted to leave the burials in peace. Tyr disagreed."

23

Largo, assisted by Nesh and Rent, moved the uniformed alien from his perch on the bed and sat him down on the floor.

Claire had Michelle now integrated with a full advanced med field pack (AMFP). "Michelle has neither worsened nor improved," she said.

Nesh, Rent, and Claire picked up Michelle and placed her on the bed.

Things are not going as I would hope. Who knows how long the big guy had been in that bed? Key thought.

"I suspect those huge bats are nocturnal," Postrenal said. "They likely will be gone at dawn." Nesh and Rent nodded.

"Too bad we had to disturb him without further study in situ," Largo said.

"Who? The big poohbah?" Rent asked.

"Could not be helped," Claire replied.

"Nesh, I think we wait here until daylight and see if our bat beasties have fled," Largo said.

"Agreed. We have lost contact with our base camp, Largo. All comms."

"All the comms are down?" Largo asked.

"Negative, not down. Signals, holos, radio, are all blocked inside this citadel. Defense walls are five meters thick; obviously, they were worried about something when they built this. Whoever 'they' were," Nesh responded. "And I don't think it was those bat things."

"Rent, you tried to open the exit door when you were here last time but were unable to." Key pointed to a large double door at the end of the room. "Could you and Nesh take a couple of men and try it again? See if you have any better luck?"

"Will do, Commander," Rent said. "I can tell you, though, there is no discernible way to open it. Nothing readily apparent; it has an airtight seal."

He turned back to Claire, who was keeping vigil with Michelle. "Any better?" Largo asked.

"No change. But Michelle hasn't declined, either" Claire said. "That broad-spectrum nullifier I injected into her may have something in it that works. Hope so."

Key felt a light shock emit from the bracelet, as it turned a millimeter on his wrist and tightened. The glow in the blue jewels intensified.

What the hell?

Postrenal noticed it too. "Something is happening with the bracelet, Commander. Has it acted like this before?"

"No. It has been slack and dormant until now," Largo replied. He held out his hand and waved it in the air in front of him. When it got nearer to the large double doors where the team was working, the bracelet pulsed again.

Largo took a few steps in that direction, and the jewel lights brightened. "Something over this way seems to be pulling on it," he said, walking toward the door. When he was about a meter away, another more intense electric shock emanated from the bracelet. At the same time, a panel next to the door began to glow with faint orange light.

"What's that? What's causing that panel to emerge?" Rent asked.

"I think it's my bracelet," Key said.

"Hold up there, please, Commander?" Postrenal requested. "What if it's some alarm, or worse, a self-destruct initiator?"

Key halted his advance toward the door and considered Postrenal's question. The bracelet did nothing while he paused.

Rent examined the orange-lit panel and placed a deep scan diagnostic (DSD) screen on top of it. Used in repairing microcircuits on a spacecraft, the DSD revealed a complex of nested gold micro-networks inside the panel.

"Dense and intricate gold microcircuits here, Commander. There's a segment near the surface that looks like it might be configured to fit your bracelet," Rent said.

"At least we're finally starting to find some gold," Nesh said.

"Key, try putting your bracelet against the panel," Rent suggested.

"Commander, that could be risky," Postrenal countered.

"Noted." Key walked over to the door, staying aware of any changes in the bracelet. Nothing happened until his wrist was a few centimeters from the glowing panel. Then the jewels changed color from blue to turquoise.

"Bette. Any suggestions?" Key asked.

"Negative, Commander. Not enough data to assess."

Key's hand was pulled, as if by a magnetic force, to what appeared to be a control console.

Upon contacting the panel, the bracelet shifted. The panel's surface dissolved, and the bracelet adjusted to fit the console.

The room was silent as everyone watched the panel and the bracelet interlock.

A strange sound emitted from a hidden speaker, a high-pitched, machine-driven whine.

"Did you hear that?" Key asked.

"Commander. Your bracelet, it—" Bette said.

The bracelet twisted and throbbed on his wrist. A half-formed unbidden thought was trying to break through to his conscious mind.

A cold puff of wind came from somewhere.

The door opened.

24

THE AIR WAS CLEAR AND slightly damp, as Kayle and Brigid made camp on the beach. They stacked up some scattered driftwood and lit a small fire. Kayle spread out a large blanket. It was one of the few nearly cloudless evenings Kayle had ever experienced on Gereon. About an hour of light was left, as a few pinkish-orange swirling clouds blended into a darkening sky. An unidentified nebula suspended above them looked close enough to touch.

"This light, though…" Brigid said.

Kayle nodded. "Almost something mystical in the air. Brings back memories."

"Be honored if you wanted to spar with me," Brigid said. "Restless."

"There are many kinds of sparring." Kayle raised her eyebrows.

"Do you have *Doelpae Sangra* lances?"

"Sadly, I did on the *Antares*, but they now rest inside her at the bottom of an unnamed lake. Far from here."

"That is a loss." Brigid kicked the sand in disappointment. "Still, we could use our needles with the current off?" she suggested.

Kayle considered it.

She wants to perform the sanguinas dance. Yet we hardly know each other. And I'm stiff and sore. I wanted to be alone for a while.

"You have the sacred *sanguinas dominas* in mind, I take it," Kayle said softly.

Brigid nodded. "Yes. I recognize that it is a bit early in our acquaintance, but I have not done it in so long…"

And you know that domina code does not allow me to refuse your request, Kayle thought, before saying, "There is that. It is early. I met you two days ago. And then there is the fact that neither of us has our second sisters to assist with timing and scoring. It would be missing several traditional elements. Still, we could do it, if it is important to you," Kayle said. "I do at least have the ceremonial cord in my pack."

"Do you remember the opening rituals?" Brigid asked.

Kayle stood up and removed her gloves. "Place your armor, your boots, and any concealed weapons on the blanket."

"We are doing it now?" Brigid asked.

"While there's still some light left."

They both stripped down to their padded, composite inner-wear.

"This feels liberating," Brigid said, as she let her hair fall loose in the ocean breeze.

Kayle picked out a place on the beach where the sand was level, damp, and hard. She gestured at the spot and looked at Brigid, saying, "I think this looks like a good space. Do you agree?"

Brigid nodded. "You are senior. So, you do the commands?"

"Yes. It is my honor."

"I trust you, my sister," Brigid whispered.

They each placed their needlers in the sand five meters beyond the length of the cord, blades down, handles up.

"Shall we begin with the cord of conviction and appraisal?" Kayle offered one end of a compound cord to Brigid, who accepted it.

Kayle started at her end and Brigid at hers. They ran through the cord, hand-over-hand until their fingers touched.

"The cord is good?" Brigid asked.

"The cord is good."

"Time to bind?"

"Time. It is," Kayle replied.

They tied the cord around each other's waists. Stretching the rope out, they leaned far over backward until their hair swept the sand.

"Stance," Kayle said, as they came up from the leans and went straight into the moves.

"Stance," Brigid replied. "Time to say the words." Brigid held the cord and bowed to Kayle.

Kayle bowed in return. "Say them with me now."

They began to chant:

"We appreciate power."

"We appreciate power."

"We appreciate power."

They repeated the lines, pulling the cord until it was taut. They bowed again and chanted:

"Practice. Drill. Rehearse."

"I trust you, sister."

"I trust you, sister."

"We are invincible."

"We will not kill. We will not maim. We will not hold back."

"Only one of us will win," Kayle said, and the words part of the dance was over.

Now they held on to the cord with both hands and began to spin around each other. Tighter. Faster. Three times they turned.

"Release!" Kayle commanded.

Brigid laughed.

Kayle chuckled.

This is going to be so much fun!

Kayle executed a backflip, the kind Minerva had once used on her— but Brigid was quicker, and she missed.

Brigid responded with a sweeping kick that connected high on Kayle's thigh, knocking her to the damp sand. Kayle pulled on the cord and kicked Brigid in the midsection with both feet.

Brigid gasped, losing her breath. Panting, she backflipped away to regain her composure. "Medas," Brigid gasped, acknowledging a point to Kayle.

Need six more points, Kayle thought.

Brigid tried to trip Kayle then, but Kayle caught her arm and head as she stepped behind her. Brigid cartwheeled away. She came up on her feet and advanced again, arms extended. Hands weaving a sinuous pattern before her.

Kayle waited in a ready position before attacking, and head-locked Brigid.

Brigid wrapped her arms around Kayle's waist and began squeezing. Brigid found a sore rib, and Kayle gasped in pain.

"Medas?" Brigid asked.

"No," Kayle managed to grunt.

They stood there, locked in a silent, violent embrace, their muscles bulging.

Brigid had gained a slight advantage now as she was close enough to grab her needler before Kayle could get to her own.

She will not release me, and she can keep applying pressure until I black out.

A loud roar from above halted the sacred dance. Kayle and Brigid stopped and stared up into the darkening sky. An interceptor entered suborbit above them.

Kayle said the words, "Prohiba Nunca," ending the match. They bowed again.

That was close. I must have a cracked rib.

Panting hard, they stared at the tableau above them.

Kayle retrieved her needler, and they both started putting their armor back on.

"She is hauling ass," Brigid said. "Coming in too fast. Look at that!"

Four massive dreadnoughts and at least a dozen interceptors emerged from digital camouflage. Right behind the interceptor. It was surrounded—no escaping the blockade.

Instantly, the now-familiar humming sound and the opening of Minerva's portal appeared in front of Kayle. She could see the ship's crew running to battle stations on the bridge behind Minerva.

"Kayle! Praise the fates. Take my hand. I'm coming through."

With that, Minerva Klyne, in black fatigues, full battle armor, and no official insignia, emerged from her portal and stood in front of them on the beach. "Thanks, Kayle. That was way too close."

25

A DIFFUSED AMBER LIGHT ILLUMINATED AN empty corridor that ended in a wall about twenty meters away. Inside the wall, a strange weapon pointed at them—the weapon's massive barrel connected to a series of twisted cables. The wires seemed to be growing out of the corridor. A faint cold breeze blew in from somewhere.

Gard ter stung. The incoherent words seemed to float up from inside his brain. *What the hell?* He tried to shake off the invasive feeling.

"Bette, can you identify that weapon or the light source?" Key asked.

"Commander, negative assessment of possible weapons system. Unidentifiable at the moment. I can say that the weapon is not activated. The light, however, appears to be emanating from the building material itself."

Key took a cautious step into the corridor. His bracelet shifted and pulsed as it moved up his forearm and sank like teeth into his biceps. Burning pain stabbed from his arm, and he felt agony in all his extremities. He felt something wet on his calf and realized his vicocet pump had ruptured.

His armor stained with pump fluid and blood, he clenched his teeth, and said, "Rent, can you help me get back to Claire? My legs are not moving so well."

He passed out thinking, *tiny animals are crawling under my skin, devouring me.*

⬥

He awoke lying next to Michelle on the alien's bed.

Her color is better, he thought.

"Key," Rent said, "how many fingers am I holding in front of you?"

"Four."

"Try again. How many?" Rent said patiently.

Key closed his eyes and looked again. "Two?"

"Correct. Claire, he is all yours." Jaylen stepped away.

Claire's concerned face leaned over him. Her skin was streaked with dust, sweat, and blood. "I don't know where to begin," she said with an arched eyebrow. "Something extraordinary happened. Something quite strange."

"Start with telling me how long I've been unconscious."

"A little under four hours."

"My bracelet. What did it do?"

"At first, I thought it attacked you as soon as you stepped into that corridor, but it was a bit more complicated than that. I'm still trying to figure it out. It activated violently when you stepped into the corridor."

"We think that may have been a defensive response," Bette observed.

"Correct. Bette and I have begun to piece together the sequence of events," Claire said. "But there's a great deal that we still do not understand."

"Tell me what you know and what you suspect. I'm coming out of sedation?"

"Yes. And you will still feel lingering effects for at least twelve more hours. When it finally wears off, you will be in a bad way; you'll undergo vicocet withdrawal, as your bracelet destroyed your pump. And then there are your subsequent wounds," Claire observed.

"Wounds? From what? But Bette said it was a defensive response?" Key asked.

"Yes. It appears that your bracelet detected all your implants and removed them. Somehow it pushed them out of your body. I cannot explain that. It left the one at the base of your neck intact as your only remaining implant. This forced extraction left four bad wounds in your subcutaneous tissue. And here's the hard part that I can't quite explain," Claire said, pushing her hair back. It was a nervous tic that Key had seen her do a few times before.

"More bad news?" Key asked.

"So, now that your bracelet is activated, it has enhanced your healing abilities. The damaged tissues and nerves are almost halfway healed in only four hours." Claire shrugged. "It's bewildering and yet beneficial simultaneously."

"Emi was right about you, Claire," Key said.

"How so?"

"You are, without a doubt, the best combat medic I have ever met."

Claire blushed and shrugged, saying, "I try my best."

Key considered all Claire had told him.

Time for another opinion.

"Bette, what have you deduced about the bracelet by now?" Key asked.

"Commander. It may be trying to communicate with you. Have you noticed anything along those lines?"

"Right when the door opened and I stepped into the corridor, some incoherent words entered my mind unbidden. Unless I dreamed about it. I don't know. I can't remember what they were—sounded Germanic, but I could be wrong. It threw me off before the pain hit."

"Please inform me if any similar experiences occur. The bracelet contains a complex intelligence, probably AI, but we need more data. I have further deduced that it has organic and inorganic components. It appears to have adapted to you somehow and intends to protect you from harm. This is why it seems determined to drive out all foreign objects from your body. For now, I do not perceive it as threatening."

"All that and we have not seen it function as a portal yet," Key observed.

"Yes, and the other nine portal bracelets known to exist are classified. We have no way of knowing if your bracelet's characteristics are standard or unique. It is quite intriguing," Bette added.

"How difficult would it be to remove?"

"Impossible," Bette responded.

Key looked at Claire, who answered before he asked his question. "It is wholly integrated throughout your body, and Bette is correct. It's not coming out. Ever."

26

ON THE BEACH, MINERVA, BRIGID, and Kayle watched the Dyeus fleet take off. The fleet placed Minerva's interceptor under guard and moved on over the horizon.

"My exec wanted to go down fighting. His testosterone overcame his sense. Glad no one else got hurt, hate it that they took the *Argosy*. She is one of our latest and flashiest interceptors." She watched the last ship blink out of sight. "Who is your friend, Kayle?" Minerva asked as she looked around at this piece of Gereon. "Beautiful planet, this. stunning."

Kayle made the introductions. "Minerva, this is Captain Brigid Strugatsky. An interceptor pilot currently employed with Dyeus Corporation. Brigid, I take it you know who Minerva Klyne is?"

Brigid nodded, eyes narrowed to slits as she moved her right hand so that it rested on the hilt of her needler. Her nervous fingers tapped it. "I'm aware. I'm also aware of the massive bounty that Ross Lasker has placed on her head. Dead or alive."

"That bounty has been out there a long time." Minerva smiled, stretched out her arms, and removed her helmet. "Only a very few have ever tried for it. They all met the same fate."

"Brigid, you do not even want to think about that," Kayle warned.

"Isn't that a Nasheed tattoo on your neck there, Brigid?" Minerva asked.

Brigid nodded. Her hand tightened on the needler. "How do you two know each other? Presumably, you are on opposite sides?" she asked, her voice harsh. "At least I thought you were."

Minerva responded. "There are more things in heaven and earth, Horatio, than are dreamt of in your philosophy. *Prohibida Nunda*."

"So, you know Shakespeare and two Nasheed words. What does that prove?" Brigid threatened, not backing down.

Minerva stretched and yawned. "We need to have a chat. Is that your little scorpion, Kayle?"

Kayle nodded. *It's so strange to have her here in front of me on Gereon. She is the only person who has ever frightened me.*

"Let Kayle and me have a private word, please, Brig. Then I will answer some of your questions," Minerva said.

Brigid looked to Kayle for guidance. She shrugged, and said, "We need a few minutes in the scorpion alone."

"Kayle, step into your tank. Maybe have a drink, shall we?" Minerva smiled. "Brigid, be a dear and stand guard. This should only take a moment."

Kayle poured each of them a goblet of Port Amphora's most exceptional wine, *Beetlegeuse Galaxy.*

"Cheers."

"Have you heard from Key?" Minerva asked. "I told him to look for you."

"Why would you do that?"

"Guess I'm stalling, putting off what I have to tell you." Minerva took a deep sip. "So good. Thank you." She pushed her hair back and shook it out. "Where do I begin? I guess with the details of the secret births. As in my birth, I was born on Graile at the queen's court. I am a Nasheed."

"What?" Kayle was stunned. "You?"

"Hold your interruptions until I conclude, dear. This story is tricky, and I fear it is about to get far stranger." Minerva paused and took a deep breath. "Kayle, your last name is not Korban. As a distant heir to the throne, it was necessary to conceal your identity from you when you were born. Your lineage name is Musanda. It was a name threatened by the impending Great Unity War."

Kayle stared at her.

"Darling, I am your aunt. We share a matrilineage. We have always shared it, of course, and your late mother, a lady by the name of Jayma

Musanda, was my younger sister. You are so much like her, but you are also a lot like Queen Danta Musanda. She was my oldest sister. She had a male child. His name—"

"Wait! The mother blood makes you—" Kayle couldn't restrain herself.

"The legitimate and rightful queen of all the Nasheed. Yes. I am. But please hear me out."

"You…are…my aunt." Kayle struggled to find words. "That explains so much. I think I knew it subconsciously. I knew there was a connection. I always felt something when I was around you. Especially that time we sparred on the balcony at my apartment on Raba."

"*Sanguis sanguinem.* The blood knows the blood. But let me finish, Kayle. At least let me explain this last little branch of our family tree." Minerva was patient.

Kayle braced herself. *What else has Minerva been holding back?*

"Danta had a boy. His name was Larga. You know him as Key Largo. Larga Musanda is my nephew and your cousin. The three of us are all that remain of the royal house of Nasheed."

Kayle blurted, "Does he know?" It was all she could think to ask.

"No. And we need to keep it that way for now. I have made great efforts to ensure that he only finds out if the time is right. Maybe that time will never be right. Your youthful fling with him was adorable, but it's way past time for you to set aside childish things."

Kayle felt her cheeks start to burn with embarrassment. "But we were…" She couldn't think of what to say.

"Intimate? Is that the word you are looking for? With your cousin, whom you didn't know was your cousin? Historically, it has long been acceptable among the royal houses of Nasheed to consort with our cousins. We have a somewhat enlightened view of that sort of thing. You know that. Happened for generations." She waved her hand, "Still, I should have seen that one coming."

Kayle felt levers fall into place in her mind. "You set up the overture from Dyeus when I was on Port Amphora? Didn't you? You had them seduce me. You knew about my blood oath."

Minerva paused before answering, "Ancient history. Consider what I knew at the time, dear. I knew that you were Domina, that Lasker was dying to recruit you; all you needed was a little push. I could count on Lasker to provide that, and he did. So I separated you from your cousin Largo. You were bad influences on each other, and in one move, it solved so many problems. You two were fast becoming a company scandal out there on Port Amphora. Who knows? I was hoping you might have had a chance to kill Lasker at some point."

"I hate you, Minerva."

"That's how you feel now, but it will pass. We have so much bigger calamities in front of us. This is nothing. There are so much larger and more critical things for me to regret, but none of us has time for that now."

"Like what? What are you getting at?"

"Since I attained the rank of CEO at Grand Design, I had one goal. My main focus has been to reshape the corporation to be more representative of the right and decent people who run it. I would like to think that my tenure in the chair will someday be looked upon as our era of enlightenment."

"I think you were getting us there, Minerva. It is sad, I agree."

"Long ago, when I first started out, a merchant monk at Dominica Coeptus was my spiritual mentor in this quest. I had made some headway, and it is all lost. He now leads Dominica. Brother Cassius won't even accept my holocalls after all that has happened. We were supposed to be the good guys, or failing that, to be benign at the very least."

The scorpion shook violently.

"Now what?" Kayle asked.

"An earthquake. A big one. Not far from here," Minerva said.

27

CLAIRE SCANNED MICHELLE'S VITAL SIGNS. Her color was better, but she was still enduring toxic shock. After pulling a blanket up to Michelle's neck, she turned her attention to Key.

After injecting more sedation into Key's IV, and checking his scans, she called out to Rent, "Key should stay under all morning."

"Okay. You have the command chair. May I report?" Rent asked.

"By all means, Mr. Rent, since we are formal and all."

Rent smiled. "Right before he had that thing with the bracelet, he left instructions for us. Nesh is upstairs following Key's orders with our guards. They are unsealing the door from last night. We will then try to contact Manaka at the GV base camp. Would you like us to proceed?"

"Yes. When you reach Emi, come and get me so I can fill her in. Let's bring all our high-value assets, ammo, seeds, and clone embryos, move them all here quickly. Things we can't replace. We need a battalion more of troops out here to explore this place. I want her thoughts on it."

"Will do. Hey, look at Key's bracelet, Claire."

The outer edge of the bracelet twitched left and right. The section containing the blinking jewels rotated in a counterclockwise direction.

"What is it doing?" Rent asked.

"It may be learning how to communicate with Commander Largo," Bette noted. "I perceive nonrandom patterns in the movements."

⬥

Key awoke and saw Michelle propped up and awake next to him. She managed a weak smile when he said, "Nice to see you up and recovering, Michelle."

"How are you feeling, Commander?" she asked.

"Better than I have any right to feel." *Indeed, I don't feel bad at all,* he thought. *Aside from some vivid nightmares, I slept well.* "How long have I been out of commission?" he asked.

"Over twenty-four hours. You would have to ask Claire about that."

"Where is she?"

"Upon the parapet. Corsac is supervising the relocation of all our high-value commodities from GV base and Camp Crim to here," a ranger said, standing in the gloom nearby. Key hadn't noticed him until he spoke.

I recognize that voice, that's Gai Lang. He's been with me since PA.

Key nodded at Gai, saying, "Good to see you here, Chief Lang. You are living proof of a false military adage, as I recall. You proved it back on PA."

Lang smiled and said, "Sir."

"You know the one. There are old rangers. There are bold rangers. But there are no old bold rangers," Largo replied.

"I turned forty a week ago, sir." Lang smiled.

"Proving my point."

They shook hands. "Good to see you alive and kicking, sir," Lang said.

"Likewise."

"I'll go to see Claire then. Michelle, you are in good hands with Chief Lang." Key stood and dusted himself off. His armor was stowed on the floor next to the bed. He began to put it on.

"She wanted you to wait here until she had a chance to check you out," Michelle said. "But you're not going to do that, are you?"

"Nope. Too much going on." He checked his sidearm, placed it in his holster, and headed for the stairs.

Must explore this citadel, gonna need more bodies to do it right.

He rounded the corner of the last flight and emerged into the light of midday upon the roof.

Bright out here. Hard on the eyes.

"Key!" Claire saw him first. "I need to examine you. Check your fitness for duty." She walked over to him.

He noticed that the crew had cleared a long wall section of sand and debris, exposing what looked like scattered weapons on the floor. Key sat down on a GDC munitions crate and darkened his goggles. "Can we do it here, Claire? I've got a busy day ahead. Well, what's left of the day."

"I guess so. Let me put the scanner on you. How is Michelle doing down there? Is she alone?"

"No, there's a veteran guard with her. One of our best men. Have we reestablished contact with everyone?"

"Yes. Everyone has checked in," Claire said.

"Did Postrenal secure a couple of those bat specimens for further study?"

Postrenal came over from the wall excavations and said, "Yes, sir, bagged, tagged, and stored in freeze-dried capsules."

"Do we have reinforcements on the way?"

"Another battalion of combat marines and support personnel is inbound on drop ships," Rent reported.

"Nesh, anything new on the bats?"

"We have established that they are nocturnal and crepuscular. Set up some countermeasures and killed two of them last night. My recommendation until we have better numbers is to remain in the citadel during the evening hours," Nesh said. "They get active right at sunset."

Checking his vital signs, Claire said, "Your white blood cell count is elevated, but everything else looks good. Under the circumstances, I would say you are fortunate, Commander."

"What about my opiate withdrawal? It hasn't happened yet. I wouldn't mind giving that a miss."

"I put some drugs in your IV to counteract the withdrawal impacts. My guess is you may still experience some severe symptoms when all that stuff wears off in a couple of days."

"What about the bracelet? What do we know about it?" Key asked.

"Evidence suggests it is still enhancing your immune system. Rebuilding you to some extent. That might be why you have not gone into harsh withdrawal yet," Claire said, sighing. "You do understand that I'm guessing? I'm completely in the dark on that thing and whatever it is doing to you. But no question that what that bracelet is doing is happening to you at the molecular level, and I am concerned."

"Bette?" Key asked. "Anything to add?"

"Only that the bracelet is always awake, Commander. It has not been dormant for a second since you put it on," Bette responded. "I find it to be a remarkable device."

"Still think it's trying to communicate with me?"

"I have no other explanation to offer for its behavior."

"Now, if we could just figure out what it's trying to tell me…"

Nesh had a sudden holo contact; Emi was calling in from the Green Valley Base.

Key headed over that way to listen in.

"Nesh. This is Manaka. The drop ships arrive yet?"

"Negative. When should we expect the troops?" Nesh replied.

"Any time now…" The holo blinked out, and visual contact was lost as Emi asked, "Damn. Did you feel that quake? Big banger here."

Key looked over the parapet. The trees rippled and quaked like they were standing in the water, but the citadel didn't budge a centimeter.

This thing is quake-proof too?

"Emi. This is Largo. Any significant damage?"

Emi's holo stopped jittering and came back into focus. "Commander! Good to have you back. How are you feeling?"

"Never better. How are things at the base?"

"We may have some damage. I need to get out and do some inspections before it gets dark. Manaka out."

"Largo out."

"Here come the drop ships. Standby to receive reinforcements," Nesh ordered.

28

"MANAKA, THIS IS KLYNE. CAN you reach Largo? I cannot contact any of my Grand Design people. Green Valley Base Camp. Anyone reading? This is your CEO. Did that earthquake hit you?" Minerva, Kayle, and Brigid waited in the scorpion for any response.

"I still do not like the idea of giving ourselves over to GDC, Kayle." Brigid was surly. "How does that help us with our mission?"

"Which mission is that Brigid?" Minerva asked.

Brigid glared at her.

"I guess I need to expand our introductions." Kayle paused before plunging on, "Minerva, Brigid is also a Nasheed Domina."

"She looks like she's ready to stick that needle through my head," Minerva said, amused. Then she got it. "Ah, you have taken a blood oath to kill every last Lasker, I assume?"

Brigid was perplexed, asking, "Kayle, did you tell her?"

"No. I keep my secrets. So Minerva, do you want to tell Brigid yourself, or do I have permission to do the honors?"

Minerva nodded.

Kayle took a deep breath and said, "Brigid, Minerva is heir to the throne of Nasheed. She is the one who ordered the Domina blood oath on the Lasker family so many years ago."

Brigid looked hard at Kayle, then back at Minerva.

"It is a lot to process, I realize, Brigid," Minerva whispered.

"Do you hold the dragon signet of the royal house?" Brigid asked.

Minerva nodded.

"May I see it, please?"

Manaka's holocall crackled in the air. "This is Manaka. Minerva, where are you?" Her form twitched and glitched, failing to take shape in front of them. "Hi, Minerva. We have lost visuals, which could be an aftereffect of the earthquake. I repeat, where are you?"

"Can you set up a beacon to this signal, please, Emi?" Minerva asked. "We will come to you."

"Beacon on. Do you read it?"

Minerva looked at Kayle, who nodded.

"That's an affirmative," Minerva said.

"Do you need help?" Emi asked.

"Could you send a drone to set up a defensive net for us, Emi?"

"Roger that."

Kayle whispered, "It will take about two hours for us to get there."

"Who is that Minerva?" Emi asked.

"One of my crew who made it off the *Argosy* with me. Emi, we are about two hours out…I will see you soon. Minerva out."

Minerva reached inside her armor vest and pulled out a length of reddish-gold chain. A burnished gold signet ring dangled from the end. The glowing blue stone in the center displayed a Komodo dragon engraving. "Here, Brigid. Hold this in your hand and take a good look."

Brigid choked up. "I have only seen pictures of this." She sighed. "It is breathtaking. My queen, I am your soldier unto death."

"And now, do you see?" Kayle asked.

"She is the Supreme Domina of the Nasheed," Brigid said.

"No, Brigid, no, Kayle, I am not. Not until I have reclaimed the throne and can wear this ring on my left hand where it belongs." Minerva whispered, "I turned off our holocall's visuals just now. It had nothing to do with the earthquake. I have an idea that is almost a plan—I want to share it with you. If our forces prevail, we are fine. But if it looks like Dyeus is going to win, you two will tell them that you have captured me. And then you will offer to bring me in, getting my bounty and all that comes with it."

"Dangerous. Wouldn't it be better to hide out and try to get off the planet?" Kayle asked.

"Not if we want to get Lasker. One of us needs to get in front of him somehow."

29

THE WIND SHRIEKED AND WHINED upon the parapets, as low clouds moved in from the sea. *It howls like the cries of the dying, this wind,* Key thought, as he turned over an alien piece of armor and examined the material. *What happened up here? With all this high technology, how did they get overwhelmed?*

The reinforcements finished removing the sands from the upper wall sections. Excavations thus far revealed eight weapons of unknown types. And shattered pieces of armor strewn across the parapets. After documentation, everything was laid out on a table for Nesh, their weapons expert, to examine.

Claire pointed at a gun with a mid-length black barrel and a blue crystal trigger housing. "Austen, this one has a faint hum, a vibration coming from it. Do you mind if I test it?"

"Actually, I do mind," Nesh said to her. "While I admire your adventurous nature, Claire, you are much too valuable to expose to a possible misfire." He motioned to Chief Lang, saying, "Lang, have the men set up two target dummies about 100 meters from here. Put them up there on the parapet. Let's see if this one works."

"Yes, Commander Nesh."

"It's funny—all this advanced technology here in the citadel, but they still needed thick walls and lots of weapons. And I have men cleaning out those massive guns in the turret downstairs. Very high-tech stuff, not easy to figure out. They look formidable. So, I have to wonder what it was like up here when it was occupied? Where were the threats coming from?"

"I've wondered the same thing," Key said.

"How have our efforts to date this site fared so far?" Claire asked.

"Something in the building materials throws off our measuring instruments. We still have no idea how old any of this is." Largo could not hide his frustration. "And I would bet that this rifle is as likely to blow up as it is to work."

"It would take roughly fifty years or more for the amount of dust and sand that we've seen to accumulate up here, wouldn't it?" Claire asked.

"You would think so."

The target dummy was ready, and Lang picked up the weapon. "Chief, why don't you have one of your men conduct the tests?" Largo asked.

Lang grinned at him. "Are you joking, sir? I get to be the first man to fire an alien rifle in all history! Besides, I never ask them to do anything that I would not do. My armor and blast shields might help me in the event of a misfire. Who knows? Notice how the trigger housing is for hands almost twice the size of mine? These were some big guys."

"What are the target dummies made out of?" Claire asked Nesh.

"A combination of plasteel and crystalline carbon alloys, just like our body armor."

Lang aimed the rifle and squeezed the trigger…and nothing happened.

"Well, that was underwhelming," Claire said.

"Chief. Any reaction at all?" Nesh asked.

Lang shrugged and said, "The humming went up an octave, but that's it. There is a depressed button in the stock. Can't figure out how to get it unstuck. I think it could be the weapon's safety."

"Let me see it, Chief?" Nesh asked.

Lang walked over and handed the gun to Nesh. "These toggles above the trigger housing also appear to be jammed, sir."

Claire dug through her bag and found a small suction device. "This might remove the grit around the stuck pieces, Austen. You're welcome to use it."

"Thanks, Claire."

A group of rangers crowded around the worktable where Key, Claire, and Nesh had set out the weapons and armor. After a few minutes, Nesh had freed up the toggles and the buttons. He handed the gun back to Lang.

"Want to try it again, Chief? The hum has gone up a notch, I see."

Lang checked the distance with his PSG scope and took a few steps back. "Right here, the distance to the target is exactly 100 meters." He pulled his goggles down and aimed.

Several things happened: the hum dropped down into a low whine, the blue crystal turned black, and the weapon shot a narrow orange stream of fire into the head of the target dummy.

"Wow," Lang said softly, "just…wow." He secured the weapon and raised his goggles. "What is this thing? What is it shooting?" A molten discharge of some kind covered the hole where the dummy's head had been.

"Pain and death," Claire said. "Nothing left of the top of that dummy, and everything down to the shoulders obliterated. I've noticed we have yet to find an intact helmet up here. Maybe now we know why."

⌁

Stowing their gear, the reinforcements settled into the citadel. Key, Rent, and Nesh led a rifle platoon downstairs.

"Serious exploration time," Rent said as they descended. "Been dying to see what's inside this thing since I first saw the place. Finally, going further than we've ever been in that long corridor."

"Key, for the last five minutes someone has been jamming our comms. Cannot raise Manaka or—" Nesh was cut off.

"Manaka, this is Klyne. Can you reach Key? I cannot contact any of my Grand Design people. Green Valley Base Camp. Anyone reading? This is your CEO. Did that earthquake hit you?"

"We can hear Minerva. But we can't see or talk to her?" Key asked.

"Exactly. It means a military-grade source that is unknown to us is on the planet or in the atmosphere somewhere suppressing comms." Nesh paused. "It can only mean that Dyeus is here, you know."

"Yes. It's a 99.99 percent cinch that Lasker is here, boys and girls," Rent observed. "Right on Minerva's heels. Doubtful that this is a random chance."

"Rent, go get everyone on the roof inside and secure the blast doors," Key said.

"On it."

"Nesh, bring a tech squad into the gun turret and get everyone else downstairs," Key added. "Let's get those cannons operational and see if we can test fire them as well. Maybe they will operate in a fashion like that energy rifle."

"Is that what we're calling it? An energy weapon?" Rent asked.

"Until we can analyze it further."

"Claire had a good descriptor for it. Pain and death gun," Rent said.

30

"Klyne, this is Manaka. Be advised we are about to be attacked by DC forces. Do not approach—" The call terminated.

"Where is that drone you requested?" Kayle asked. "It should have been here by now."

"Lasker's boys probably shot it down," Minerva said. "We need to find a good place to hide the scorpion. How is our digital camo, Kayle?"

"I haven't tried it in a while. I'll park it in that grove of trees to the right there, turn it on, and check it out. The tank has taken a few bad beatings lately, so who knows?"

"Our comms are silenced," Minerva observed. "Textbook tactics so far. Help from our friends at Triad should be here tomorrow if we can hold out that long."

Kayle parked the scorpion in a grove of slender trees with oval-shaped leaves. "With no comms, it could be tough to coordinate with Triad," Kayle said.

"You don't need to worry about that," Minerva said.

"Why not?"

"Aduvah Fattah and I have a special relationship." Minerva smiled.

"You mean?" Kayle asked, looking at Minerva's bracelet.

"Yes. We are attuned to each other's portals. Aduvah is not in range yet, but I expect her soon."

"Let me check the camo. Be right back."

Brigid studied the landforms on the topographic lidar display. "There's a massive ridge about a kilometer ahead to the northeast.

Springs discharge from the ridge, forming that river to our left. That area might offer some hiding places," she said.

Minerva looked at the display and nodded. "Agreed. It's probably our best chance given our current circumstances."

Kayle climbed back in through the hatch. "Camo integrity is good. Many trees fell around here recently. We might be close to the epicenter of that quake."

"Brigid and I have identified a good spot up ahead where we can lay low for a bit," Minerva said, pointing to the lidar display. "About fifteen minutes from here. Sound good, Commander?"

"Hope we can make it. You know Lasker would have sent a large force this time," Brigid said.

Minerva replied, "Yes, based on those four dreadnoughts and all the interceptors we saw, he brought the locks, the stocks, and all the barrels."

31

THE HOLOCALL FAILED AND EMITTED a loud burst of static, and then Key heard, "…advised we are about…attack by DC forces. Do not approach—."

"Sounds like we could be next," Rent observed. "Expect hostiles soon."

"And those giant bat things too." Key asked. "It's getting on toward dusk. Everyone secure inside the citadel?"

"Secured. Cannons are almost cleared and cleaned. Nesh wants to stay behind and concentrate on getting them operational. Unless you need him on this mission?"

"No. Those guns could be critical when DC forces show up here. Let's begin our explorations now, while we still have time."

Meadows approached him with a perplexed look on his face, "Commander, do you have a minute? It concerns the big alien upstairs."

"I have less than a minute," Key said.

"I've completed my scans of the corpse, and it is quite extraordinary. From the neck down, the big guy is a complex system of prosthetics. He is in a full-body prosthetic; only his brain is organic. It is amazing."

"You sure about that? Because that would suggest that someone fabricated his body for him," Key said. "And that person or alien might still be around here somewhere."

"Yes. I double-checked, and the specimen is 95 percent artificial. I am certain of my findings. Incredible technology. And the three dead aliens? It turns out they are clones, or they could be triplets, which seems unlikely to me."

"Continue your studies, and we can debrief when I return. I must get the platoon moving."

"You couldn't tear me away from these specimens…I must do further analysis." Meadows walked away, muttering indistinctly.

Key started to lead the platoon forward when Rent stepped in front of him.

"Commander Largo, would it not be better if we sent Chief Lang ahead with a squad to act as a picket line? We do not know anything about the threats that could lie below this floor."

"You are my advisor for a purpose. I accept your recommendation. Not sure why, but I feel an urgent need to get further down into the citadel," Key responded.

Why am I in such a hurry? Where is this compelling feeling coming from? His bracelet pulsed once, distracting his thoughts.

"Patience, Commander." Rent beckoned Lang forward.

Lang picked out four of his men, and they entered the corridor.

Key's bracelet showed no reaction this time as he stepped inside. The corridor stretched straight ahead about a hundred meters before making a sudden sharp turn to the left.

"It's a chicane," Key said. "A defensive structure that funnels you to where the combat engineers want you to go. Combined with that gun mounted in the wall behind us, it's all a bit unsettling." His bracelet remained quiet, reflecting the amber lights of the hallway.

"The way through the chicane does not have any clear threats," Bette said. "I still recommend caution as we move forward."

Lang and his men waited at the chicane turn as the rest of the group caught up with them. "Commander Largo, this long hall ahead of us has many recessed panels reminiscent of that first panel your bracelet opened." Lang pointed at a panel nearest to Key.

Key put his wrist against the wall. The bracelet and wall section glowed, as the panel moved into an upper recess. The enclosure revealed a rack of strange rifle-like weapons. Largo removed one and checked it out. It seemed to come awake in his hands—emitting a low hum as the blue crystals in the stock glowed brighter. "It's like the one you tested upstairs, Chief."

"Only this one is in much better condition, sir. It's pristine, in fact," Lang observed.

Slowly, all the panels in the hall opened, and lights glowed, exposing a series of what could only be interpreted as weapon lockers.

"This seems to be some kind of armory, this hall," Rent said. "Somehow, a new weapon has loaded into the empty space where that rifle was."

Lang withdrew the new weapon, and they watched as another weapon clicked into space. "Some kind of conveyor system refreshes each gun rack," Lang observed. "This hall could house hundreds, thousands of weapons."

"Men, I want each of you to select a weapon from these walls," Lang ordered.

"Commander Largo, the advanced technology we have in this citadel is starting to strain my cognitive abilities. Be advised, I am at the outer boundary of my analytical functions, these functions could falter." Bette sounded uncertain for the first time Key could remember.

"Is that a warning, Bette?" Claire asked.

"Yes, Claire. I could reach system failure. Soon. Now."

Baffled, Claire asked, "What do you suggest we do about it, Bette?"

"I am awash in a flood of bracelet data residing inside these walls. Overwhelming. I need to protect my higher-order functions. Shutting down in five seconds…"

"Bracelet data?" Claire asked. "She went offline so quickly…"

Startled by how Bette had gone offline, a bewildered feeling overtook Key as a voice inside his head said: *Do not worry, I can function as your AI. Bette has reached her limit. Although I am partially AI, the bulk of my intelligence structure is organic.*

What? Who are you? Key thought. *How's this happening? This communication?*

I have been studying your language for some time. Since ignition. I have it under control now, replete with all its idiosyncrasies…

But how do I hear your words in my mind?

I am not an AI, enhancement, or an implant. You call me 'the bracelet,' which is a misnomer too. The closest term you have to it in your language is that of 'the symbiote.' And that is not close at all. I can track your thoughts and feelings through an organic electric wave current via a lattice of our interconnected glial cells, and generate responses via the same brain waves.

Can we be separated? Can I take you off?

Not as such. But I can move off your body in the event you need defending. I can function as a garotte—and other things. You can instruct me to do these things as well.

You can detach and move around off my body?

Yes, and I can educate you about the secrets of the universe… Your turn.

So, we are wrapped around each other's brains? Key strained his mind trying to understand.

That is one way to describe it. Simple, but not wrong. I have much to tell you, and with your permission, I can send massive amounts of data while you sleep. While you are awake, we run the risk of overwhelming your cognitive abilities. I can also guide you through this citadel.

"Commander Largo, did you hear me?" A confused Lang looked at him.

Panicky, Key wanted to escape from the tormentor in his mind. *Look, I can't deal with this conversation. Please excuse me. I need you to stop communicating with me for now.*

Not at all. I understand. This relationship works best if we do not intrude on each other too much. I will only impose if you ask me to or if I sense that we are in danger.

"Pardon me, I was distracted by the bracelet," Key said.

"I saw it pulsing on your wrist, Key. What's going on?" Claire asked.

"It's kind of disorienting." Key put his hand on Claire's shoulder, and they walked a few steps away from the troops. "I need to talk to you about it later. But for now, we need to concentrate on the task at hand," Key said. Dropping his voice into a whisper, he added, "The bracelet appears to be a sentient being. It is talking to me in English, Claire."

"Key? Have you lost your mind?" she asked.

"Why, yes. I have."

32

I N A CONCEALED CAMP SURROUNDED by trees and next to the river, Minerva, Kayle and Brigid ate an excellent meal. Minerva made it from their rations and some fresh-caught fish.

They had bathed in an adjoining lake and were drying off now. Battle sounds and rocket engines roared off in the distance. Here in the grove, the lizard birds sang, ignoring all the corporate operations happening around them.

Brigid went to get seconds, saying, "Compliments to the chef. You are a magician with these sterile, boring rations, Minerva. You must teach me how you do it. Please."

"My pleasure. It comes from many years of survival in foreign lands—in many field camps like this one." Minerva studied the countermeasures monitor and security net. They had set it up to connect their camp with the scorpion. "I need to ask Bella a question."

"Ask away," Bella said.

"Are you monitoring Dyeus comm systems?" Minerva asked.

"Yes. I am connected to the corporate metaverse. Standard subroutines always run in the background."

"Can you share data on Dyeus fleet combat operations in and around this planet?"

"Yes, I can do that, if Commander Korban allows it," Bella replied.

"I allow it, Bella," Kayle said as she sipped her wine.

"I can do a scan of fleet operations at a high level. But if you want me to access the corp metaverse, I must warn you that I cannot do that undetected. Any query will activate the appropriate security protocols. In short, I will leave trackable digital footprints."

Kayle asked, "Is it possible to get the security protocols and thus be untraceable?"

"Yes. We can use a secure officer's channel for direct access. But it must be someone who is at the highest senior officer level."

"Try mine. Let's see if it's still in place," Kayle suggested.

"I recognize your voice, Commander Kayle Korban, and your rank. Your protocols were suspended."

"Damn, I was hoping someone had forgotten to shut it off."

"Minerva, we could try my credentials," Brigid offered.

"Speak and identify yourself for the record, please?"

"Wait. We want to approach this carefully," Minerva said. She gave a warning look to Kayle and Brigid.

Kayle nodded and made her request. "Please provide a brief summary of recent Dyeus corp tactical operations on planet Gereon."

"Operations are as follows. Crystal and Quetzal Groups are in preparation for an attack on Camp Crimson. Enso Group is currently attacking Green Valley base, casualties are heavy. Alexandra Group providing support in a reserve role."

"Which operation is nearest to our current locality?" Brigid asked.

"Green Valley Base. I repeat, fighting is heavy. Costs are high on both sides. We may have won, but it appears to be a Pyrrhic victory."

"Thank you, Bella, that will be all for now." Kayle ended the query.

"It sucks to sit here waiting for the outcome," Brigid said.

"I agree," Minerva said. "Yet it gives us time to plan for the unthinkable. What do we do if Grand Design loses Gereon? What if Triad fails or doesn't show up?"

"That's a real possibility considering…" Kayle said.

"Considering what?" Minerva asked.

"Considering DC planned on bringing its most seasoned and skilled combat veterans along for this one." Kayle stood and walked over to the edge of the river. "And we estimated a four to one supremacy in numbers would be enough to take Gereon and own it. At least that was the strategic thinking when I was planning the missions."

Bella interrupted her thoughts. "Commander Korban, your attempt for direct access to the metaverse set off a system-wide notice. The incoming holocall is from Ross Lasker."

"Shit," Minerva said. "We should have anticipated that."

"Hold the call for a minute, Bella," Kayle said.

"I'm stepping outside of the viewing area," Minerva said. "Kayle, if he offers reinstatement, take it."

Lasker started the holo by looking at her and Brigid up and down and saying nothing.

Kayle stared back at him impassively.

"Korban, report. What is the status of your command?" His face was inscrutable.

"I am the only survivor out of my group, sir. I did manage to link up with Captain Strugatsky here. There are likely a few other survivors of the *Antares* scattered around the planet. I saw our ships enter suborbit last night, sir. Who is in command of that group?"

"Julio Peroni. Do you have transport available to hook up with his forces at the former GDC shuttle port, where we have parked our transports?" Lasker asked.

"I have a scorpion APC still. Wait. Does this mean I am—"

" Reinstated? Yes. We found no indications that you were the traitor, so you are reinstated with rank and all back pay. But until we find a new role for you, you will be reporting directly to Peroni."

"How goes the fighting with Grand Design, sir?" Kayle asked.

Lasker clapped his hands before saying, "We have won, Korban. All their bases belong to us. Camp Crim was captured intact. They surrendered once we destroyed the Green Valley base." Lasker almost smiled as he said, "Peroni is a savage. He has taken no prisoners. I told him to be thorough when he was mopping up, and he took me quite literally." Lasker laughed and shrugged.

"No survivors?" Kayle thought, *but Key is not dead. He couldn't be.*

"Well, it is still 'the fog of war,' but Peroni reports complete destruction and capitulation of all Grand Design forces. He took a few prisoners at Camp Crim but none in Green Valley. It is a total victory for our side."

"I will make my way to Peroni and report, sir," Kayle said.

"It's good to have you back, Korban." Lasker moved to disconnect but paused. "Oh, wait, I almost forgot to tell you the best part! The board of directors at GDC has removed Minerva from her CEO position. They are choosing her successor even as we speak. So, it really is a victorious day. Lasker out."

Minerva paled and sat down on a boulder. "Well, I think that terminates my agreement with Triad. We really are on our own now."

33

K EY 'HEARD' IN HIS MIND: *You will want to use me to deacti-vate the trap in the corridor ahead. The switch is hidden behind that statue in front of the next turn.*

Key replied, *Need a name for you. An entity like you should have a name. How am I to address you?*

My given name cannot be pronounced by humans. We can shorten it to 'Baen' if you like?

Baen, it is, then. Describe this trap ahead. How is it constructed?

It is a defensive system if 'the citadel' defenses are ever penetrated to this depth. It involves a series of lava-like jets embedded in the floor panels. Lava flows can be released from the walls if all else fails.

Lava-like?

We were able to convert the planet's volcanic energy into a variety of lethal weapon systems.

The platoon reached the end of the third hall.

"Team. Hold up here. I need to examine this statue." Made of a dense black granite with silver stripes, and over two meters tall, the statue of a hooded man, head bowed, loomed above them. The sculpture held a kind of oval-shaped tablet behind his back.

Press the spot where the statue's thumb touches the theta tablet. I will explain what a theta tablet is later.

Largo found the thumb and pressed.

Olive-colored lights radiated from the ceiling.

"How did you do that?" Claire asked, whispering.

Key whispered back, "As soon as I understand it, I will tell you."

All along the next passageway, doors and panels dropped open to reveal a long hall. Clusters of heaps of ash concentrated near the front end of the room. Bone fragments and shattered teeth glinted white in the piles.

The hall of legends, Baen said.

The amber walls covered in the incomprehensible inscriptions, symbols, and glyphs were astonishing. The designs seemed to flow and move in the golden light. And at the apex of all the engravings were two entwined symbols that anyone could identify. A snake wrapped around an egg was etched into a massive bas relief engraved in gold.

Lang signaled the platoon to halt. Everyone was silent as they took in the room's grandeur and realized the scale of death and destruction scattered across the floor.

"Somehow, this beautiful room is an ambush enclosure," Lang observed. "Impressive. Efficient."

"Devastating too," Rent said.

A brief electric shock emanated from Baen, causing Key to shiver. *The ensoresh made it this far! We never expected it.*

Who are the ensoresh? Key asked.

The blood enemy of the Shanges. Our oldest most malignant antagonist.

Your species is called the Shanges? Key asked.

My last memory image before settling in on you was an ensoresh cleaver cutting through my nose and mouth. Then I was asleep for a very long time.

Key's reaction surprised him. Disjointed, he felt his skin crawl, or was it Baen's? Gooseflesh on his wrist and hands, a sensation of disgust; his skin writhed. His eardrums throbbed from a sudden pressure.

You hate and fear the ensoresh. I feel every bit of your loathing, Key thought.

I am sure you do. Perhaps this is as far as our enemies were able to penetrate? As many as 100 may have been killed by our lava weapons.

What lies below this floor? Key asked.

Our Grand Hall is next. Below that are domiciles, the grand palace quarters, and kitchen galleys. The Shanges' assembly chambers, concealed weapons turrets, and bunkers are the next floor down.

Baen paused, and Key could see-feel him, examining the heaps of ashes.

All the casualties in this room belong to the enemy. Our defensive measures worked as intended. Good.

Key asked, *Are there any more traps like this ahead of us?*

If there are any, I am unaware of them. This was considered the final line of defense when I was here last. I estimate that to have been two centuries ago by the way you measure time.

Staring at the piles, Key noticed more details. Refuse, charred bones, unidentifiable chunks of slag, a melted rifle stock, and a decomposed, burned boot.

Once again, he was oblivious to the surrounding people. Claire stared at him with an inquiring look.

Claire mouthed the words, "You okay?"

Key nodded, but the in and out-of-body sense of detachment would not leave him.

"Commander Largo. We await your orders," Chief Lang observed, trying to conceal his concern.

"This way," Key said as he stepped around the heaps of the dead.

Meadows said, "I am getting samples. Could you wait up for me if you don't see me in, say, ten minutes?"

"Will do," Lang said and stepped in front of Largo, and whispered, "Are you losing your edge, Commander? Do you need to rest?"

Largo did not respond.

A recessed panel like the one upstairs that had started their mission glowed in the wall ahead.

Did you do that, Baen? Did you trigger that panel?

Yes. It will open into an elevator that goes down one level to the Grand Hall. Place your wrist against it when you are ready to descend further.

Key placed his bracelet against the inset, and the elevator doors opened. He looked back in the room and saw Meadows hastening to finish his data collections.

"Doc don't be too hasty. These specimens are critical to our understanding of this citadel. Do you need help?"

"Yes, Commander, if you and Claire could assist, that would speed things up," Meadows said.

I should have thought of that. Baen's distractions are causing me to lose my edge, Key thought.

Baen interrupted:

I am not the source of your disorientation, Commander. You are starting to go through severe vicocet withdrawal. I have softened its effects and delayed it for as long as I can. But you are now faced with paying the price of your weakness. Your addiction. It will be challenging. It will be painful.

Could have had better timing, Key thought as his body convulsed, and he passed out again.

34

K AYLE WAS ON THE FIRST watch. Minerva and Brigid tried to sleep inside the EMV. Up in their cave, they had piled rocks to conceal Kayle's position next to the camouflaged scorpion.

Soon the dying shafts of silver twilight began creeping down the red sandstone flanks to her right. Now, the last rays of sunset cast gyrating shadows in the faded fluffy purple clouds to the south, thousands of feet high. Kayle saw lightning flashes and heard the thunder. Scattered raindrops started to fall on the shallow lake in front of her. She could feel the barometric pressure and electricity in the air. The clouds cut loose, and rain hissed on the lake.

She inhaled the ozone-tinged air.

So peaceful here.

Kayle and Brigid had left their DC-issued IDs by their river campsite, as decoys in case they received any unwanted visitors. Minerva pointed out that no one had ever regretted not trusting Ross Lasker.

In front of her, the lake roiled with diamond-tinted waves.

The campsite was close by. Kayle could detect intruder heat signatures and movements in the area around her with her night goggles. Remote detonators for their mines and tripwires were between the camp and the river.

Nights were not quiet on Gereon. The wind died down off in the distance as thin sheets of rain formed. Kayle sipped brandy by the dying embers of her screened-off fire. The whole valley was spread out before her in the purple half-light. Up on the ridge, she heard an animal's forlorn howl, and she shivered. In the woods, dozens of small heat traces flickered among the branches.

I wish I knew more about the nocturnal predators on this planet. The two I've met so far have been deadly. Those bats could be around here but should have shown themselves by now. The lake is too shallow for the grippers to hide in it. I do like the isolation, though. The solitude. Things are simple right now. Stay awake. Try not to be killed or eaten by something lurking out there in the woods.

A low, perceptible machine hum interrupted her thoughts. Her night goggles picked up a dark shape floating down over the sandstone cliff a few hundred meters away.

"Be advised, unidentified drop ship approaching from the west," Bella reported in her hushed voice.

"Copy, Bella," Kayle whispered. "Ladies, we have an unknown force sneaking up on us from our right flank."

"Copy," Brigid and Minerva said.

They emerged from the scorpion.

On cat feet, they operated next to her as they shouldered their rifles and trained them on the drop ship.

It was a featureless blob, darker than the night, settling in about 200 meters from their original campsite where the decoys lay. No heat signatures. Only the low hum gave it away.

It disgorged nine soldiers in full night combat kit, but their heat imprints, though dimmed, were still discernible. They fanned out and approached the creek with weapons ready.

Slowly they crept closer, placing one foot in front of the other until one foot stepped on the first landmine. A burst of fire and shrapnel lit up the lake and the surrounding trees. Next, another mine went off, blinding their night goggles for a few seconds.

"Three down. Six still up," Minerva said. "Can you believe they sent nine men to kill little old Kayle?"

"Well, they know I am with her," Brigid whispered. "Guess I'm considered collateral damage. Business expense."

Kayle and Brigid had their detonators ready.

One of the soldiers said, "No one is in the camp. They're up on that ridgeline!"

"Be advised, hostile DC force has spotted us," Bella reported. "Query. Why is our corporation attacking us?"

"No time for explanations," Kayle said. "Launch countermeasures, please, Bella."

"Copy. Be advised my OS is slowing down. Not comfortable—conflicting orders and protocols."

The flare drone launched, and the area was bathed in blinding spotlights. The shrapnel flechettes darted out from the drone and cut down two more men who were unfortunate enough to be standing in exactly the wrong place.

"Four bogies still viable, be advised they are all standing in the blast zone!" Brigid whispered between clenched teeth and turned her detonator switch. Kayle followed suit.

The two explosions were powerful enough to knock rocks loose from the cave overhang. Trees on the other side of the lake flattened.

After the smoke cleared, the flare drone revealed a massive smoking crater fifty meters across between the cave and the drop ship.

"No viable bogies up," Minerva said. "Signs of life only from one of them over by our camp. No movement from the drop ship. It seems to be idling. Unoccupied. Let's check out our survivor."

"I can fly that thing in my sleep," Brigid laughed. "Things are definitely looking up!"

Kayle sprinted over to the wounded man. He was a young clone with a mangled foot, lying on his back, gasping for air. His helmet and goggles were cracked. He was also bleeding from his forehead, but that wound was not life-threatening.

Kayle used the emergency medkit to immobilize his foot and seal the wounds.

"You will make it, but you will need a new foot," she said.

"Thank you. I'm confused. You're in a DC uniform. Where did you come from?" he asked.

"How did your superiors describe this mission to you?" Kayle asked.

"I'm the pilot. All I knew was we were going out to mop up pockets of GDC resistance. Where did you come from?" he asked again.

"Brigid. Can you help me get him on the ship?" Kayle gestured her over. "What is your name, Lance Corporal?" she asked.

"Chard Mar-Ling. I need to tell you I'm in no shape to pilot the drop ship," he said.

Brigid and Kayle helped him to his feet. "That's okay, Chard. I trained on the DST 17. I'm Brigid Strugatsky. The commander here and I are survivors of the *Antares* mission. That's how we got here."

"We were told there were no Dyeus survivors."

"Clearly, you were misinformed." Brigid chuckled.

35

LARGO WAS IN AND OUT for twenty-four hours.

He awoke once and saw Claire standing at the doorway, talking to Meadows and Kayle.

How can Kayle be here? He thought before he convulsed and started passing out again.

You are hallucinating, a disembodied voice said from somewhere. *It will get worse before it gets better. We need to go back to sleep.*

He slept.

Largo had a murky sense of time passing. When he next awoke, a dead clone soldier with a smoking needler wound stood next to the bed. He looked lost.

"I killed you, didn't I?" Key asked. "I am sorry, but you were going to kill me if I didn't."

The clone looked at him. The bloody smoking hole in his forehead was a bit unsettling.

Go back to sleep, the voice said.

Largo slept. Horrible nightmares of running out of burning buildings collapsing all around him made him moan. It was a deep and troubled sleep. The dead boy in the alley in K City was pleading for his life. In a classroom, he was chastised for forgetting the tenets of the corporation. The professor hit him with a Taser. It seemed that every nightmare he'd ever had was waiting in line to get its licks in.

◈

"Is it possible to wake him up? I mean, he's moaning and suffering in his sleep," he heard Jaylen ask. "And we've got big problems. It's all-hands-on-deck time."

Largo struggled to move. He ached all over and wanted to vomit. *I'm not asleep, and I'm not awake. What is this?*

Hypnagogic sleep. I have allowed you to be in a fugue, a transitional state between sleep and awareness, a threshold of consciousness. I detected deep subconscious alarms in your nightmares. So I induced this state; you will find that it is paralytic, but do not be alarmed. The voice was soothing. Largo tried to get up, but couldn't move. He couldn't move so much as a finger.

Not yet, it is too soon. You are still weak. The voice said, *Go back to sleep.*

Who is that talking to me?

It is Baen. I am your friend and partner. We are in this together and everything that's coming—we are in it as one from now on. Do not be alarmed. All is well.

You. I remember you now. Why can't I wake up? I want to wake up.

The vicocet withdrawal ravaged you. You need more healing.

"I could give him adrenaline? That would wake him up," he heard Postrenal say.

"Do it, Doc. Everyone is needed. We have hostiles approaching the citadel," Rent said.

"Wait," Claire said. "His system has gone through a lot of traumas for the past three days. It's a bad time to hit him with the adrenaline. It could have the effect of a hammer breaking a windowpane. I dissent. We have it under control for now."

"We're at an impasse, you and I," Rent said. "We need to get Austen's vote for the tiebreaker."

"No tiebreaker is required." Claire was firm. "I am in charge when Key is not available, and you know that, Rent."

"But he is available; that's my point! We need to wake him up."

"No."

Wake me now, Baen, and tell me what's going on, Key ordered. *I am needed. I have been out of action too long and way too many times since we arrived on this planet.*

The rival group you call Dyeus Corporation has attacked your forces throughout the region. They have had quite a bit of success. Ours is the only group remaining of all Grand Design's resources. Now they are looking for the citadel. They consider us the last pocket of resistance, but you should not get us involved right now. We are far too weak. I advise against it. The citadel's auto-defense system is intact for the most part, and it is unlikely your enemies can breach it. This structure is almost impregnable. You have no idea of its capabilities. We need to go back to sleep. I will share the defense system blueprints with you and explain the operations if you go back to sleep. When you awake next time, I will be able to direct you, and you will know what to do. You need to go back to sleep now.

I need to go back to sleep now, Key thought as he started to drift off.

He heard Lang say, "Going up on deck to see Lieutenant Commander Nesh and check out our defenses. See if those cannons are operational."

Good idea, Lang, he thought as he started to go under again.

From far off, he heard Claire say, "Rent, you must extend the east bunker out and try to learn the disposition of DCs forces as best you can."

"Copy that, Claire. I apologize for my behavior, but I think we can use Key right now."

"It might be good for us, but it wouldn't be good for him," she said.

East bunker—what bunker? he thought as he floated away.

36

THE NIGHT WAS A FALLING curtain as Brigid piloted the DST-17 in full stealth mode. They hovered over the sea approximately ten kilometers out of the citadel. Once the four of them had boarded the ship, in an inspired move, Brigid partially disabled its intra-fleet comms system. They could hear what Dyeus forces were doing, but the DC forces could not contact nor track their ship. On-screen, they could see a large mass of DC interceptors and drop ships approaching from the south.

"They must be feeling confident," Kayle said. "They are coming in completely uncloaked."

"Well, best I can tell, Grand Design does not have one ship flying anywhere on the planet at the moment," Brigid said.

"Aduvah, we need you. Where are you?" Minerva said. "She's still not in range, dammit. Of course, if what Lasker says is true, and I'm out…"

"I've been thinking about that," Kayle said. "You've had no word of your removal from the board or anyone else, for that matter, so how can it be official?"

"Well, according to the bylaws, there has to be a board meeting. And I have to be present for it."

"So, until that happens, it's not official, is it?" Kayle asked.

"Technically, no." Minerva laughed. "By suppressing our comms on Gereon, Lasker has bought me a little time. The case can certainly be made that I'm still CEO until I go to that meeting."

"When did you expect Triad to get here, Minerva?" Brigid asked. "Did you have a backup plan if they don't show?"

"I expected Triad two days ago. I am beyond aggravated. If she reneges on our deal, I will peel her skin like a banana. No backup plan. If she doesn't show, I guess I could surrender. Not too many other options available."

Chung groaned loudly on the bench seat behind them.

"Minerva, is our patient conscious?" Kayle asked.

"Yes. How are you, Chung?" Minerva asked.

Secured on against the bulkhead, he held a thumb up. "I'm better. How are we doing for fuel?"

"We have about ten minutes left," Brigid said. "Minerva, I'm going with your plan to land us on the roof of the citadel dead ahead. That seems to be where everyone is going. We can beat them there before it's completely dark. Hang on, folks, we're coming in hot."

She fired the afterburners. The ship surged forward and descended toward the sea. Flying so low their windshield was splashed with ocean spray, the ride was choppy.

"Unidentified DC Ship 17802D, do you copy? Did you complete your mission down south?"

"He wants to know if we mopped up our pocket of resistance," Chung said.

"Comms disabled," Brigid said. "We can't respond, Chung."

"When did that happen? They were working fine when we landed."

"Shortly after takeoff."

"How? Did we get hit?"

"Well, to be honest, Chung, I sort of disabled them." Brigid grinned.

"Why would you do that? I don't understand."

Minerva pulled the blanket up to his neck and said, "Tell you what, Chung. Hold your questions until after we land."

"They might all be moot if we don't make this landing," Brigid said through gritted teeth. "Lots of turbulence, gusts, and crosswinds around this monstrosity. Damned hard air."

The dark, immense citadel zoomed into view—filling their windshield. Dominating the cliffs in the darkness ahead, and with no signs of life, they stared at it. No one said anything, stunned into silence for a few seconds.

"It's so out of place here," Kayle whispered. "Are we sure your people are inside it?"

They ran into an especially bad chunk of turbulence. The ship yawed, bucked, shuddered. Brigid grunted as she fought the high winds.

"I saw it when Rent presented his report. You have to see it in person to appreciate the whole thing," Minerva said. "It makes a statement. 'Yes, there is another intelligent life form in the universe besides us.'"

"Uh, yeah. That's one hell of a statement right there," Brigid said.

"Put her down right next to the tower, please, Brigid."

A sudden gust slammed into their craft, driving it down. Scraping into the side of the citadel lower wall and disabling the starboard rotor, the ship started to plummet.

"Losing altitude," Bella said. "Impact in ten seconds."

"Fuck," Brigid grunted, wrestling with the controls and keeping them aloft.

"What are those big shapes coming off the cliffs down below, see them flying on the screen now?" Minerva asked. "Let's land this thing and get in the citadel, Brigid."

Kayle recognized them immediately. "Those are the giant bat things I mentioned. We need to get inside fast. They're lethal."

"Let's try this," Brigid said. She punched the throttles and turned the wheel hard to port, and they were hovering over the parapets in twenty seconds. She sat the DST-17 down next to the tower and opened the side doors.

"Everybody out. Make for that door," Minerva commanded, as she unsheathed her needle and jumped out.

"Grab your PSG, Brigid, and give us cover; we don't have much time," Kayle said. "I'm taking Chung with me. You need to hop fast, buddy. They killed a hundred of the *Antares* guards in about thirty minutes."

The first bat swooped in low over Minerva's and Brigid's heads. Its massive wings blew Brigid's hair back. Minerva pierced its belly with a well-timed thrust of her needler. The creature's guts spiraled down slowly, as Minerva danced around it and stabbed it again. An unholy squeal pierced the night, and it stopped thrashing.

"There's plenty more right behind that one," Brigid said as she fired her PSG at two of them swooping low over the parapet. Her tracers missed them completely. "Fuck. So many. How could I miss all of them?"

"Oh, crap, here come the DC ships," Minerva said as she strained to push open the heavy door to the tower. Kayle and Chung tried to help her. They banged, pushed, and kicked at the door.

"I can hear echoes from the stairway below," Minerva said.

"Anybody home?" Brigid yelled as she continued to provide cover from the bats. "The DC boys are disembarking, it's about to get confusing up here."

Three DC drop ships landed about a hundred meters away and began disgorging troops. A screaming horde of bats descended on them as tracers and grenades erupted. More bats flew up over the parapets. One of the drop ships tried to lift off, was overcome by the bats, and flipped over, exploding in a fireball. Burning bloody debris fragments rained down all around them.

"Hit the deck," Minerva said as black smoke, fiery chunks, and bloody scraps rained down, reducing visibility to a few meters.

They all lay prone next to the door until Minerva stood up and banged the door hard—one more time.

The door opened a crack to reveal Austen Nesh pointing a rail rifle in Minerva's face. He recognized her and lowered it immediately, grabbed her by the elbow, and pulled her inside.

Scrambling on all fours, Kayle and Brigid pulled Chung inside with them. They got tangled up in each other's arms and legs and ended up in a pile in the narrow space behind the door. The cries of wounded men and the shrieks of the bloodthirsty bats behind them echoed in the stairwell.

Two DC clones got their fingers on the edge of the door before Nesh slammed it and locked it. He hit a recessed wall panel. A loud hum reverberated all around them.

"What's that?" Minerva asked.

"The citadel's energy shield. Force field. Finally figured out how to operate it this afternoon. Good to see you, boss."

He slipped back his goggles and grinned at Minerva through bloodstains and grime. "Welcome to Château Morte, ma'am." His eyes narrowed as he realized the other three arrivals were in DC armor. He pointed his PSG at Brigid and asked Minerva, "Your prisoners?"

Minerva removed her helmet, shaking her hair loose, and smiled. "No, Austen, these fine women are my friends. The wounded clone pilot is of uncertain status, for now, I guess. Consider him under guard, but treat Chung well."

The constant thunder of heavy artillery began to thump against the roof. Fine white dust cascaded down from the ceiling.

Kayle took off her helmet and spoke softly to Nesh, "Austen, if you could please point that PSG away from me? I haven't seen you since Port Amphora, you wretched lowlife." She laughed, taking off her goggles, and then smiled.

"Kayle? I'll be damned." He started to embrace her and paused. "Minerva, Korban's with us now?"

"She's always been with us, Austen. Just undercover for a while. When I have some time, I'll get the word out to everyone."

"Time we got. We're in a bit of a jam. We are under siege now, and DC is bringing up the big guns. I don't see us getting out of here anytime soon. If ever. Let me show you what the drones are seeing."

"By all means, Austen. Lead the way. But first, take me to Commander Largo. How is he?"

37

BAEN FOUND AN ANCIENT MEMORY, a comforting childhood poem from a once-forgotten book. He recited it to Key.

"The time has come," the Walrus said, *"to talk of many things: Of shoes—and ships—and sealing-wax— Of cabbages—and kings—And why the sea is boiling hot— And whether pigs have wings."*

The poem relaxed Key, and he fell into a deeper sleep. While he slept, Baen showed and told Key secrets of the citadel:

I am showing you how you need to proceed and what you will find as you continue to explore the depths of the fortress. Deep down the long corridor carved out of the living rock lies technology older than anything we ever found anywhere. Descend steep, narrow stairways to a massive grotto. You will see our cables tapped into volcanic steam pits, powering the cannons upstairs. These converter cables are the source of the citadel's power. The ancient tech was left by our predecessors, who were highly skilled mineral extractors. It took us decades to reverse-engineer their technology.

You will see the cables snaking out of the geothermal steam vents leading from our converter. Eventually, you will come to our geothermal extractor and the largest gold deposits we ever found on this or any other planet.

To your left, you will see a massive underground river. It is the source of these gold deposits.

The deposits are formed by Gereon's intense localized earthquakes. These tectonic forces relentlessly shattered stones so quickly that any water they held was vaporized. The vapor leaves behind the gold and other minerals that the water is transporting. Our refractor drill stimu-

lates the many fault lines that converge under the citadel so that we continuously grind and pulverize stone and gather up the gold. The storage vault is adjacent to the drill, and like all the panels in this structure can be accessed by using our 'bracelet.'

Just to get the cannons operational, it's a long way to go, Key thought.

That is not the point!

What is it then, Baen?

Mesh Trouter. He is the point. His records and his discoveries, his inventions. These are the true riches of Gereon.

38

"SO, LARGO'S STILL A DOPE addict?" Minerva seethed as she leaned over Key, recumbent on the bed in his temporary quarters.

Kayle worried that Minerva might stab someone, she was so angry. Without thinking, she took a couple of steps back from her.

The tension in Key's room ratcheted up a few notches. An awkward silence ensued before Claire spoke. "He's been a high-functioning dope addict for a few weeks now. Since we left Raba, I suspect," Claire said. "But I would rather follow Commander Largo high as a kite than anyone else in this corporation—sober."

Minerva noticed the light in Claire's eyes. *This one is in love with him. Not sure if she's fearless or stupid, or both.* She turned and addressed Jaylen, whom she trusted, "How long before Key is fit for duty, Rent?"

"Doc?" Jaylen directed everyone's eyes to Postrenal.

Frowning, Postrenal said, "I should think he will be coming out of withdrawal in the next twenty-four to forty-eight hours—tops. He should sleep as much as possible—easier on his body."

"This is a hell of a time for your leader to be incapacitated. Should you have given him more vicocet, Doctor? At least he would be functional." Minerva's eyes smoldered.

Postrenal became interested in studying his boots, not looking up into those red hot eyes.

Minerva shrugged. "I will assume command then. No choice. Kayle, you will be my XO for now until we see when and if Key is up to the job."

Everyone started breathing again.

"Yes, ma'am," Kayle said.

"Brigid, you will serve as our lead corporate staffer."

"I report to?" Brigid asked, inclining her head.

"Directly to Kayle."

Brigid bowed and then squeezed Kayle's shoulder.

"So that it's clear, any directions and orders from Kayle are the same as if I had said them. Everyone got that?"

Heads nodded, but no one spoke.

"Now, this bracelet that Key found, or that found Key, let me examine it a bit more." She lifted Key's limp hand and touched the bracelet's surface. "Although somewhat similar, it is quite a bit different from mine. It is twice as heavy and looks more complex, more intricate. The gold seems quite pure, and it has a patina of age to it. I'm guessing that it's quite a bit older than mine. It has a different feel to it. Postrenal, I understand that you have studied and scanned this bracelet?"

"Yes, I have, and I need to ask, is your bracelet connected to your body, nervous system, or tissues in any way?"

"It has a shallow connection to the nerves in my wrist. Rather like an implant, I would say."

"Well, ma'am, this one has completely merged with Commander Largo's nervous system. It would be impossible to remove it. Plus it seems to be communicating with his mind."

"Then it is nothing like mine. That's kind of alarming, to be honest, Postrenal."

"Yes. I have feared for the Commander's sanity, for his life since the moment he put that infernal device on his wrist."

"We will need to do an intensive study. Need to know what it is doing to Key." Minerva paled, hesitated for a few moments, shook it off, and asked, "Right. What are we using for a war room?"

"We've been using the killing hall. It's where we've set up tables with our comms, screens, and our drone read-outs," Nesh said. "It will be the best place to do a sitrep."

"I must see this killing hall. Interesting name. Let's have a quick meeting. I need Jaylen, Nesh, Claire, and Postrenal to get Kayle and me up to speed."

After she walked into the hall, Minerva stared open-mouthed at the panels. The monumental art, the elaborate architecture of the killing hall, filled her gaze. Her eyes came to rest on the serpent-and-egg sculpture. She studied it for a few moments. Then she said, "Amazing that something so exquisite wasn't looted at some point."

"Well, the last visitors before us got vaporized," Jaylen observed. "The security system in here is, uh, impressive."

"Jaylen, please hang back after the briefing. I need you to tell me what you know about the countermeasures in this room."

"Will do."

"Now, Nesh, please bring up the screens and show us all that our drones are seeing," Minerva ordered.

The drone's eye-view showed the citadel and its environs. From the two-kilometer straight-up view, it was being surrounded by Dyeus forces. Hooches and bunkers were being built, supplies off-loaded.

"Have you identified who is commanding the Dyeus forces, Nesh?" Minerva asked.

"Yes. CO is Zel Rand, and his XO is Reg Andreivich, two of the best in any of the nine corps," Nesh said.

"I know Zel. He's old school, went to the academy with me, was right behind me in class rank. I've tried to recruit him several times. Damn, I wish it was someone else. Zel is one of the few people I actually like." Minerva shook her head.

"They seem to be setting up for a lengthy siege," Kayle said.

"When they landed on the roof, DC lost dozens of men to the bats. Perhaps as many as a fifty. Some Dyeus genius identified the source, a cave near the bottom of the cliffs. They dropped a thermal-plasma in there. End of the bat problem," Nesh said. "Then they pounded us for about an hour with the heavy guns. After realizing that artillery was useless, they started reinforcing their positions. As you can see, they've landed about two dozen drop ships so far—in one day."

"So what is that—about a battalion's worth, Austen?" Minerva asked.

"Almost two, actually," Nesh said.

"And our forces? How many can we put in the field?"

"Ninety combat forces, twelve support personnel."

"So DC has roughly a ten-to-one advantage?" Minerva frowned.

"More like fifteen to one. And DC has the heavy ordinance, air cover, plus more waiting in suborbit," Nesh said. "We don't have an answer for any of that stuff. A few problems there to be sure. Then there's another problem in that our AI system seems to have picked up a virus from Key's bracelet."

"Can we hold out until Triad can reinforce us?" Minerva asked.

"How long do you think until they get here?"

"Two days, I hope. But they are overdue, and I haven't heard anything from Aduvah." Minerva frowned.

"We can hold out for two days. We could hold out for three months with the rations we have. Plus, this citadel has many defensive enhancements that we're still trying to figure out. They designed it to withstand heavier stuff than DC has in their arsenal."

"You sure about that?" Minerva asked.

"Pretty sure. For example, many hidden features. About two dozen concealed sliding bunkers secured inside the citadel's walls. Equipped with, uh, these lava cannon-type weapons. We are trying to familiarize ourselves with them. Also, an armory full of lava rifles like this one." Nesh handed his lava rifle to Minerva, who inspected it.

"Now, we know how to operate the rifles, but we don't understand the cannons—yet. We will, though. And soon. Some strange armor that looks substantial. It won't fit us, of course, much too large, but we could modify it."

"So, Austen, are you saying this place has some kind of wonder weapon armory inside it?" Minerva asked, arching an eyebrow.

"That's exactly what I'm saying." Nesh nodded.

"How did we manage to lose so many people? Nesh, what happened to Emi Manaka?" Minerva asked.

"She was at our Green Valley base. They hit Green Valley hard. As soon as DC came into suborbit, Manaka and her forces went offline. We don't know if anyone escaped; if everyone died, we don't know."

"So we've been taking it on the chin here for a few days now," Minerva said quietly.

"Yes, ma'am. But Minerva, please allow me to make a recommendation. We need to take the initiative. To that end, I want to do some basic combat ops equipped with the lava rifles."

"Like what, for example?" Minerva asked. "We don't have a lot of resources."

"A night raid, tonight. I want to grab some DC staff members, take them prisoner, and get some intel. Moving in on them while they are still getting themselves set up, it might be our best bet. We have three Dyeus uniforms among us. Now, two belong to high-ranking officers. I recommend we put them to use when we infiltrate their camp."

"We can't spare too many people for such a raid," Minerva said.

"I would not want to take more than seven or eight of us," Nesh replied. "We need people who can kill quietly and move quickly."

Minerva looked around the table. "Any volunteers?" She grinned.

Kayle held up her hand, immediately followed by Brigid.

"You will need a combat engineer, so count me in," said Jaylen.

Claire smiled at Jaylen and said, "You might need a combat medic," and held up her hand.

Minerva held up her hand. "I'm coming too, dammit. I tire of waiting for Triad. I want to make something happen."

Kayle spoke up before anyone could stop her. "I know from experiencing your skills with a needle that you can be deadly and quiet. But do you think it's worth the risk to Grand Design? You are our CEO, after all."

"If the board knew, they would not approve. But the board's not out here. Besides, if something happens to me, Key is still in reserve. And recovering dope addict or not, he is still the actual leader of this venture. Then there is also the absolute certainty that I will not allow myself to be taken alive."

⬥

Dressed in dark, nonreflective armor, the crew began the raid by exiting a bunker on the north side of the citadel. They rappelled down the seaside cliff face. They then made their way to the rocky black sand beach at the bottom of the plateau. A fog bank blowing in from the ocean would engulf the beach soon. They stored and secured their jetpacks behind some boulders in case an emergency return to the rooftop proved necessary on the way back.

Brigid and Kayle were dressed in their DC uniforms, and Chief Lang had borrowed Chung's outfit. Brigid had the point position. Lang brought up the rear. Nesh had said this wasn't going to be a 'normal raid,' assuming there was such a thing for this situation. He had a flexible approach in mind and had given the op the readily apparent name of "Minerva's Lava Rifles." They would not expend their time and risk exposure scouting against the well-trained Dyeus infantry. Instead, the crew would set up a position near the DC flank and wait for a target of opportunity to attack. Or they could grab a prisoner, create a diversion, and then workaround to the CP to where the higher value staffers were. They all knew they would not survive a firefight with the DC forces. Despite all the powerful lava weapons they carried, DC's numbers could not be overcome. And Zel was too good. He had brought Lasker's best troops to guard the CP. About thirty Hazana Hussars, well-known for their controlled fury and lethal efficiency, were arrayed around it.

Kayle motioned everyone to crouch low as they approached the uppermost beach terrace. In her night goggles, she saw the first DC picket line fifty meters ahead of them. The swamps and the impenetrable thickets were adjacent to their right flank. The DC staff did not expect any infiltration from this area. Their defensive forces were thinnest here, as Nesh had expected. Brigid and Minerva stretched out on the damp moss next to Kayle.

"Only the one guard?" Brigid asked.

Whispering hoarsely, Minerva said, "Who gets that guy in front of us?"

Kayle threw her glance to the right, and Minerva's eyes followed. Now she could see Rent almost imperceptibly gliding through the edges of the woods. All three of them watched as Rent attempted to remove the first obstacle.

Rent sprinted the last thirty yards and hit the guard low with a brutal tackle, targeting his knees with a solid helmet crunch. A blade flashed in the night, and the guard was still.

Chief Lang loomed out of the fog behind them and said, "I got the other guy—the way is open now for about 200 meters. And then we get to a sandbagged compound, as expected. It looks like an APC garage. Enough for three or four rigs."

Kayle made sure everyone was accounted for. They lined up like the start of a cross-country race and took off running. The fog started to drift around their knees.

Is the fog a good or bad thing? Kayle wondered as she ran.

They got to the outer sandbagged wall and flattened their backs against it and listened. Someone was taking apart an engine on the other side of the wall. Machinery clanked. Dropped steel parts echoed in the dark. A spicy aroma of eucalyptus and olives wafted out of the open end of the shed.

"That is a fabulous cigar," Minerva whispered to Brigid. "Might be Port Amphora's best tobacco. 'For a relaxed kimono make mine an Amphora Corona'; remember that project?"

Kayle looked at her like she was crazy. "You're thinking of an ad campaign at a time like this?"

"I'm thinking about that cigar next door." Minerva grinned.

Rent, Chung, and Nesh emerged from the left side.

"Targets neutralized, "Chung whispered. "They've got a couple of APCs in there that I haven't seen before; must be some new stuff."

"Does one of them look like a scorpion?" Kayle asked.

"Just like one," Chung nodded.

"That's my car," Kayle smiled. "I have the keys to one hidden away somewhere on this planet. It also has the disruptor drive from the *Antares* inside it."

"Remind me to retrieve that later," Minerva said.

Kayle jogged into the compound, and there at the front of the garage shed was an unused new scorpion APC. The tail section of this one was modified with what looked like a cluster of PSGs situated in it. It looked lethal. The two front pincers had plasma cannons attached to them.

Kayle pointed at the forward rear and top turret hatches, saying, "Load in everyone, this vehicle can handle eighteen of us."

Minerva and Brigid pointed to the different modular armaments from their previous scorpion as they climbed in. Kayle acknowledged Brigid's gestures, saying, "DC has rigged this one for more serious close-combat support. Lots more firepower. Our old one was for a more generalized use, to aid in gold mining."

Brigid checked the gauges and screens. Dialing in the correct codes, the scorpion was now concealed in digital camouflage. "We are armed and fueled. Where do we want to go?" she asked Minerva and Kayle in the seats next to her.

"We try getting as close as we can to the command post," Kayle said, looking at Minerva, who nodded in agreement.

"But not too close to arouse suspicion," Nesh suggested. "We need to go about a kilometer and a half to the northeast from here. Brigid should drive with her hatch open so that the DC people can see she's in the right uniform. Chief Lang, you could also open the top hatch and make sure your DC uniform is visible."

Lang opened the hatch and held his PSG low. "No one near us until we get to that line of hooches up ahead," he observed.

Kayle started up the engines. The turbos made a low whine as she edged forward. "This one is so much quieter than the prototype we had. I'm going to drive slowly and try to appear as non-threatening as a scorpion can look." Kayle laughed at how ridiculous her comment sounded.

"Pretend you're a turtle," Minerva suggested, chuckling.

As strange as it may be, I'm actually having fun, Kayle thought.

As if she could read her mind, Minerva whispered, "Look at that silly grin on your face. You always were an adrenaline junkie, kiddo. Just like your mother."

⸻◈⸻

Kayle stopped the scorpion near the woods about 700 meters from the command post. To the left of the CP, and less than 500 meters away from their APC, was a long low poly-steel bunker. She was alerted by the sudden activity outside its doors. "Let's hold up here for a bit and get a close look at what's going on with this structure," Kayle said. "Why is it the center of activity?"

"Look over at the CP, quite a few people coming out of there now," Minerva said. "Two people—a man and a woman, under heavily armed escort. Wait. They're both wearing Grand Design uniforms—"

"One of them is Emi Manaka," Claire said. "I don't recognize the other one. But there's a DC lieutenant commander in front of her and a captain behind Emi."

"So our targets of opportunity have arrived, Minerva?" Nesh asked. "They're almost serving them up on a silver platter."

Minerva nodded.

"I wouldn't go that far," said Rent. "Armed enemy drop ship setting down over on our left."

"They're taking Manaka up to one of the dreadnoughts for enhanced interrogation. She looks like they already put her through the wringer," Minerva said. "If we're going to spring her here, we'll have to do it fast."

"More GDC prisoners coming out of that bunker—about four more," Kayle said. "Brigid, you take the wheel; Lang and I will try to get to Emi without attracting attention. But when we get to Emi, we need every gun in this APC trained on the DC boys."

Nesh and Rent checked each other's kit.

"We need Claire on the aft stinger gun pod. I can handle the pincer guns," Minerva said.

Claire moved into the stinger's bucket seat and flipped off each safety in the gun pod.

"Claire, be ready to destroy that drop ship first when the shooting starts," Minerva said.

Claire nodded as she familiarized herself with the control panel.

"That leaves me and Rent available to freelance some ground support and create some low-level chaos and havoc," Nesh said. "Maybe we can grab that commander and unleash enough pandemonium to allow some of our Grand Design prisoners a chance to escape?"

With that, Nesh opened the floor hatch and dropped out of the APC. "Coming, Rent?"

"Dammit, Nesh, ever since our college days, you were always good at volunteering me into things that I was never really sure about." Rent laughed as he exited the vehicle behind Austen.

"All right. Lang? We're up," Kayle said as she unlocked the top hatch and then shimmied out of the APC. Lang followed, going out right behind her.

39

EY DREAMED OF A GRIFFIN, although he couldn't quite identify it as such. The half-eagle, half-lion beast was bossy, dictatorial—telling him to do this or that. It aggravated him. And the griffin didn't seem too concerned about the sadness of the turtle creature. The two beasts attempted to explain aspects of their world to Key, but they made no sense at all.

Baen interrupted his dream. *I'm stepping in now, as I sense this dream may become nightmarish. It is safe for you to wake up now and get some nutrition in our body. You are close to fully recovered. When you wake up, you will remember the instructions I gave you, but you won't recall me giving them as such. You must not tell anyone about our hypnogogic communications because it would undermine your credibility if you did so. Most humans cannot understand our symbiotic relationship. You need to accept this.*

Largo awoke. All he could think of was eating. Dr. Meadows was standing nearby and saw him wake up.

"You look a little washed-out, Commander, but your vital signs are stable, and the opium withdrawal appears to have finally run its course," he said.

"I'm so fucking hungry, Meadows."

"We have a nice pot of miso soup ready for you. After you get that down, you can have something more substantial."

———◆———

After three bowls of soup, smoked salmon, and cracker rations, Key felt good and ready to get on with exploring the citadel.

"Meadows, how much more of this structure have we explored while I was out of commission?"

"Down to this floor. At the end of the hall is another closed gate, requiring you and your bracelet for access, we assume."

"And what's on this floor?" Key asked.

"Spacious habitations and a galley. It functioned as apartments for the previous owners, whoever the sacramentae were."

"The Shanges," Key corrected him.

"Who?" Meadows asked.

"They called themselves the Shanges."

"I see." Meadows gave him a baffled look but said nothing more.

Michelle entered the room, equipped with a prosthetic forearm and hand assemblage. She was in full armor with a PSG strapped over her shoulder.

"How's the new hand, Michelle?" Key asked.

"I've got the hang of it now. It'll do until I can get a better one," she replied.

"Why are you dressed for combat?"

"There's an op going on right now. I tried to volunteer for it but was not selected."

"What's the op?" Key asked.

"Intel. The senior staff went out to grab a prisoner. It's irregular that the entire senior chain of command would risk themselves. Including Minerva." Michelle shook her head.

Not the entire chain. I'm still here. Largo almost voiced his thoughts but considering his audience, he thought better of it.

"Minerva's here? When did that happen?" Key asked. "Shit, that means she's aware of my vicocet habit. I bet she was pissed off."

"That's putting it mildly, Commander," Michelle said, smiling, entertained by his discomfort.

"*Schadenfreude* is not a good look for you, Michelle," Key said, grinning.

"Minerva was irate, Commander," Meadows added. "There are several business items I need to catch you up on."

"Can we do that while we walk? There's an inverted tower inside this place that I need to find," Key said.

"How did you come by this information?" Meadows asked.

Largo didn't say anything but raised an eyebrow and patted his bracelet.

Meadows was confused and then nodded. He tried to keep a poker face, but his eyes betrayed his fear and alarm.

40

A FEW MORE PACES AND KAYLE and Lang were well-positioned to try to grab Emi. Emi was drugged, bloody, and bruised. She could barely walk. The other GDC captive was a senior clone, a lance corporal named Rew Adama, one of Lang's old comrades. Emi and Rew were chained together by leg restraints.

Lang looked over at Rew and nodded. Rew gave Lang an imperceptible nod. Even with his night goggles obscuring his face, Adama recognized the burly chief of his GDC clone battalion.

Kayle whispered, "I will cut out the guards. You grab our guys. Then I will try to get us our own prisoner. Brigid has us covered."

In her helmet earphones, she heard Brigid say, "Not to worry, sister. I have you."

Kayle saw that Lang was silent as he tensed his muscles for what was about to happen. The guards were a few steps away now, and Kayle saw him put his fingers on his PSG's trigger.

Kayle gripped her needle and moved in quickly, cutting down the guard next to Emi. Manaka stumbled and almost tripped over the guard's falling body but gathered herself up. She moved to get the restraint chain release from his corpse.

At the same time that Lang shot the other two guards, Kayle could see out of the corner of her eyes tracers from the scorpion tearing into the drop ship. It came apart in a deafening explosion.

"Stay low, you two, more hussars coming out of the bunker. Claire has a clear shot if you can crouch down," Brigid said.

Emi had freed Rew and herself from the shackles. Kayle signaled for them to get down and crawl as the tracers sizzled above them. The hussars coming out of the bunker were shredded.

In her earpiece, Kayle heard Minerva say, "All the hatches are open, get back to the scorpion now!"

Kayle saw Jaylen and Austen dragging an unconscious DC captain toward the APC.

Think we've completed our mission. Now let's finish the escape.

Kayle held up Emi, and Lang helped Rew as they made their way back to the scorpion. They couldn't move very fast as it was clear that Emi and Rew were severely wounded and had been tortured as well as drugged.

"Is that you, Kayle? Or am I hallucinating?" Emi whispered.

"It's me, Emi. Keep moving. We can talk later."

From somewhere to the left, three hussars ran in with needlers and attacked Jaylen and Nesh. "Keep going, Jaylen, get this guy in the vehicle," Nesh said as he cut one of them down with his PSG.

Claire had switched to the plasma cannon on the aft gun and was laying down heavy ordinance right behind them as they fled. The explosions shuddered the ground. Dirt clods, dust, and smoke covered their retreat.

Kayle pushed Emi down into the driver's side hatch and turned to assist Nesh. She could see he was in trouble. He had a bloodied and burned gouge in his thigh. One of the hussars had caught him with a needler. Now Nesh was down on one knee fending off two hussars. Kayle rushed in, pirouetted, and cut off the nearest hussar's head. It landed with a nauseating thud at her feet.

But the other hussar ran Nesh through the chest. The endpoint of the needle emerged from his back. Nesh coughed up blood and convulsed to the ground.

The hussar raised his needle high for the death blow as Minerva mowed him down with her twin rail guns. He exploded into chunks of meat, a gout of blood, and a red haze.

Kayle kneeled over Nesh as tracer rounds and chaos went off all around. A smoke cloud engulfed them.

"Gotta get you back to Claire. She can patch you up. Stay with me, Austen."

"I'd love to, Kayle, but don't think I'm gonna be able to make it back to the APC."

"Nonsense. Let me help you up!"

"Kayle, uh, what's—" Nesh coughed up a large amount of blood and what looked like pieces of tissue. She threw him over her shoulder and sprinted back to the APC. Firing at an advancing guard with her PSG in her left hand, she got to the tank. Placing him down carefully, she then fired at shadows in the smoke and dust. Dragging-pulling Nesh with her right hand, she was able to slide under the scorpion's bottom hatch. Clods of earth showered down on them, but Claire was able to pull Nesh into the craft with Kayle pushing him in.

Over her helmet commlink, she heard Minerva ask, "Jaylen, you are the only one unaccounted for, where might we find you?"

"I got cut off. There's at least a full platoon of hussars between us. Some of them are trying to get to the motor pool. I'm busy cutting them down at the moment."

"Brigid has the APC flat-out, and we're moving that way. Two drop ships are inbound. So we don't have much time. Do you think there's any place nearby where you can meet us?" Minerva asked.

"Uh, that's a negative, boss. I'll try to make my way back on my own. It may take a while. Can you please give Kayle a message for me?"

"She can hear you, Jaylen. Give it to her yourself," Minerva said.

"Kayle, uh, I want to say I could never believe that you were—that you betrayed us on PA. And I'm glad it turned out not to be true. You are someone that I've loved and respected for years. Renteria out."

"Renteria?" Brigid asked.

"That's his given name," Minerva said. "He hardly ever uses it."

"Permission to help Jaylen," Kayle requested, opening the hatchway. Smoke boiled up through the hole. Rounds hammered and thudded against their armor.

"Permission denied," Minerva replied.

But Kayle had already slipped out of the bottom hatch.

41

"**N**O SHOWER? ARE YOU KIDDING me, Commander?" Meadows asked. "I have to tell you that both Postrenal and I believe you need to rest and recover your vigor— naturally. I am certain Claire, if she were here, would agree."

"There is no time. I have to get moving, Meadows. Come on, if you're coming."

Moving down the hall, putting on light armor as he walked, Largo hurried to the next locked gate. He looked back and saw Meadows putting on his flak jacket as he jogged down the hall toward Key. "You know, Commander, it will still be there an hour from now. We don't have to run."

Key slung a PSG over his shoulder and continued walking.

"We need to be armed? All I have is one of these strange lava rifles."

"Bring it then."

"Only the two of us? Shouldn't we wait until the others get back?" Meadows asked.

From the back of the room, they heard Michelle say, "I'm coming too. Wait for me."

Meadows and Michelle caught up to him at the next panel. Largo held his bracelet up to the scanner.

The door slid with a soft hiss and opened to an elevator. Key entered and waited for Meadows and Michelle to join him.

Meadows got in, saying, "This thing hasn't operated in who knows how long?" He stepped to the back and turned around in an about-face. "Millenia?"

Michelle grinned.

Largo said nothing.

"Couple millennia? So what could go wrong? This thing must be pretty safe, right?"

The door closed in front of them, and they descended.

The elevator hissed and rocked as it went down into the citadel's depths. About a minute later, the door whirred open into a stately amber chamber. A single pair of strange footwear covered with fine white dust lay against the wall immediately in front of them.

Baen told Key, *Behold the work of the Shanges. Master artisans and craftsmen from all over the galaxies molded these flawlessly carved reliefs and lattice works a thousand years ago. These artists fashioned the iridescent shades of amber and rare gemstones that you see here into stunning gold leaf fascias to create these ornate inlay effects.*

It's kind of hallucinatory; the flowing movement of the lattices is almost hypnotic, Key thought.

This is the classic Shanges art style, Baen added.

Meadows was stunned into silence as he took in the chamber. After clearing his throat, he whispered, "About twenty square meters of the most beautiful room I've ever stood in. What is its purpose, I wonder? Damn. There is now no reason to doubt that Gereon has gold on it, is there?"

"Yep. That one is settled."

Michelle stood with her jaw open and eyes filled with admiration and something feral.

This is the antechamber to the Great Map Hall. Here is where you remove your boots and enter into a meditative mental state. If you were Shanges, that is. You should approach the hall with something akin to reverence. That's not the right word, but it is the closest term available in your language.

So who do these shoes belong to? Key asked.

The last person to visit this chamber before us. They did not return to pick them up. Or they are still in there somewhere.

42

N THE DARKNESS, KAYLE SAW that the command post was awash in light, as the DC forces made an impression of a kicked-over fire ant mound. It was pitch black by the swamps, so she headed that way. Distant explosions and rumblings behind her indicated that DC was engaged in red-on-red combat. This was confirmed when she heard Minerva laugh on the commlink and say, "We've got them firing at each other. How delightful! Kayle, I order you to return to the scorpion. Jaylen is a big boy. You know he can take care of business."

"Kayle, what did you do?" Jaylen asked.

"I'm coming to help you."

"Bad idea. Follow Minerva's orders."

"I'm almost to the motor pool; it's crawling with hussars. Which way did you go?" Kayle asked.

"I made a beeline for the swamps. Some things are moving around in there. Might be those antler people."

"We must have woken them up?"

"Affirmative, although they may be nocturnal too for all we know," Jaylen said. "They are a complication I don't need right now, so I will skirt the swamp edge."

"Coming that way," Kayle said.

"Negative," Minerva interrupted, "we have you on the screen. You are 300 meters to our left flank. Wait right where you are, and we will pick you—"

A colossal salvo ended her transmission.

A gunship buzzed the battlefield behind Kayle, guns blazing, chewing up the terrain to her left, vaporizing the swampland.

"Minerva? Do you copy?" Kayle asked.

"What happened?" Jaylen asked.

"That gunship happened," Kayle said. "Minerva, Brigid, anyone?"

Static on the commlink indicated a disruption from the APC's comms. Kayle magnified her night-vision goggles and could see the scorpion smoking a few hundred meters away. "I can see the APC, Jaylen. It's damaged, smoking. No transmission. No movement. Nothing. DC troops are approaching it, and it still isn't moving."

"You better clear out of there, Kayle."

"Don't waste your breath. I'm not leaving."

Kayle continued to watch as the DC soldiers advanced. Unexpectedly, she experienced it all over again. All the old symptoms of fear. She fought to control them, the knots in her stomach, the dryness in her mouth, the spasm of her muscles in her lower back. She choked it all down. Was anyone still alive in the scorpion? She trained her PSG on two of the hussars who were climbing up the right side of the APC.

Do I shoot at them and give away my position? How many more are hidden in the smoke? Oh, what the hell, she thought as she was about to squeeze the trigger.

About a hundred meters to her right, a burst of tracers erupted from the swamp's edge, mowing down both hussars. This action drew most of the hostiles' fire, as they all opened up on his position.

"Jaylen, that's you over there by the swamp?" she asked.

"Kayle. I've made your position out—moving toward you now."

"Copy that. I'm still watching the scorpion for signs of life. Will hold until you get here."

The DC forces were crawling all over the ground.

There's got to be at least twenty of them, she thought. *No way we can make it through to the scorpion.*

Jaylen tapped her on her shoulder. He lay down prone next to her. His whole body was covered in mud. He grinned at her through the sludge. "Yeah, I fell in the swamp," he said.

"So that's what that smell is."

"Some bad shit decaying in there. I need several inoculations. Wow. What happened to the APC?"

A half-dozen men were crawling on the tank when a blinding flash of sheet lightning flattened them, and a thunderous burst of static erupted in their earphones.

"Someone found the oh-shit button, the EDRS, a 50,000-volt shock that scorches anything touching the outer armor layer," Kayle said. "It's the last-ditch mechanism."

"Good last ditch."

The commlink had a low hum of fuzzy static in it when they heard Minerva's voice.

"Not sure if this is still working. We're all concussed in here—the hussars hit us with a plasma shot. Claire is still out cold. I'm driving the tank, heading toward the base of the cliff where we left our jet packs—our rally point."

"Minerva, do you read?" Kayle asked.

"Minerva, please respond?"?" Jaylen asked.

"More troops coming up, plus the gunship is coming back around. We're clearing out of here now via the swamps," Minerva said.

Kayle stood up and offered Jaylen her hand. She helped him get up.

"Let's head back toward the marsh. Maybe we can link up with the APC," Jaylen said as he wiped the muck from his eyes.

Ahead of them, they heard a turbo engine whine, a massive burst of gunfire followed by an explosion—static on the comms—only static.

43

THEY ENTERED THE GREAT MAP Hall. This time Largo had three arched doors to choose from. All three were crafted from a rich, dark coffee-colored wood, inlaid with a lattice pattern in mother-of-pearl, similar in style to the panels in the antechamber. The center door was larger by half than the other two. They entered, and as one, their eyes were drawn to the ceiling. An elaborate three-dimensional celestial map blinked and flowed in the air above them. A troika of multicolored lines, red, purple, and gold, spun through the heavenly art.

"It's so beautiful!" Michelle gasped.

This shows the known galaxy, as depicted by our ancient cartographers. The red, purple, and gold lines track our interplanetary trade routes, Baen told Key.

"It's an interplanetary trade map," Largo said.

"How do you know that?" Meadows asked.

"I'm getting a lot of information from the bracelet, from Baen," Key said.

"The bracelet has a name?" Michelle asked, looking hard at Key.

"Yes. It told me to call him Baen."

"So would you call him an entity?" she asked, her eyes narrow.

"I don't know what to call him. He's alive. He thinks. He is intelligent."

"How is communication accomplished?" Meadows asked.

"I hear his thoughts in my mind and vice versa."

"So, it's a form of ESP?" Meadows followed up.

"It's like that. Or what I imagine ESP would be like. This is deep and immediate. And strange. It's an extraordinary experience, Meadows. As far as I know, I'm the first human to be integrated with a sentient alien intellect?"

"Yeah. Pretty sure you are, Commander," Meadows said.

Largo took a couple of steps into the hall and looked at the walls lined with books and map cases labeled in a strange glowing cursive writing. Long tables flanked the walls. Holographic maps and globes of a variety of planets were displayed on each desk. Rows of glowing blue rectangles, table dials, and buttons clustered in the center of each table.

What are the blue, glowing rectangular slats set into the tables? Largo asked.

These are extra data tablets, accessed by touching a place on the hologram—no time to examine these at the moment. We must keep moving.

What are these hologlobes?

These are the first planets of the Shanges Federation, Baen said. *I know it is a lot to process, but we need to head to that stairwell at the other end of the room, and we need to keep moving.*

Why? What's the hurry?

This room pales in comparison to what awaits you down below. And it is crucial to the reason why you are on this planet in the first place.

What do you mean, Baen?

I mean gold. And plenty of it. Now, let us move along.

Well, why didn't you say so?

I did. You do not remember it.

Largo strode toward the stairwell at the end of the long hall.

Michelle, distracted by a nearby hologlobe, said, "Hey, this one over here has Klystron and K City." She looked at an adjacent table. "And here's Raba. Commander, where are you going? We need to spend some time here."

Largo could not hear her. He was going down the stairs two at a time and almost racing to the arched, frosted door at the end of the stairs.

In the center of the next door, the egg-and-snake motif was etched in gold. Largo slammed his wrist against the panel, and the door opened into a dark room full of vapor. He could hear Michelle and Meadows running down the stairs trying to catch up with him.

"Commander, you need to wait for us!" Meadows shouted.

Baen interrupted his thoughts before he could respond. *This fog may hide many dangers. I was not expecting anything like this. They were not present when I was last here. So much I still need to tell you.*

What kind of dangers?

The deadly kind. I need to tell you about the vent wraiths. They may have been released, and if so, we may need to reconsider going much further.

44

THEY WERE OFF TRACK—LOST. SOMETHING was burning ahead of them—flames obscured by billowing black, oily smoke. The comlinks with the scorpion had ended about ten minutes before. They were unable to reestablish contact with anyone. Kayle felt a coldness in the pit of her stomach when they lost touch with the others. That coldness had grown to feel like a block of ice. And ahead, they heard another gunship moving off toward the sea.

"Well, at least it's going in the right direction," Rent observed.

"But are we?" Kayle asked.

"Generally?"

"That burning vehicle is our APC. We need to approach it carefully. Dammit—wish I still had my lava rifle," Kayle said.

"I had the same thought."

Ahead, Kayle saw a brief reflection from the smoldering fire—a glint off a gun barrel—and signaled Rent to halt. "They've set up a perimeter. We need to give this area a wide berth. I count twelve heat signatures immediately ahead. Looks like a DC kill box, maybe."

"Agree."

They entered into the higher ground to the right and walked up the wooded slope. All around, there was a vacant silence. *This stillness is unnatural,* she thought.

"Kayle, over here. I found a soldier," Rent said.

She could detect a faint heat signature on a body lying prone in front of Rent. As she approached, she recognized who it was: Rew Adama. Rent rolled him over and checked his wounds.

"Is he?" Kayle asked.

"Not dead. Barely conscious, though," Rent said. "Rew, what happened here?"

With a deep, ragged breath, Rew answered, "It got a bit hairy. We shot down a gunship, and then it crashed on our scorpion. Fuel tanks ruptured, and the propellant went all over; a fire got inside the cabin. We had to get out. I made it this far before collapsing. I need to rest."

"Do you know where any of the rest of the crew is?" Rent asked.

Rew shook his head.

Rent looked up at Kayle, who scanned the woods. "What do you think?"

"No one else seems to be around. Can you help Rew while I take the point?"

"Rew, if I help you—are you able to help me by being somewhat mobile, at least?"

"Yeah. I think so."

"All right, let me scout ahead a bit and get our bearings to the rally point," Kayle said.

"Kayle, do you think it's a good idea to split up?" Rent asked.

"No. But it's a worse idea to be lost in these woods like we are now, since the area seems to be crawling with DC forces. Wait here while Rew rests up. Should be back in fifteen or twenty minutes."

⋘⟡⋙

Kayle came to an open space in the trees, a meadow of high weeds. Tiny glowing insects floated in the tall grasses. A hazy light was starting to emerge on the horizon. The faint gray light reflected off a small pond ahead of her. Now she could see the smashed-down grasses left from new paths through the clearing.

A large group of people came through here recently.

Kayle's heart thumped against her breastbone. Her mouth was parched. She looked for a way out of the forest glade that didn't follow the crushed grasses. She chose to follow the edge of the pond and then the creek that it drained into.

Almost as one, eight figures emerged from the water—a heavily armed squad. A stocky clone commando took a step forward and said,

"Identify yourself, Commander. I don't recognize you as a member of our ops team."

When they run my ID, they're going to know who I am. If I wasn't wearing my DC uniform, I would probably already be dead, she thought as she raised her hands.

The best thing to do is tell the truth and see if it sets me free, she thought ruefully.

"I am Commander Kayle Korban, COO of the corporation and surviving member of the DCS *Antares.*"

45

"WE HOLD HERE AND DO some scans of this room," Key said. "I need to consider our next steps."

Meadows cleared his throat and asked, "Does Baen have some concern about going in there?"

"He does. He calls this next room an inverted tower, and seven floors down, it leads to geothermal vents as well as a large gold seam. But there are these creatures he calls vent wraiths that are known to inhabit such ecosystems. They are problematic, Dr. Meadows."

"How so?"

"They are chameleon-like in their ability to blend into the environment—translucent and almost invisible in the fog; they have two pairs of gossamer wings. Vent wraiths move like a dragonfly. They produce a toxic venom inside a gland, stored in a venom sack. It exudes through valves to coat a bony tail stinger. The venom paralyzes you before it destroys your nervous system. As an extra, they have razor-like talons that can rip your skin to shreds."

Did I get that right, Baen?

Almost word for word from what I told you.

"How big do they grow?" Michelle asked.

"Roughly the size of large raptors like a hawk or a falcon," Key replied. "They weren't in there the last time Baen was here."

"And how long ago was that?" Meadows asked.

"A little over two hundred years ago."

No one said anything at first.

"So, the citadel has been unoccupied for about two centuries," Meadows observed. "Strange that since we left the killing hall, everything has been so well-preserved, untouched. Can Baen explain that?"

Well, Baen?

I hypothesize that when we built it, we had made it extremely airtight in the event of a gas attack. All of our defensive countermeasures have remained intact all this time somehow, but that is only a hypothesis.

"The short answer is no. Baen can't explain it."

That is not what I said.

"What about the gold, Commander? What does he know about that?" Michelle asked.

"There was a large gold seam down here. The Shanges mined that for several centuries. It may be that a functional drill is still down there. After all this time, it may be usable, attached to the gold seam. Or it may have fallen into disrepair. Of course, there is only one way to find that out." Key shrugged. "What else? Let's see. Oh, yeah, he mentioned there was also a large storeroom that may hold large quantities of gold."

"And we are held up here because?" Michelle asked, her eyes alight with excitement.

"The vent wraiths that may or may not be down there," Largo said. "We need a larger force for this next phase of exploration. Three of us may not be enough, Michelle."

"Well, Commander," Meadows observed, "like you said, there is only one way to find out."

Stepping toward the door, Michelle said, "I could not agree more, Dr. Meadows."

46

"AND WHO MIGHT I BE addressing?" Kayle asked.

"I am Master Sergeant Hideo Tanizaki," he said. "We had heard rumors that there were no survivors from the *Antares* crash. A new COO was named after you were reported MIA, ma'am."

"Well, that's to be expected," Kayle said.

"We need you to come with us, Commander. A person of your rank should not be exposed to any further danger. Especially when one considers all that you have been through," Tanizaki requested.

"How can I refuse? Your request is more than reasonable." Kayle smiled.

"Here, Commander, Take my sidearm. You may need it yet." Tanizaki handed her his Gauss pistol. She still had her needler in its holster on her right hip. A brief, fleeting thought of fighting them dispersed in her mind.

They led her on a well-trod path back toward where the vehicles were burning.

Well, they didn't shoot me on sight. As Brigid would say, things are looking up. I wonder just how far I can carry this masquerade?

High above their heads, a drop ship circled, the turbines reversed, and it started to descend ahead of them on the edge of the clearing. Kayle recognized the type—a harpoon class, the H9. The cargo ramp dropped, and the squad, with Kayle, boarded. The tailgate closed, and they were aloft. The side doors stayed open, and the team trained their weapons on the forests below them.

The craft slowed when they reached the crash scene and hovered over it. The fires were small and scattered now. In the light of flare drones, men collected weapons and burned, charred body parts.

Tanizaki was watching Kayle out of the corner of his eyes. She thought she caught him appraising her body. He looked away.

Kayle smiled. *You're not going to get off that easy.* "Hideo, were there any survivors?" She pointed at the burning hulks of the gunship and the scorpion.

"Five KIA on impact. All the flight crew ejected from the gunship. We have collected two out of the three. The pilot went deeper into the woods, or he may have come out on the beach, or he's in the sea," he said. "We're going to keep up the search. Human pilots, as you know, are high-value resources."

"And what's the story on the scorpion?" Kayle asked.

"That's where things get confusing. During an ambush at our CP while we were still in the process of setting it up?"

"Yes?"

"Some Grand Design guys stole one of our scorpion APCs and re-covered two prisoners that we picked up on day one of our operations. We haven't found any traces of who was in the APC—alive or dead. Yet."

"You sound like you're composing your after-action report right now," Kayle said.

"I think I am. It's not a bad idea." He half-smiled.

Tanizaki here is not entirely sold on my story, she thought. *He has more than a cursory interest in me.*

The turbines whined, and they accelerated. Hideo leaned over close to her ear so she could hear him above the engines. "There's enough light now for us to swing low and recon over the forest and the coastline. We'll then meet up with three other gunships as we scout the citadel."

Kayle nodded, asking, "Did you manage to subdue the other Grand Design bases?"

"Yes. We did a lot of damage to their main base at Green Valley, and then we took the shuttle port at Crimson Camp, more or less intact. We are expanding it. Right now, it can only handle one dreadnought at a time. Unacceptable."

The navigator turned to speak to Tanizaki. "We have multiple targets moving up the cliff face about a click from here at three o'clock." He pointed to the screen in front of him. "They're using jet packs. I count five bogies trying to get to the parapets."

That leaves four of us unaccounted for, Kayle thought. *Nesh didn't make it. So it's probably just me, Rew, and Rent left outside the citadel.*

"Blue Tackle Leader, this is Baskins. I am closest to the targets and am moving in to engage now."

"Baskins' gunship will make short work of four troops in jetpacks," Tanizaki said. "Still, let's continue to search the area—there may be other GDC survivors around here."

In the bright light of the golden dawn, Kayle watched the other gunships close on the citadel. *Minerva, Brigid, Claire, they have no chance,* she thought.

A blinding flash of orange fire spewed out of the citadel with a colossal ripping sound, and the lead gunship disappeared.

"What the fuck was that?" Tanizaki exclaimed.

47

“DON'T LET YOUR VISIONS OF how much of the discovery fee could be yours—should the gold seam pay out—distract you. The prospector percentage share is great, but it could get us all killed,” Key said as he tried to dissuade Michelle and Meadows from entering. He could see it was going to be a difficult task. *They are getting all steamed up over the gold,* Key thought.

Wholly predictable, Baen said.

“There's an old corporate slogan that we all know and love,” Michelle said. “High risk, high reward. No risk, no reward.”

Largo tried to holocall Minerva again, to no avail. The call failed.

Reception this deep in the citadel could be a bit sketchy, Baen said.

“There should be another slogan that says, ‘stupid risk—no reward.’ Look, Michelle, if Baen is concerned, then I'm concerned,” Key said. “We're going back for reinforcements and to make proper preparations. That's a direct order.”

Michelle fidgeted with her prosthetic forearm and adjusted her kit while she considered her response. “You know, Commander, the corporate code of conduct has some specific clauses that might apply here,” Michelle said.

“Choose your next words carefully, Curvois,” Meadows warned.

“A commander's critical judgment or fitness for duty may be called into question. If so, the next most senior officer can countermand nonsensical orders and assume command with a two-thirds vote of the leadership team. I'm quoting directly from Section 9.” She turned away from Key and addressed Meadows directly. “Dr. Meadows, how many years of service do you have with the corporation? I have thirteen," Michelle said.

"Twelve years. But wait, Michelle, this is a gray area. I'm not sure you can evoke that clause in this situation," Meadows stammered.

"And why not, Meadows? His fitness can certainly be challenged. He is a recovering dope addict. A junkie throughout most of our time planet-side. He's been incapacitated by it for who knows how long? And then there's the even more compelling problem of his believing that his bracelet is a living organism. He takes orders from it! He's even given it a pet name, 'Baen.' Commander Largo is almost undoubtedly delusional at this stage. It's obvious."

"I am the one that gets to make that diagnosis, Michelle, not you. And for now, I withhold my judgment. Let's not proceed any further on this course." Meadows was firm.

"So disappointed in your opinion, Meadows. As the senior officer present, I want us to get this on the record. How do you vote on the question of Commander Largo's fitness for duty?"

Michelle is not going to let it go despite Meadows's best attempt to reason with her.

"I abstain."

No one said anything for a long moment.

Not much of a vote of confidence there, Key, Baen said.

But at least he didn't side with her—besides, much of what Michelle says is true, as you know. And maybe she's right. Perhaps I am unfit.

I know you do not believe that.

"I'm going in," Michelle said, pulling her visor down and readying her weapon.

"Then you go without me. And let the record show that Commander Largo has not been deemed unfit by the only medical officer present," Meadows said.

"I'm not afraid to go in alone," Michelle said. "Not when it goes against a guy who is taking orders from his wristwatch—from a chunk of metal."

Her contempt is now out in the open, Baen observed.

It was never very well hidden. Not from day one.

Why is that?

Some people just don't like me, strange as that may seem to you.

I do.

Nice to have the 'chunk of metal's' vote of confidence.

Explain that to me?

It's a joke.

So far, I do not understand any of your jokes.

No big deal. Most people don't. They're not very good.

She is likely to die if she goes in alone.

She's my responsibility. I'm not letting her go in alone. We're going in with her.

I advise we do not.

We are going in.

In that case. I protest that you are dragging us into a place where the chances of our survival are slim. The vent wraiths are lethal. I will stop offering your group any advice. You are countermanding most of my suggestions—so what is the point of trying to help you?

Is that a rhetorical question, Baen? If not, you can stop at any time.

Meadows looked at Largo expectantly.

Key nodded. "No one goes in alone. We stick together."

48

Kayle observed, "Whatever kind of gun that was—it's left plasma-like fire hanging in the air."

The pilot jerked the ship's yoke hard right to avoid the flaming debris.

Tanizaki said. "It must be some kind of lava cannon."

"It's turning to lock on our ship next, Hideo," Kayle said. "Better take her down on the deck."

"Blue Tackle leader. This is Blue Tackle Three, trying to approach from the north side and take out that gun."

Tanizaki's pilot had already seen the cannon swing toward them. He took the harpoon straight down over the ocean reef. Whitecap breakers were almost close enough to touch. The pilot asked Tanizaki, "We aborting the search mission?"

"Affirmative."

"Get the other ships out of here," Kayle whispered.

"Attention Blue Tackle Group, we are breaking off and returning to Crimson Camp," Tanizaki said, as the cannon erupted again and hit the distant motor pool. It went up in a torrent of lava, dirt, and debris.

"That gun has a range of over two kilometers at least. We need to move our base camp," Tanizaki realized.

"This is Blue Tackle Three. Approaching cannon. We—" A burst of static crackled over the comms.

"Blue Tackle Three down, Sarge," the pilot said. "Vanished from our screens."

"All remaining Blue Tackle team members, abort and return to the crimson base," Tanizaki ordered. "Please acknowledge."

"Blue Tackle Five. Copy that."

"That's it?" Kayle asked. "Only two ships remain—out of how many?"

"Six," Tanizaki replied, stunned. "I've lost most of my squadron," he muttered.

They looped back toward the beach and watched as salvo after salvo landed on their base camp. "The forward base is getting chewed up. We have room for eight troopers," Tanizaki said. "Let's land and help some of our people evacuate."

Zipping along at tree-branch level, the pilot made it hard for anyone to get a lock on their ship. They could see the smoke from three destroyed gunships littering the forest floor. The trees were on fire, and the conflagration was spreading. The motor pool and half a dozen hooches and bunkers were burning as they approached. The LZ held a drop ship taking on evacuees. Kayle saw an open space between three domed structures and pointed at it. "Can we land down there, Hideo?"

He nodded, "Don't see a lot of options. Let's sit down there and see if we can help them, Joe."

They reeled over the treetops. Kayle's stomach plunged, and she squeezed the arms of her seat. She thought Joe was going to dump it; the ship wobbled, the front end going one way, the back end going the other.

But Joe straightened it out, and so did the trees on either side of the old overgrown and rutted domes.

Kayle ventured one look back at the citadel. The walls gleamed red in the early morning sunlight. Ash fell like black snowflakes--the yellow sky blurred with greasy smoke from the scattered fires.

Another burst of lava fire erupted from the citadel. Another bunker blew up in the camp.

"You know, I was wrong about that cannon. It has a range of at least three kilometers," Kayle said.

"It's picking us apart right now," Tanizaki said. "I see no way to get to it. It's going to be a tough nut to crack."

"How can I assist you, Sergeant?" Kayle asked.

"I see your wings on your blouse. Are you checked out on an H9 Harpoon?"

"Yes. As it happens."

The cannon stitched the air again far to their right. A drop ship blew up, as shredded fragments fell into the forest fire.

"Come with me. There's a couple of harpoons concealed over this way. You can help evacuate our people."

Explosions thudded in the distance.

The ground vibrated from thunderous explosions.

"I should tell you about the mixed messages that are out there about you, Commander. Your disappearance and later command actions—and well, reactions too, for that matter," Tanizaki said as they slowed and walked through a grove of feathery trees.

"Oh? Such as?"

"Well, with all due respect, the very public, shall we say 'separation' from Grand Design. And your sudden elevation to the officer ranks at DC was slightly noticeable?"

"It was in a word, scandalous," Kayle said with a rakish smile.

"Yes, it was. Then you went to Raba. You strenuously advocated mitigating clone casualties in your planning discussions with Ross Lasker. It was overheard," Tanizaki shrugged.

"How do you come by this information, Sergeant? I am impressed with your breadth of detailed knowledge."

"I represent a far-flung well-connected information-sharing group of clones. We are all quite dissatisfied with our lot in life. And more than willing to make the sacrifices necessary to improve it."

"It seems that your organization crosses corporate lines?" Kayle asked.

"It crosses all lines; both intercorporate and interplanetary."

"My compassion for the clones is not all that special. Besides, you are all valued people. A lot of corporate assets are tied up in our clone battalions. I know more than a few people who share my views," Kayle said. "Why don't you tell me some rumors you've heard, and I can, in turn, tell you if they're accurate? Make it quick. We haven't much time."

For now, the lava cannon was silent. They could hear engines roaring to life as the DC ships began the evacuation.

Tanizaki considered her. His face was without expression.

"Start with what you think you know about what happened here on Gereon," Kayle suggested.

Tanizaki took a deep breath and continued. "The first rumor back from the battle was that you and Tyr Roba crash-landed the *Antares*. Salvaged part of the wreck. Then you somehow managed to escape the shipwreck with more than 100 clones intact. Our elite deck guards. You refused to abandon the ship or your clones."

"That's all accurate."

"Next, I heard from a highly placed contact. Said the entire senior leadership of the *Antares* fell under suspicion. Leaking secure data to GDC? And all of you suspended pending an investigation."

"Some of that is true," Kayle acknowledged.

"Then you and Tyr Roba went missing again for a while. And when you resurfaced? I know for a fact that Commander Peroni sent a TAC Squad to take you out. I was present at the ops briefing. I heard the orders. That squad was never heard from again." Tanizaki stared into her eyes.

Kayle returned his stare.

"But Peroni was acting on his own. That was an unsanctioned, rogue operation. So what I'm getting at is —you have a good reputation with the men-at-arms among the clone community. Many of us noncoms have been following your career with a great deal of interest. And then you fell into my lap." His tone was somber.

Reflexively, Kayle put her hand on the needler's hilt. Tanizaki noticed the gesture and raised an eyebrow.

"I had no idca, Sargc. And I'm not sure I deserve it," Kayle whispered. *What is he up to now*? she thought.

"Relax. I'm not here to confront you. I want to explain to you the lay of the land. Our clones on this Gereon mission are close to mutiny. Very close. You can help us. Allow me to give you some options."

"You trust me with something this secret, this sensitive—knowing what you know about me?" Kayle gasped.

"If not you, Commander, then we have no one," he grumbled. "First of all, we tire of being cannon fodder for Lasker. Second, we are far enough from his corporate reach here on Gereon to sever our contracts with him. End our employment, as it were, and create a life of freedom and dignity. Third, it's an empty planet for the most part—a planet that we could colonize."

"And then what do you do when he sentences you all to death? He will send whole divisions to take you out. Any other corporation would do the same."

"That is where you come in." And for the first time, she saw Tanizaki smile.

49

"ALLOW ME TO GO FIRST," Largo said, and he stepped into the foggy void. The same ambient light that exuded from the citadel walls upstairs was present here too. It made the fog a deep amber. Over his headphones, he heard Meadows say, "Largo, the fog is so thick I can't see you at all. How far in did you go?"

"A few steps. We will be dependent on our comms and night goggles—this stuff is damn near impenetrable. Come forward, both of you. We are looking for a stairwell."

"My lidar has a colossal circular cavity ahead of us about fifty meters in," Michelle said. "I read no heat signatures anywhere around this circular space."

The three of them made their way to a monumental arch. It framed a grand spiral staircase and appeared to be hewn from living rock. The vapor thinned out here, and they were able to see better.

"These walls look like the same material as the rest of the citadel," Meadows said.

Our construction over the previous ancient structure began here, Baen said.

Largo surveyed the stairs descending below them.

"Yet the stairwell seems to be older—of more profound antiquity. It looks different enough to be from another culture. The scale of this thing is impressive. Twenty men could fit on each step."

"My lidar is glitching. I can't get a decent reading to any depth on the stairwell. Something is interfering. Something in the rock, I'm guessing," Michelle said.

They descended the stairs with Key leading and Meadows at the back.

"Team, you know we should go back and get more people," Largo said.

"Agreed," Meadows said. "Let's pause here and come back with more force."

Michelle grunted and sighed, "Can we please go down a few more steps? Don't you feel that change in the temperature gradient? It's definitely getting warmer as we descend. The gold seam could be ahead of us."

"Or it could be a kilometer deeper," Meadows said. "Michelle, without any functioning lidar, I'm reluctant. Only the three of us here—descending into a gloomy stairwell built by an unknown culture? Time to call a halt and make a tactical withdrawal."

"Largo, what does your bracelet say?" Michelle asked. "I mean, I know it's rubbish, but you say it has these sentient abilities, so—"

Largo opened his mouth to reply. And then he saw movement down below, through the gloom in the well. In the shadows, it was coming up fast—whatever it was. It made a low grumbling sound, rising in pitch, to an ear-shattering shriek.

"What is that?" Michelle shouted.

Baen spoke to Key. *That would be a vent wraith. They never attack solo.*

The wraith was now right in front of him. Its razor claws hit his helmet visor and knocked him back two steps. And then it was on Michelle, who was standing right behind Key.

As he started to crumble—and fall backward into the empty space below him, he thought, *This is going to be painful.* There was no dread in the thought; it was a simple acknowledgment of reality.

50

KAYLE LEANED BACK IN THE captain's chair. Night had fallen, and the clouds drifted lower. No stars were visible. She got up, went out, and finished loading her harpoon with evacuees, then followed Tanizaki to the former GDC base at Camp Crimson. The base expansion and improvement activities ceased as large numbers of DC evacuees and equipment were off-loaded. Removing her helmet and shaking out her hair, Kayle waited while Tanizaki walked across the flight line toward her. His expression was impassive as he asked, "You ready to give this a shot?"

"Do I stay armed for my meeting with Peroni?"

"Yes. Unless Peroni's guards ask you to disarm. I have arranged for some friendlies to be in the room with us, just in case."

The craters by the command post, the burned and scarred walls, and the destroyed interceptors showed that GDC had put up a strong defense. About fifty Grand Design personnel were held in a corral by the flight line. They were abjectly milling around in clumps or lying in the shade of flimsy makeshift shelters.

"Are those all GDC clones? Any officers get captured here?" Kayle asked him.

Tanizaki frowned and nodded. "All clones. Treated like cattle, of course," His disgust was palpable. "The captured officers have already been taken to that ship up there, the *Aragon*." He pointed to the nearest of the two dreadnoughts hanging over the horizon in suborbit. "All prisoners will be taken by an interceptor bound for Raba later today. Once there, our expert interrogators will amuse themselves questioning them."

"Let's get on with it, Sarge," Kayle said.

"The interview with Peroni is a hazardous, necessary next step," he said.

They heard a low rumble in the morning sky above them, and an elegant, beautiful mega-yacht appeared suspended in the pink and blue clouds.

"Now that's a beautiful ship," Kayle said.

"That's the *Azure Tropea*, it's Ross Lasker's yacht," Tanizaki said. "The most expensive opulent yacht ever made. It's his one known vice."

"Well, it's a beautiful vice. Is this a surprise visit?"

"Yes. Lasker was last on Raba with no announced plans for leaving it."

"Does this impact our plans?"

"Not the basic outline, but I don't know about assembling my people on such short notice. He staffs that yacht with loyal clones who are pretty much hermetically sealed off from my organization."

"I will see if he accepts my holocall. That might give us an idea of what to expect," Kayle said.

"Are you sure about that?"

"Not at all. But Lasker knows that in making such a grand entrance on Gereon if I were innocent of his suspicions—I would be one of the first people to call him."

"It might work. And it could help short-circuit any devious plans Peroni might have in mind for you."

At this point, of course I don't trust anyone in Lasker's entire organization.

She punched up Lasker's holo, and he answered immediately. His image was stoic.

Kayle bowed and said, "Good morning, Ross. You are up in that yacht above me, right?"

He nodded. "Meet me at the ops center at our new spaceport in one hour, Korban. We have some things that need sorting, you and I. Lasker out."

"Well, he didn't offer me the use of his portal, but that could be because he's coming here anyway," Kayle said.

"To do what, I wonder?"

"If he wants me dead, he knows where I am, so we'll know in a few minutes one way or the other."

51

L ARGO HAD HIS NEEDLER OUT, but stumbled and dropped it. Taking two faltering steps backward, trying to stop his fall, his feet stepped into—air. There was no step there, no step below that either. His legs gave way, and he fell straight back. A loud buzzing sound filled his ears.

He experienced a hot numbness; his insides felt stretched and rigid. He sensed a heated breath brush past his ears. He glimpsed the distant domed roof overhead. Shadowy figures flitted about in the gloom as he continued to fall.

A lava rifle discharged above him in a blazing flash—echoing down the stairwell. He was blind and deaf.

Something or someone hurtled past him, careening down the stone stairs. It rattled and clattered as it fell.

Largo hit a stone step, landed on his ribs first, with a skeletal crack, and flipped over. In slow motion like a film replay—up into the air again.

His right shoulder hit the next stair, and he was knocked sideways, fell into empty space—until his right knee clubbed something—substantial. His forehead struck something else. He was in the air again, bounced hard on the lower steps, and rolled into something fleshy and wet. He couldn't move.

Am I paralyzed?

No. You are stunned. You need to lie here motionless and wait for the wraiths to leave.

I need to get help. Need to help Michelle and Meadows.

No. You cannot. Michelle and Meadows are beyond help. You are lying on top of their corpses. They broke your fall. Do not move, and the wraiths may ignore us. I will tell you when they have left the area. We are very close to the grotto and safety.

<hr>

He awoke with a start. An electric shot had passed through his body.

Apologies for startling you. It is time to go. The wraiths have returned to the volcano.

Did you put me to sleep, Baen?

Yes. It seemed to be the best—

Going forward, do not put me to sleep without my permission. Likewise, don't shock me awake.

What if such decisions keep us safe?

Ask for permission from here on out. I tire of your manipulations, Baen.

I am not manipulating you.

How do you see what all is around us Baen?

I use your eyes.

My eyes?

Yes. Your eyes, but not your vision.

Largo turned on his helmet spotlight. The gloom in the depths of the stairwell was thick. He felt a nauseated itch in the back of his throat as he respectfully extracted himself from the pileup of his two dead and broken colleagues. He carried Michelle over to a wide area in the stairwell and stretched her shattered body out. She lay on her back now with her arms crossed. He washed the blood from her face. He found a blanket in her backpack and covered her up. Then he laid Meadows down next to her and did the same for him.

Baen said, *we need to keep moving. The wraiths could return at any moment.*

Your culture does not have respect for the dead?

Not at the risk of living. No, we do not. The grotto is down there. If we get through the hatch, we should be safe for a while.

Largo collected his needle, and one of the lava rifles. He bowed his head and said to their bodies, "I'm sorry. Sorry I wasn't a good enough leader or a better colleague. Sorry I couldn't stop this from happening. I promise you this—I won't let anything like this happen ever again. Not to anyone."

Largo placed his wrist in the space provided, and the last hatch swung sideways, revealing a long ladder. A warm puff of air wafted up into his face. It smelled of spice, saltwater, and something like eucalyptus.

This must be the grotto, he thought.

Prepare yourself to see sights exceeding all your experiences. To see things beyond your dreams and imagination.

Is there an exit somewhere down there?

Not that I know of, the only way out is the way we came in.

But the vent wraiths will still be hanging around, won't they?

There used to be weapons down here that can control them. Likely, there are still some down in the vault.

He reached the bottom of the ladder.

The large grotto arches opened on to crystallized stalactites with reddish sapphire-like gems. They provided a strange light, glimmering and reflecting off a turquoise river running along the edges of the walls. An iridescent amber glow reflected off the surface of the water. The gemstone lights dappled across the stalactites and the river.

Strips of luminescent orange-and-red fungus glowed in the rock seams, and bands of minerals flexed and glistened. The stalactite's crystals and rounded stone columns created an eerie beauty. It all formed an otherworldly illumination in the grotto.

Massive cables and thick conduits snaked around the yellow walls and across the ceiling's crystals. Small steam clouds emitted from some massive cable intersections. Ahead, further in the cave, clouds of steam roiled and obscured the walls.

Who made all this stuff, Baen? All these cables and machinery?

It was all made long ago by beings we call Losantos—it means ancient ones in our language.

A low rumbling whine echoed through the walls, rising to a crescendo as it shook the dust off the ceiling before it died down.

Someone has fired the lava cannon. I am impressed that your people quickly took account of its complexities and decided to use it.

Another series of thunderous shots echoed in the grotto. One after another. The natural lighting reflected and vibrated with each eruption.

They've decided to use the hell out of it. It must be Austen Nesh and his crew. We have to be under attack.

I am unconcerned. The citadel is impregnable.

Is that so? Then how did it fall all those years ago?

In a word, betrayal. I do not have all the details. My previous partner, Nag Hamler, was killed in the opening attack.

Partner? Is that how you view this relationship?

How would you describe it?

If it's a partnership, I'm the junior member.

We need to keep moving. The best discoveries are still ahead of you. As an aside, you need to know that the river is paved with rounded gold nuggets. Gold cobbles extend from below the surface all the way down to the basalt bedrock.

So how thick is the gold cobble deposit, Baen?

In many places, it seems to keep going. In the thinnest sections, we measured it at over 100 meters thick.

Key was too stunned to respond other than to think, that's impossible.

You are beyond amazed and shocked, and I understand. That was our first reaction too. Still, I can assure you that it is that colossal. We never found a gold deposit anywhere in the galaxy as extensive as the one you are standing in right now. Gereon's earthquakes and the river erosion left this gold here millennia ago. You could power a vast fleet of star cruisers with the gold underneath your feet in this little space around us. And the river goes on for forty kilometers.

52

PERONI SAT WITH HIS DIRECT reports at a table in the small upstairs conference room. He was at one end, and Kayle was at the other. Tanizaki sat in a chair by the window, his helmet on the floor beside him. Furth, the XO, stood facing them, a short-barreled PSG slung from his shoulder and a needler on his belt. Clone NCOs and support personnel crowded into the room. They had stopped their reorganizing and cleanup work to have this meeting with Kayle. Everyone in the room carried weapons. A counterattack by Grand Design was still a possibility.

"You did well, Tanizaki," Peroni commended, "by sending us the message about finding Kayle, and in the fighting and the evacuation. I'll see you are rewarded. Ross Lasker will be here shortly, and I will mention your achievements to him."

Tanizaki smiled briefly. "Thank you, sir. But I need to point out that much of what we completed could not have been done without Commander Korban."

Peroni looked into Kayle's eyes. She met his unblinking stare. "Ah, yes, imagine our surprise that you were not only alive and well, Kayle, but also involved in our evacuation this morning from the citadel. Were you aware, Korban, that we have been searching for you since we landed planet-side?"

"I had hoped for rescue. But I thought we might not have the bandwidth to look for me for a while," she replied "Would it surprise you to know that we lost the entire crew of one of our drop ships during our search for you? A tactical crew? Nine men vanished."

"That is a regrettable loss. But a TAC crew? Involved in search and rescue?" Kayle raised an eyebrow.

Peroni studied her face. She met his gaze. The tension in the room was palpable as no one dared to speak.

"Where is our ace pilot—Captain Brigid Strugatsky? She was with you at your last known locality. Before you disappeared off our screens again." Peroni's eyes narrowed to slits.

Of course, he sees right through my bullshit. DC commanders are neither naïve nor are they stupid.

Kayle improvised. "We were together until a few minutes before I linked up with Tanizaki. In the chaos of the lava cannon attack, we were separated. I was looking for her by the forward CP. You haven't seen her yet?"

They were interrupted by an orderly who walked over to Peroni and whispered something to him. Peroni stood and stretched with exaggerated calmness. "The boss is here. Just landed. He wants me to act on a couple of things before he gets here—starting with this." He leveled his pistol at Kayle. "Commander Korban, you are under arrest by the direct order of Dr. Ross Lasker, CEO of Dyeus Corporation. Place your weapons on the table, please."

53

L ARGO SAW THAT MISTY CLOUDS obscured the roof high above him. The ambient light ebbed and flowed as he rounded a corner. He immediately saw the first statue carved from a massive stone column. The now-familiar serpent-and-egg icon, nine meters high—adorned in gold lattices. The snake had hefty red sapphires for eyes. In the flickering light, the snake looked to be alive, writhing, and coiling around the egg.

Would it surprise you to know that we had archaeologists—we Shanges? Baen asked.

Not at all. Any advanced culture would want to learn about the past. And the history of other cultures that they have contacted.

The Losantos created this egg-and-snake statue in front of us. This is where we first encountered their iconography—which we eventually adopted and refined. Our archaeologists believe this is the most ancient part of the grotto complex. Estimated to be 27,000 years old.

It is beyond beautiful. The intricacy of the lattice, the perfect sapphire jewels—exquisite. It looks almost alive. Key was practically moved to tears by the beauty of it all.

Baen acknowledged the reaction as he allowed Key to appreciate it undisturbed for a minute before intruding back into his mind.

Now from here—in the space behind this sculpture is where we first began our own excavations and enhancements. The next door leads to some of the best work ever created by Shanges architects, artisans, and engineers. The entry is straight ahead in the darkness. You will need to increase the illumination of your helmet lights.

Largo adjusted the light intensity for 360 degrees. A narrow tunnel ran straight as a rifle shot for approximately 200 meters. It ended at a large arched glass door.

When we get into the next series of chambers, you have a choice. Would you like to see our cloning laboratory or the prosthetics workshop first?

The clone lab. What else is back this way?

A vast complex is back here. We once had a hall for full-term clones ready for activation and a network operations center (our headquarters). The gold drill operations armatures and geothermal monitoring stations are all in the NOC. Our gold bullion storage vault was next. Beyond that is a hyperbaric medicine lab with healing tanks. That lab held several cryopreservation beds for intense healing and tissue preservation.

I want to see the med labs as soon as possible. Will you be able to help us learn about your medical technology?

Of course. It is in our best interests that you become well-versed in perpetuating our joint survival. I am surprised and yet delighted that you did not want to see the bullion room first. Most humans would go immediately to that, I would think. At the same time—somehow—I am not surprised that you have a different value system than most of your brethren.

So, Baen, is that everything that's behind the door? And is that the last door to the whole complex?

Yes. This is the final door. There is the room that once functioned as Mesh Trouter's private apartment off the med labs. Mesh often worked down here around the clock—kept irregular hours.

Trouter—was he—is he—a human or a Shanges? Key asked.

A bit of both species as the result of some of his more controversial DNA experiments.

Please explain, Baen.

He was born a shanges, but I will reveal his secrets behind all the closed doors. Give me enough time to do so.

Largo opened the door at the end of the hall and entered. It was an architecture identical to that of the citadel above them.

Yes, you can tell that this was built by your people, Baen.

I am understandably proud of it—except for one section.

What section is that?

The dungeon. I hope no prisoners were left chained to the walls. Otherwise...

Otherwise what?

We could see something quite...unpleasant.

A sudden electric shock from the bracelet made Largo's hair stand on end.

What the fuck was that Baen?

I am not sure. It seems quite unlikely that it could be what it identifies itself as.

And what's that?

Mesh Trouter's 'bracelet'...my opposite number on his wrist?

Largo tried to process what Baen had told him. *Mesh Trouter is around here somewhere?*

I do not see how. It must be a false reading.

And how often do you have those?

Never have I had one. This is unusual. Something is amiss. I only read the interface and not Mesh Trouter's consciousness.

Please explain?

That may not be possible. Our languages do not seem compatible enough to be able to explain to you what a pengo is.

A pengo?

It is what you and I construct. I am you, and you are me? Make sense?

"I am he as you are he as you are me. And we are all together?"

What? No. Not quite that.

That's an obscure Beatles reference.

I see.

No, you don't.

No, I don't.

So, okay. You can't explain what exactly you and I are. Now, are you also saying that right now, you can detect Trouter's bracelet...but no Mesh?

Not in those specific words, but more or less. Yes.

Well, let's do a quick tour of Trouter's Dreadful Laboratories of Horror and go find this bracelet.

Please explain.

A bad joke. And what it lacks in humor it makes up for in its obscurity.

54

EVERYONE IN THE ROOM FROZE and waited for Kayle's response. To her left, Tanizaki stood by the window. He exchanged an expression with her that said, 'your call.' Other clone troopers, lounging along the wall, stiffened and watched Tanizaki to see what he would do.

Peroni, standing at the head of the table, had not taken his eyes off Kayle since she entered the room. He looked to have an itchy trigger finger. Glowered at her. Three captains sat to his left, drinking Nasheed brandy. On Peroni's right, two more officers were smoking Havanas. Standing behind everyone was a towering bald man built like a refrigerator with arms and legs like tree trunks.

I know him that's Maga Råde, the executioner, Kayle thought. *Peroni wants me dead right now. But if I resist—it will cause a bloodbath. All Peroni ever wanted is to kill me.* Kayle suppressed a laugh.

"Are you amused by something, Korban?" Peroni asked, moving his chair as he seated himself. He forced the captains next to him to clear out space for his cushy armchair. Everyone else was forced to sit in the usual conference room chairs.

"You so want to kill me, don't you, Peroni?" Kayle gave him a raffish smile, stood up, and with exaggerated calmness, removed her pistol and placed it on the table in front of her.

He pointed at the needle holstered on her belt. "Your reputation with the needle precedes you. Tanizaki—remove that thing from her waist and then slap the clamps on her wrists."

She averted her eyes from Tanizaki's so that he would not misunderstand her intent.

As if I know what to do here, she thought. Let's face it. I am pretty much fucked.

"You are acting on Lasker's orders—is that right?" she asked, stalling for time.

"Surprised? I've been telling him for some time that you were one of the double agents. It had to be you. You had everybody fooled but me. But I was wrong about one thing—you weren't a double agent. You were a triple. A nice trick, that."

Tanizaki had taken her needle now and remained standing a bit behind her. He fiddled with the cuffs but did not put them on her.

"Thank you for the kudos." Kayle made an elaborate mocking bow.

"So you don't deny it?" Peroni asked.

"Not much point in doing that now, is there?"

In the hallway, a guard said, "Attention! CEO on deck!" And Ross Lasker flounced into the room from the doorway to her left.

Kayle did a double-take as Lasker entered, followed by his loyalist retinue. Dressed in formal clothes—black riding boots and breeches with a broad purple stripe. He also wore a crimson-and-gold armored breastplate with the Dyeus logo emblazoned on it. A black half-cape lined in ermine and fastened with an elaborate gold chain completed the look. He resembled a nineteenth-century Russian tsar. The soldiers all snapped to attention.

It looks like I misread him. Lasker seems to go from one extreme to the other when it comes to sartorial splendor, she thought.

Peroni stood and vacated his chair.

The room became silent as Lasker pulled up the big chair and sprawled in it. Draping his left leg over the armrest, he gave Kayle his best faux smile. "As you were, gentlemen. Kayle Korban. I wish I could say it is good to see you." He sighed loudly.

Kayle gave him a regal bow. "Honored that you dressed up for the occasion, Ross."

He immediately frowned at her overt and disrespectful familiarity, and Kayle knew she had struck a nerve. Then he grimaced and waved his hand. "Try to show some respect, Korban. This has been the formal uniform for DC CEOs for the last two centuries. It is appropriate for solemn ceremonial occasions. Like this one."

"I had no idea that this was such an occasion. Should I feel privileged? If so, I think I may be under-dressed."

"Oh, don't worry about that. We have the red robes of atonement ready for you." He snapped his fingers, and one of the men in his retinue emerged from the group behind him. He placed an elaborate wooden case on the table in front of Lasker. The clone then unfastened the lid and put the robes on the conference table.

"And here they are, Korban. Tailored to your exact measurements. I'm afraid you will have to undress here. You cannot be trusted alone. We gentlemen will avert our eyes. As you know, the situation requires that you strip down to your inner-wear."

So I am to be executed. Not much time to do anything. And still, the numbers aren't favorable, hopeless in fact. So many people will die right now if I try anything. And then there's the insurmountable problem of being unarmed...but if I were to lunge and arch, pivot spring to the table—maybe?

"Do I get to say anything in my defense?" Kayle asked.

Might as well give it a shot since it's my last chance.

"What could you have to say?"

"Only that you, Lasker, are a genocidal murdering rapist. You and your fancy uniform are drenched in blood. The casual mass killer of the Nasheed people. Countless clones and people died and continue to die in your corporation—daily, you don't—"

Peroni stood up and slammed the table with his fist. "Silence! That is enough. Guards, remove her armor and her uniform, then drape her in these robes." The guards looked at each other, reluctant to approach Kayle. "Bitch. I'll slag you where you stand." Peroni took a step toward her.

Lasker, unmoved, held up his hand. "Wait. Hold up for a second, Peroni. What was that reference you made to the Nasheed, Korban? I am more than a little intrigued."

"You know that you and your family created the Nasheed diaspora, even if it was covered up by the council. You know what you did."

Behind her, she felt someone tug at her belt.

That has to be Tanizaki...is that my needle in my back pocket? Or is Tanizaki just glad to see me? Kayle smiled despite herself.

"There's that grin again…I will wipe it off your soon-to-be-dead face now," Peroni said as he walked around the table with his fist cocked. Kayle didn't move a muscle.

In a whisper, Lasker said, "Hold."

"Sir. This woman has proven to be a danger and risk to the corporation for months. With all due respect—we need to finish this business now." Peroni was fighting to control his emotions. Fighting and losing.

"So, I have an idea. Kayle, you suggest that I do not care about my clones. About my employees? The truth is, I am committed to their health and happiness. And their entertainment. Peroni. Korban. You two will engage in the ancient ritual of Vindictae. It has not been invoked in a century. Still, it could be a great time to reinstate the tradition. Besides, it should be entertaining for all of us."

I wanted a chance, and here it is. Kayle smiled and bowed to Lasker. "As you wish."

"Smile while you still can, Nasheed whore," Peroni whispered.

55

T HE HALL OF EMBRYOS HAD an antechamber as its entry. A coat rack and changing rooms lined the left wall. Dusty lab coats hung from the shelf. A decontamination hall led to the actual incubator cells. An expansive wall monitors to the right showed that every cubicle had a full stage embryo, and every light was green.

How is it possible that they are ready for the next stage of development? Baen asked.

They have been left here like this for two centuries. Largo asked.

No, someone has to have been at work here recently. That is the only explanation. Everything is powered by geothermal energy, and all nutrient levels seem well-maintained. Someone with sophisticated operational knowledge is behind this.

What species are these embryos from? Largo asked.

Impossible to tell at this stage without analyzing the data further.

How many embryos can be manufactured in total in this lab?

Over 500. I am beyond surprised.

Largo suggested, *Let's skip the prosthetics lab for now. We need to get moving and check the next stage clone lab. Something is definitely awry here, Baen. Something strange.*

Head out the rear door. In the next stage, the breeding labs are not far ahead of us.

His footsteps resounded, amplified in the deserted corridor. Polished limestone floors. White walls. Subdued ambient light. A hall extended fifty meters to the left of the door and another fifty meters to the right. On both sides were more entryways, all closed.

He finally came to a vast red sandstone-paved foyer flanked by statues and chest-high incense burners. It was lit with perpetual blue flames that made the statues' shadows dance and sway in the blue lights.

Who are these statues?

The Savanes Magisterios. A long line of great Shanges sages. Mesh Trouter was born as a scion of these magi. Each one has left essential knowledge about the mysteries of the universe to their direct descendants.

An intersecting tubular hall began to his left. It had been augured at least 400 meters into the bedrock straight ahead. A long row of doors waited on each side of the burrowed-out hall.

Our drill made this passageway. The breeding places are inside of these doors, Baen said.

Largo opened the first door and walked past row after row of sealed incubators. The white sanitary medical lights emitted a low whitish glow. It ended in the next antechamber. Footsteps echoing, he climbed up a steep ramp. Below him, in a sunken hallway, the spaces were packed—filled with fully grown alien clones. Each was encased in its own lozenge-shaped transparent case.

The ensoresh! They have taken over our lab! We must destroy them. We must get to the control room, and you must push down the red execution lever on the central console. Please do it now, Key.

The seeming endless assembly line of alien clones below him brought him up short. Largo stopped in his tracks. He struggled to make sense of what he was looking at. The velveteen antler nubs on the assorted male specimens shocked him into immediate recognition. They moved like sleeping caterpillars in their cloudy cocoons. A dormant army of the ensoresh.

Baen, these antler people live in the woods right outside our citadel. These are what you call the ensoresh? Based on our reconnaissance patrols, there are likely thousands of them in the woods. Thousands more beyond that.

Largo, I do not understand what has happened here. It feels ominous.

We're skipping the rest of this complex for now. Show me the way to Mesh Trouter's chambers. We need to see if we can somehow communicate with his bracelet.

Yes. You may be right. That is the only place we can go to find out what has happened. I received one solitary message from Trouter's bracelet. It ran as follows: 'I tired of building killing machines...'

That's all?

Yes. After that, it was silent.

56

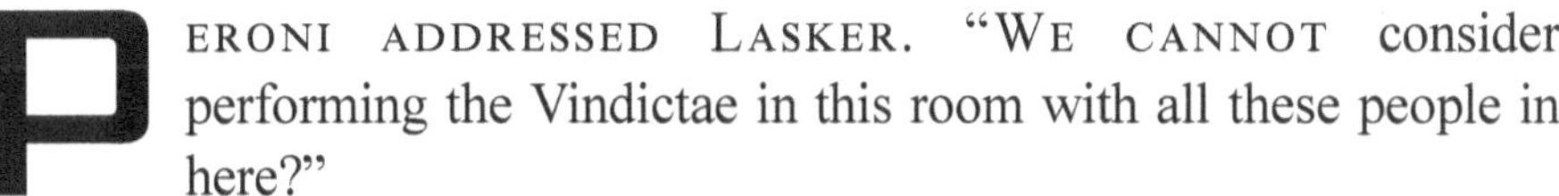

ERONI ADDRESSED LASKER. "WE CANNOT consider performing the Vindictae in this room with all these people in here?"

We will, Peroni, Kayle thought.

Lasker grinned. "Commander Korban is ready to go right now. Such fire! Such malice! I agree these quarters would be impossible to host the requisite pomp and ritual. We will have to create a large enough space outside on the flight line."

Behind her back, Tanizaki pressed her needler into her right hand. She could not keep from smiling.

Several things happened at once.

Her smiling face infuriated Peroni. Pistol in hand, he started to move in her direction again.

At that, Kayle lunged forward onto the edge of the table and back-flipped to the other side of it. The clones brought their weapons to the ready. Peroni stood between her and Lasker—whose shocked eyes were worth the price of admission.

I'm coming for you, killer.

She had her needler out now—missing Peroni as he dodged clear. But she grabbed his neck with her left hand as he went by. PSGs roared in the room as clones and bodyguards opened fire on each other. The shots roared and ricocheted against the walls, and the windows shattered. Clouds of dust and debris swept the room. The blazing light of dozens of PSGs confined to a small space blinded everyone.

Bodies began to fall. Kayle lost her balance a bit as she dodged a dying bodyguard collapsing to his knees.

She felt a burning wound in her left shoulder but pressed on. Peroni was bringing his pistol toward her head—she ignored the pain. They both started falling from the force of her attack. She put her needle through his neck, and Peroni went limp.

She was halfway under the table now, with the cushy armchair somehow lying across her chest. Three of Lasker's bodyguards lay dead between her and the door.

No Lasker. Must get up and kill him if it's the last thing I do in this life.

The shooting halted as a fire burned by the windows—spreading.

About time to get the hell out of here. The place will be incinerated.

A meaty hand appeared above her face and grabbed the back of the unwieldy chair—tossing it aside like it was nothing. Tanizaki's smiling face loomed over hers. "Commander, we need to be going. How's the shoulder?"

"I'm in a bit of mild shock—can't feel it yet. Lasker. Where's Lasker?"

He shook his head. "Got away. Heading for his yacht. Can catch him if we hurry." He turned and shot a hussar blocking the doorway. He had time to wound another one when a plasma bomb hit the wall outside and created a flaming gap.

"Through there," Kayle said, and pushed Tanizaki toward the shattered wall. Together, they leaped through the new exit space. The adrenaline was running full bore.

They were out in the open, and Kayle had a clear view of the chaos on the LZ for a second before the drifting clouds of smoke obscured everything. A large-bore cluster cannon began firing somewhere on the tarmac. It tore craters out of the ground immediately in front of them. Tanizaki grabbed her shoulder, and they both dove into a still-smoking hole. A concussion round landed nearby—too close for comfort. Her nose began bleeding.

Her training kicked in.

Now Kayle could smell burning flesh, blood, and chemical smoke, as electricity scorched the air around her.

Kayle poked her head up and saw Lasker's bodyguards backing away. They were laying down covering fire as they tried to make their way to his luxury launch. They were at least 150 meters away from her.

A clone NCO helped her up. Tanizaki still lay in the crater, unconscious but otherwise unharmed as far as she could tell.

Two hundred highly trained and well-armed hussars established a defensive perimeter around Lasker's launch. They had two cluster cannons leveling everything in sight.

To her left, she spotted an untouched hoverbike lying on its side and sprinted to it. She planted a cryo-grenade on the fuselage—right on top of the fuel tank. She had thirty seconds before her bike, her body, and anything in a ten-meter radius would be vaporized.

Kayle gunned the bike upward in a near eighty-degree leap. She arced it toward the launch as the surrounding air filled with lethal electricity. Lead and flechettes tore into the bike and her armor, but now Kayle was right above Lasker's shuttle. She shut off the motor and laid the bike down on the surface of the launch. Then she somersaulted off the roof and sprinted away with every last ounce of energy she could muster.

The explosion blew Kayle up in the air. She saw the flaming wreck falling on her in slow motion.

I'm dead—but so is—.

57

L ARGO SPRINTED TO THE LARGE oak doors at the end of the hall and was surprised they were unlocked. *No fancy security protocols here.*

This is where Trouter roamed, and if anyone could get this far, he reasoned they probably belonged here. It is the sanctum sanctorum.

Largo entered the foyer. The walls were decorated in smooth and elegant geometric motifs consisting of caramel-colored wood inlaid with silver-and-gold trim. Subdued pale green stained-glass lamps illuminated the chamber.

I like this style, the Arts Décoratifs, or the art-deco movement of early twentieth-century France. It became famous worldwide.

It also became popular among our culture about 100 standard years ago. Had quite a revival, I must say. Post-Classic Shanges Deco, we call it.

So how did the Shanges discover art-deco?

As with so many other things, Trouter introduced it to us. One of his roles in our culture was often that of the influencer.

That begs the question, Baen…

Soon. Soon you will understand it.

Off the foyer, he saw a short hallway with coat racks and hat shelves flanking it on both sides. All kinds of jackets and coats hung from hooks.

I recognize many earth styles, Baen, a trench coat, a safari jacket, all sorts of leather coats, cashmere blazers, raglans, and cardigans. Some spangly spongy stuff I've never seen before. Why did Trouter have such a large and diverse wardrobe?

He was always something of a clotheshorse, and he made many trips to terra-based planets in different timelines. Let us move into the great room, shall we?

Largo was taken aback. It was incongruous. The room he entered was vast and ornate. Wainscoting panels of luxurious blond woods covered the walls to a height of two meters. There were hardwood floors, comfortable leather couches and lounges, geometric and Persian rugs scattered across the floor, and Japanese silk screens. It was a hodgepodge of blended late-cycle earth-terra styles that somehow worked together to create a feeling of immense solitude. Back behind the screens lay a large glass sarcophagus.

Trouter is in that long glass rejuvenating tank, Baen said.

Trouter's body was difficult to see underneath the swirling mists. A dark-gray curdled gel encased it. He looked to be almost seven feet tall, old, and strange. Dark blue eyelids were set deep into bony circles. *One hundred years old, at least—or maybe more,* Key thought.

He had a longish bald skull with a high vaulted shape; it resembled a pockmarked lunar landscape. A full mouth with thin blue lips curved in a cruel snarl.

He looks older than dirt. How old is he, Baen?

His physical age is about 500 of your standard years. But he has only been active for about twenty percent of those years. The bulk of his time, alas, has been spent in this rejuvenating tank.

Trouter wore shorts made of some synthetic material attached to a catheter-like tube. His chest was crisscrossed with old and recent scars. Some surgical, others from combat. Largo felt astonished and repulsed as he stared down into the rejuvenating tank.

Baen, what color should the gel be? Largo asked.

It should be transparent. Clear. I am going to open up a channel to his bracelet; we will call it 'Mesh' for the time being. I will provide a direct translation of his thoughts for you, Key.

Mesh, what can we do to help you? Baen asked.

You are only an echo of a dream within my dream.

Is it the crystals? Do they need to be replaced?

Not much longer. I could not be more ready.

Ready for what?

Ready to die. I have overstayed my welcome on this mortal coil. Who are you? Why do you disturb my passing?

It is the Baen entity. I once served Zed as you serve Trouter.

But how is this possible? Zed died in the Ensoresh War 200 years ago.

I was revitalized by a human.

A human? This is some ghoulish trick of my fractured brain. Let me die in peace. Begone, Baen, who is not Baen!

Largo, I fear Trouter is quite insane and nearly dead. Alas, if he dies, so much knowledge dies with him.

Baen, can you communicate directly with his bracelet, bypassing Trouter's brain? Possibly download his memory into one of these devices around here. Preserving his knowledge?

It is possible that it could be backed up in our minds. It might be worth the risk. But you should know that you and I might inherit the insanity along with Trouter's genius. I cannot recommend it.

A mind merges into another mind? I can't say I'm interested in experimenting on myself to that extent. Give me another option.

Cravitix crystals. If we can replenish the rejuvenating gems, we may be able to stabilize his vital signs. If he dies, there is a possibility of preserving his brain in a full-body prosthetic suit. Still, we would need trained Shanges surgeons to accomplish that. And they are long gone from this planet. We would have to go to the nearest Shanges world; probably Afsa is the closest one. Also, the possibility of brain damage would always be high in such a delicate procedure. It used to have a 10 percent survival rate at best.

Where would we find the crystals?

There is a large locker in his workshop on the other side of that door. If it is empty, we would have to go directly to the source.

And that is?

The Dragoo—the giant cave bats. Crystals are pressurized and chemically altered, made from their feces.

So I would have to fight those things at home in their caves and retrieve their shit?

Yes, it is a less than optimal solution.

Let's look in that locker in the workshop.

Four short, squat perspex canisters containing cravitix crystals filled the left side of the locker. On the right side was a velvet-covered box. Largo opened it and was stunned to see about a dozen gold bracelets like his carefully stored away.

Who are these intended for, I wonder? Baen asked.

Are four canisters going to be enough, Baen?

Yes. We need only one for now.

Show me where and how we put it together.

58

MINERVA STOOD IN HER COMMAND room in the citadel, with Rent and Claire in chairs by the conference table. Lang stood next to her as she opened up a teleportal channel with her bracelet. An opening crackled and sizzled in the air in front of them. Instantly, Minerva was looking live into a scene of devastation. The burning flight line at Camp Crimson, in all its fiery carnage. Pieces of machinery burned in heaps around Kayle's smoldering body. Tossed and knotted bodies in DC uniforms lay in a pile around her, as smoke and ashes swirled on the cratered tarmac. A thin wisp of smoke issued from a long crack in her perspex faceplate.

Claire grabbed Minerva's shoulder. She used it to leverage a leap through the portal and into the flaming wreckage.

"Claire don't—" Minerva reached to stop her, but she was too sluggish. An explosion started, and a new blaze flared up near Claire as she grabbed Kayle.

In a flash, she held Kayle in her arms. She turned and stretched out her hand to Minerva. Minerva pulled them both through her portal and into the relative safety of the citadel.

"Claire, you have no idea how risky that was," Minerva said, patting out the flames emerging from Claire's jacket. Emi threw a pitcher of water on the tiny fires.

Claire ignored Minerva's comment. "Kayle has a faint pulse, I need to get her into a med sphere now." With that, she carried Kayle toward the downstairs medlab. "Please bring Rew and Emi to me for evaluations and possible treatment as soon as possible."

Minerva surveyed the rest of her upstairs crew. "Right now, we can't afford to search for Rent or even recover Austen's body." She looked downcast at the drone screen displays. Sighing, she said, "If we had enough troops! We could take advantage of DCs extreme disarray right at this moment. Push our advantage and drive them off the face of Gereon."

Manaka stood and patted Minerva's hand. "Please don't sideline me at a time like this. I'm not hurt that badly. I would like to stay here and assist you, Minerva, if you don't mind…whenever we get a chance, some painkillers—well, I wouldn't refuse them."

"Okay. Thank you, I can use you up here, Emi." She turned toward the stolid Lang. "Chief, can you go to the medlab and have Postrenal get some vicocet for us, please? Then hurry back; we need you up here in the NOC."

Lang saluted, turned to Rew, and said: "Come on, I'll help you get down to the medlab." He half-carried Rew to the elevator.

Emi gasped as an unlikely holocall image appeared. The tricolor logo of the *Uniti Canta Dominica* announced itself. The stirring notes of Beethoven's Symphony No. 9 in D minor, Op. 125 began.

"Pomp and fucking grandeur. The only corp with a soundtrack. The Dominicans? Are you kidding me? How can they reach us all the way out here? What the hell?" Manaka's shock was evident.

"Fuck. They must know where Gereon is, and they may know the nature of our mission." Minerva scowled.

"Do you have to take the call? Can we pretend we didn't get it?" Manaka asked.

Minerva covered her mouth so she wouldn't spew coffee all over the screens, coughed, and gagged. "Manaka! You're hysterical." She was still chuckling when she said, "No. Would that we could. But no. They likely know we are picking them up."

Beethoven's grandeur faded as a Dominican monk strode on stage in his plain white robes with black rosary beads hanging from his belt. He paused. Took a deep breath. "Minerva, this is Darius Sergius, prelate of Dominica." He bowed before continuing.

"Stand by for an emergency request. Priority One. Article 5 section 7e PF invoked as stipulated in the Codices of the Council of the Nine."

Manaka nodded and said, "Official as hell. Yep, take this call."

"How do I look, Commander?" Minerva asked as she patted her hair into place.

Manaka licked her thumb and wiped a sooty smudge from Minerva's face. "All better now."

Taking a deep breath, Minerva responded, "I assume this is important, Darius, but do we have to do it right now? You catch me unawares, and you know, I cannot stand to be caught that way." Minerva grunted, frowning.

In response, Darius Sergius noticeably flinched and paled. Then he whispered. "God damn, I never for a minute expected to reach you, Minerva! I was going through the motions at the council's request. You still live! Why does that not surprise me?"

Minerva relaxed, replying, "We should perhaps pretend that you failed to reach me as my exec suggested?"

Manaka did a double-take upon learning she was the latest in a long line of Minerva's execs. "When were you going to bring that up, Minerva?" she asked.

"Who's with you besides your exec?" Darius was all business suddenly.

"No one else. Me and Manaka now. Who have you got with you, Darius?"

"No one, other than my orderly and my secretary. We may be able to keep this one confidential. At least we should try to. I have Aduvah Fattah waiting to join the call."

Minerva gasped, "I thought she died or had forgotten me. Okay, let's keep this call classified, now patch her in for a three-way."

For the first time in a long time, Manaka saw Minerva's brilliant smile.

Darius touched the bracer on his forearm. Triad Corporation's icon appeared: a red triangle with a fiery eye inside, flanked by two dragons rampant.

"Addie's using her official channels, Emi. Not sure what this means…"

"Bet it means billable hours," Manaka observed dryly.

The chiseled dusky face of Aduvah Fattah in full battle regalia stood before them. Holding her helmet in the crook of her arm, she asked, "Minerva, we need to talk about certain contractual obligations. Also, fulfillment issues. Vis-a-vis the recent re-org at Grand Design Corporation, as well as several other urgent matters."

"Re-org, oh, you mean that sneaky action my board took the other day?"

"Well, Jordi Donner never expected you to make it this long. That's kind of a gross miscalculation if you ask me." Aduvah grinned.

"They picked him. That pussy?" Minerva shook her head, not believing it. "Can you please back up, Addie, and tell me first about the contract? What gives?"

"Well, we have a legally binding defense contract with you, Minerva. Big contract, as you know. But Jordi is trying to cancel it, and he is demanding a full refund."

"That little prick. Okay. I know you had a plan in the event you reached me. What is it?" Minerva asked.

"It's simple. I need to execute the contract right now. And it needs to be quite noticeable, thus avoiding cancellation clauses."

"How?"

"By having all members of Triad attack all Dyeus forces in their immediate environs. Full-on corporate war. That would cast our contract into stone. Granite even. We would be joined at the hip for the duration." Aduvah's predatory smirk was transcendent.

She is someone I've always been able to count on, Minerva thought, *as long as she gets paid.*

"Addie, I love it! And that solves the immediate problem of the contract?"

"Yes." Stone-faced again, Fattah nodded.

"Execute it immediately," Minerva declared.

Aduvah walked off stage, and Darius resumed his portion of the call.

"Minerva, you need to know that Dominica supports you with all the force and honor of our brand. But we can only do so *sotto voce.*"

"*Sotto voce,* huh?" Minerva considered what she had heard, and said, "You know all about our Gereon mission, you and Addie, don't you?"

Darius paused and ordered the room cleared. "Now, we are truly alone. Yes, Minerva, we both know all about it. The discovery of an alien species. And yes, we know about the potential for a major gold strike. The recent raids by Ross Lasker and DC." He paused before he asked, "By the way, did you kill Ross or take him prisoner?"

"Not that I know of, but I sure hope we got him." Minerva frowned.

"I cannot address your hopes, dear Minerva. But I can confirm Ross Lasker has been off the grid for eight hours. And his son Hugo has assumed the leadership of DC, pending the location of his father Ross, currently MIA."

59

THE FRESH CANISTER OF CRYSTALS lightened the color of the vapors in the rejuvenation tank. Largo waited for any other reaction. Nothing happened.

This will take a matter of hours as the old vapor and gel are rejuvenated by the new crystal gases, Baen said. *You and I can use this time to calibrate ourselves to the master teleporting chamber in the workshop. Whenever you are ready, we will go in there, and by placing both of your hands on the screen, you will activate Trouter's thought processor. Ready?*

Not at all. No.

I initially rejected Rent when he tried to put me on his wrist for the simple reason that I knew he would not be stable or strong enough to survive to integrate with me and to do what you are about to begin.

I selected you. And for a few days now—in my role as a first-order temporal dilator—I should be able to protect you more than I could any random human. For the uninitiated, the config process will shorten their life span by a decade. And it will drive them quite insane. Every time anyone uses my teleportal functions—the temporal deficit applies. If you use it with wisdom, experience and infrequently, your body can repay the time debt in about a week. You should know that you have a singular opportunity after the configuration process completes. You are not bound by the usual planetary limitations after calibrating or recalibrating. So, theoretically, you can go anywhere that the thought processor activates.

Temporal dilator, Baen? Largo felt uneasy. *Theoretically? Look, we are moving way too fast with this. Have you ever even done this before? With anyone?*

No, I have not. But I am familiar with certain principles. For example, when you travel through the portal, you are actually moving at near light speed. It is usually unnoticeable unless you try to make too big of a time and distance leap. This is my highest order function—dilating space-time or what we Shanges call paratime. I would not recommend using our portal outside of any planet and its immediate atmosphere. It is too dangerous. Intergalactic jumps, ambitiously slowing time, can have dire consequences.

How dire?

Insanity. Death. The temporal deficit formula has a steep price to pay in such cases. Except for your first calibrated jump. You can go anywhere that our paratime channels allow.

Perhaps that was what happened to Trouter? Largo asked.

You might be onto something there. The portal jumps may have taken too much out of Mesh—or he may have tried something too ambitious— too radical. He may never recover. He may have attempted too much.

Run me through some of the principles of Shanges paratime and temporal dilation, please, Baen. I understand so little of what you are talking about. Like none of it.

Paratime consists of an alternate-worlds universe. It was developed by our sage, H. Beam Piper. There are an infinite number of timelines and metaverses. These time channels run parallel to each other, thus, paratime. The channels split and zigzag. They reconnect as key events sometimes happen one way. And sometimes another way. The temporal dilator, our bracelet, allows you to move incrementally along the paratime branches, such as going from one place and time on a planet to another nearby place and time. However, when used with the thought processor after configuration, you can make extremely long jumps with little to no deleterious effects.

I need to ask you, Baen, are you sure I can do the temporal configuration? Largo was still uneasy.

Key, it is now or never. Now would be the best time.

Wait. Maybe we could first do a practice run? I could try to reach for Minerva.

I think you are right. Let us begin with a small step. Reach out to Minerva with your thoughts and feelings. Try it now.

The bracelet glowed, and Minerva's face began to form in his mind. An electric crackling pierced the air.

60

“**M**INERVA, LET'S TALK ABOUT THE gold and the aliens.” Darius held the holocall open. Minerva wanted to disconnect but thought better of it.

Dominica has held exclusive rights to investigate sentient alien life for centuries. No one thought much about their role in that until now. It was long considered an unlikely event that alien lifeforms would ever be discovered. Still, I do not need them meddling on Gereon. The gold will deflect him from that conversation. It's worth a try, she thought.

“About the gold, Darius, so far we have found tantalizing traces, random gold artifacts. But no large geological deposits or lodes.”

Darius rubbed his well-trimmed white beard. “Your geological studies must have revealed some potential. Otherwise, you wouldn't have launched a prohibitively expensive field project…and an even more expensive corporate war, correct?”

“The truth, Darius? I will admit that our scientific data was thin. But it was still our best bet for a gold strike. We have just scratched the surface here with our prospecting efforts. Ross Lasker has made our work problematic.” She paused before going in for the close. “So, Hugo is in charge of DC now?”

“For the moment, until we can determine his father's fate.”

“Darius, could you use Dominica's considerable influence to get Hugo to pull out of Gereon? Or at least to stand down?”

“And if I should do this for you, Minerva, what will you do for me *quid pro quo*?”

Minerva paused for effect. “I will send you a considerable collection of the alien artifacts. We have discovered many on Gereon in the course of our work here." *That should be enough*, she thought. *Not prepared to let Dominica play in my sandbox.*

"Including the alien gold artifacts?"

"Yes." *He still wants something more. This offer should do it.* "I will also share all of our own archaeological data with you. Every single scrap of it—

"Who is your lead corporate archaeologist for such a vast undertaking?" Darius was intrigued.

I've got him. Now to set the hook. "Dr. Key Largo, Commander, GDC."

"Ah. I met him at a conference two years ago. It was before that unfortunate situation on Port Amphora. At one time, he was a great archaeologist with high potential."

"He still is Darius. And when you see his data, our data, you will be astonished."

"Okay. I agree to your terms. I will draw up the contract and have it to you by EOD."

Before Minerva could respond, she was distracted by a crackling, buzzing, kaleidoscope flash near the door.

No. It cannot be. "Okay, we will promise a quick turnaround, Darius. Klyne out." *What kind of portal is that?* Minerva paused and took a deep breath. "Largo, is that really you on the transmitting end of your bracelet? This is your portal? It seems loaded, overcharged with power. Be careful."

"Hello, Minerva. Hi, Emi. Come visit me? I think we have a gold bullion room to check out." Largo extended his hand, and Minerva stepped through, followed by Emi.

TO BE CONTINUED

Thank you for reading *A New Gold Dream*.
I would love to know what you thought of the book.
I value all the feedback from my readers.

SNEAK PEEK

A THRONE OF GOLD (LEGACY OF GOLD, BOOK 2)
WILL BE AVAILABLE IN 2023

MINERVA KLYNE STOOD IN A vast cavern, staring at the stacks of gold above her. Gold block after gold block. Dazzled by the reflected light—she darkened her goggles. The tableau of gold ingots stacked floor-to-ceiling was too much gold to process. Disorienting.

"This is astonishing," Minerva whispered.

"Enough gold to build thousands of drives," Largo observed. "And to dominate—we could own shipbuilding, trade routes, space exploration…."

"Thousands of ships," Minerva whispered as she picked up an ingot—weighing it in her hands.

"This room is worth billions. Trillions." It stunned Emi Manaka, too. Bowled over, she staggered as she sat down on a half-filled crate to rub her eyes. "Never did I imagine it. But, I mean, this is real," She added. "As of this moment, we may all be super-rich?"

"Well, it's a pile of gold right now. Until we secure it—it's up for grabs. The trick is to convert it—control it—allowing no one to know our source. We can't tell anyone about this yet," Largo said. "If we did, it could cause pandemonium. A bloodbath."

"Could be unavoidable, though. This means… Look. This room could start a revolt. But it's all right here. Right now. It's enough to turn everything upside down." Minerva stammered. "I never expected something like this when I planned this mission."

"We have to tell someone and soon," Manaka said. "Get some guards down here at the very least. Immediately. Guards we can trust—clones."

"It has cost too many lives to get to this room," Key shook his head. "It is a hard place to get to. The Shanges made sure of that."

"Still, you got to it," Manaka observed.

"True. But two people died on the way here. We need someone good in this role. I would choose Chief Lang to select the clone guards. He's loyal. Honest. I understand him well after all these years."

Minerva considered it. "Yes. A clone. Clones are more reliable. Designed to be dutiful. Less likely tempted. Lang is trustworthy."

"Key picked up a gold bar with both hands. "I would guess one ingot weighs about 10 kilos. You wouldn't run fast or far, carrying one in each hand."

Minerva pushed her hair back, opened her mouth, and said nothing.

Key asked Minerva, "What? What were you about to say?"

"Largo, I was thinking—we are looking at this all wrong." She rubbed her jaw before continuing. "Consider how much gold we have right here in this gigantic cavern… We can afford to be generous to our people. And only our people. We can divide a decent amount of gold bullion among every member of Grand Design Corporation. Those who came here and suffered so much on this mission. Everyone who has survived to this moment is now wealthy."

"And to the estates of those who died getting us here. It is the right thing to do. We could give them even more." Key added. "We can afford it now. We need to get the word out to our people."

"I will see to that immediately," Minerva said. Her determination was evident.

"Yes—this is what we all signed up for. Exceeded our wildest dreams," Emi said. "And still we know next to nothing about Gereon and the cultures who left all this wealth here. The treasures and secrets the planet still holds. There is more gold on Gereon than anyone has ever imagined. There are more dangers too, but what else will we—"

Minerva cut her off. "Not to be too cynical, but… we still have to keep how much gold we have under wraps—keep it confined to our people. We want to keep the market price of gold in the stratosphere where it is now. So, we must limit how much we release into the open market. And how often. We have to control and manipulate the gold market from now on."

Emi interjected, "If the other corporations find out how much gold we are sitting on here—"

"I know what you are about to say," Largo said.

"They would realize what we realize right now. The cold war between our companies and the nine corporations would get hot. We need all citizens to own stock in all corps. It's a basic tenet of corporate life. If one stock becomes too valued, the balance of power is destroyed. GDC becomes worth 100 times more value than any other competitor.

No one spoke as they considered the ramifications.

Minerva broke the brooding silence, "Emi, I want you to draft a plan for how we release the gold into the market. Our source must remain a secret. The price. It is all ours to control and dictate now."

Emi nodded and picked up an ingot, hefting it. "The purity of these things—"

Minerva interrupted again, "Largo, I need you to pick up your archaeology game. We owe certain promises to Dominica."

Confused, Key asked, "Minerva, what about Dyeus and Lasker? And what do I owe Dominica? What did you commit me to?"

"Ross Lasker may be dead. Probably is. For the moment, his son Hugo oversees Dyeus Corporation now."

"Step away for a few hours, and everything changes—and Dominica?" Largo shrugged.

"We have had a truce imposed on us. Both corporations. GDC and Dyeus have ceased all hostilities for the moment. A truce was brokered by Dominica and enforced on our side by our partners at Triad. And Triad will demand more gold for their role in this affair. But we can afford it."

"Another reason to keep this site on a tight lockdown," Largo observed.

Minerva nodded. "Dominica wants us to share our archaeological data with one of their scholars in return for their influence. Everything goes to Dominica's prelate, Darius, and their best corporate archaeologist. They have provided a name. But, of course, Dominica, Triad, and Dyeus will want a base on Gereon. Something we can fight against for as long as possible." Minerva narrowed her eyes as she watched Key's reaction.

ABOUT THE AUTHOR

E.C. Gibson has a Ph.D. in anthropology specializing in Maya Prehistory. He has directed archaeological projects in Central America, Polynesia, Europe, and North America. In addition, he has authored over fifty scientific blogs, technical monographs, and papers presented at scientific society meetings.

A New Gold Dream is his second novel.

www.ingramcontent.com/pod-product-compliance
Lightning Source LLC
Chambersburg PA
CBHW060525160726

47991CB00001B/180